No Small Dreams

By

Katrina Lyman Jones

Table of Contents

Dedication

This book is dedicated to my family:

My parents, who were my first cheerleaders;

My husband, my constant source of strength, support, encouragement, and love;

My children, who repeatedly asked, "Mom, when are you going to publish your book?!!";

And God, who gave me a thirst and passion for writing, and has always lit my way.

Acknowledgements

Many thanks to my mom, who was my first (and continues to be my reliable) editor. My heartfelt thanks to all who were my beta readers over the last 20+ years and helped this novel improve, from family and friends, to teachers, to fellow writers. This book is better because of you. I am also very grateful to the friendly historians in Oberlin who were happy to answer my many questions several years ago, and show me around the historic sites there. Lastly, a big thank you to all who have made available historical information, pictures, and explanations about life in the early 1900s, which helped me understand and more accurately visualize that exciting time period.

Dream no small dreams for they have no power to move the hearts of men.

-Johann Wolfgang von Goethe

PROLOGUE

Oberlin, Ohio—September 1901

Will he ever come back?

Samantha stood at the library window, wondering the question she had asked herself for months. She tried not to dwell on it, tried not to let the not-knowing dig into her like a persistent burr stuck in a stocking. But it kept returning as if it had a life of its own.

Redirecting her thoughts, she looked out at the maple tree which would soon feel the cool nights and withdraw its sap into slumber, remembering looking out this very window one cool autumn day as a young girl. Spellbound by the deliciously bright colors of the maple's fall attire, she had noticed that each leaf was somehow miraculously different from every other, each color and pattern a little different.

Bundled up in a sweater and knit hat, warm stockings under her dress, Samantha had gone outside–alone as usual–to play in the leaves. The brilliant yellows, oranges, and reds that fell in mesmerizing irregularity, individually or in swirling groups, beckoned her to join them. Their visual cacophony and joyous chaos of color thrilled something deep inside her. She had always loved playing in autumn leaves, but that day she decided to bring her favorite leaves inside to further enjoy them. Father would never notice and Mrs. Dolittle would not mind. So Samantha proceeded with determination and delight, trying to choose the very best ones. It was a surprisingly difficult choice, and she wished she could bring them all in together!

In the end, she settled on enough leaves to fill a large bowl from the kitchen. She took great pleasure in arranging and rearranging

1

them in rows on the table, enjoying each bright treasure, unaware of Mrs. Dolittle's chuckling and headshaking at the sideboard as she cooked supper.

That night Samantha went to bed fully expecting to be able to play with her beautiful leaves for weeks. But she soon learned that they quickly faded and dried into brittle things that barely resembled their former glory.

Returning her mind to the present, she smiled wryly at her younger self. She still remembered the pleasure and happiness of that wonderful afternoon, along with the pang of regret the next morning when she realized the leaves wouldn't last forever. Was that how she would always remember her time with Sterling, as well? Joy tinged with sadness? Something wonderful that came and went, like autumn colors?

She shrugged and let her arms drop to her sides, turning back to the table to clear the pencil shavings from her recent writing session into a dustbin. Sterling might not be here any longer, but her memories with him were still vivid, and what he had taught her would continue to grow and strengthen as she kept building on what she had learned. But was that enough?

It would have to be. After all, things did not always go the way one wanted. She would just have to make the best of circumstances, as she always did. Sitting back in her chair, she picked up her pencil once again and started where she had left off. But her thoughts kept trailing back to that day almost four months ago, when she and Sterling first became acquainted…

CHAPTER 1

AN AWKWARD ACQUAINTANCE

May 1901

Sterling first saw her at a church picnic on a Saturday afternoon in mid-May. She stepped lightly in narrow, scuffed boots, and her brown, faded cotton dress appeared too large for her thin frame. There seemed nothing remarkable about her, yet she still caught his attention, the sun glinting against the two gold braids that dangled down her back and shimmered with a hint of auburn. The straw hat she wore tipped down with her head, hiding her eyes. All he could see of her face was the profile of her slightly upturned nose and the metal of her wire-rimmed spectacles lightly cupping her ears.

The young woman walked unconsciously among a group of peers with whom she exchanged no word as far as he could see. She seemed pretty unconcerned with making any impression on anyone or catching up on town gossip, unlike the young women of his acquaintance. Perhaps that was what had caught his attention: Instead of putting up a front or trying to glean attention from the male members of their party, she just *was*. And she seemed comfortable with her differentness. Slowly she made her way with the group to a place between two trees, carrying a large book in her arms.

A few of the young men and women spread blankets over the ground and opened picnic baskets, which spilled forth a delicious variety of foods. Everyone settled around, and the girl leaned back against a tree as if against an old friend.

3

Fifty yards away, Sterling, too, seated himself on a blanket and graciously accepted the plate of food offered him. He was quite hungry and went to with gusto. But his ear was only half tuned to the conversations around him.

He knew he should not look at the young woman in the brown dress so intently, and expected her to sense his gaze and turn to find him. She picked at her food in disinterest for several minutes, still an outsider to any conversation, then turned to the book he had noticed earlier. Even from a distance, he could tell the volume was old and worn. The young woman soon became engrossed in it, and he continued studying her. She barely moved; the glasses and delicate nose turned down into the pages, the long braids rested against her thin chest.

He was not entirely certain what he saw in her, but there was something...

She sat against the tree for a long time, seemingly unmoving except for the slight movement of her right hand as she turned a page. From the look of her intensity and concentration, she devoured each page as if filling her appetite with words and knowledge instead of the food in front of her. Perhaps half an hour later, someone tapped her on the shoulder, and she slowly looked up after putting a finger on her place. She focused her eyes on the girl before her, but her expression indicated that her mind was still in the book.

"I asked if you are going to eat or if I should clear it away," the other young woman asked a bit impatiently, indicating the small plate of picked-at food.

The young woman with the book did not respond, her eyes far away again, so the other girl tried once more. "Shall I dispose of it?"

This time she nodded as if to say, but of course! And returned to her book.

When the picnic drew to a leisurely end, Sterling's companions drifted away, and the young woman's associates began to depart as well. Several young women busied themselves by shaking out picnic blankets and folding them away. Sterling decided to take the chance while he had it and turned to the last young man in his company to leave.

"Tell me: That young woman under the tree there, what is her name?"

The other man raised his eyebrows and smiled, looking where Sterling pointed. He started to make some quip about scouting out eligible young women until his eyes rested on the girl, and his smile faltered. He shrugged. "That's just Samantha Jennings. Daughter of Basil Jennings, one of the old Oberlin College professors."

"I see..."

"A pupil for you, you think?"

"Perhaps."

Sterling's associate looked at him momentarily, at Miss Jennings, then shrugged again. Murmuring something about "the eye of the beholder," he walked away.

After a few more minutes, Sterling picked up his suit jacket and placed it over his arm, then made his way through the few mingling people to where Miss Jennings sat. She was unaware of him, though he stood only three feet from her. After a moment of consideration, Sterling sat and waited for her to look up. He knew that was always the final indication: the eyes.

He cleared his throat, and in a moment, she raised her head and glanced at him, still lost in another world, her blond brows knitted together in confusion at the interruption. He looked into her gray eyes and saw what he was looking for but remained puzzled. Those eyes lacked no depth or intelligence, which was easily apparent, but there was something else he did not understand--some kind of barrier he had not encountered before.

Miss Jennings continued looking at him, then blinked several times to clear her head.

Sterling coughed. "Excuse me, Miss Jennings? I'm Lee Sterling. Most people just call me Sterling. You may have heard of me...." He hoped for a spark of recognition in her eyes, but there was none, so he continued. "The people of your fair town call me 'the teacher of modern writing.'"

"How did you know my name?" she asked in a low, musical tone.

No *hello, nice to meet you,* just *how did you know my name.* Of course, he supposed he had given a rather abbreviated introduction himself. "I asked someone," he answered with a smile. "I wonder if you might take a turn about the gardens with me...? I have something I would like to ask you."

Two young women asked if Sterling and Miss Jennings were finished so they might put away their blanket. Both girls looked at Sterling with a mixture of admiration and interest, then at Miss Jennings, perplexed.

"Yes, we are finished. Thank you," he said, standing.

Miss Jennings looked at her book--rather wistfully, he thought--folded back a tiny corner of the page, and closed it. It was thick, he noticed; very thick, perhaps over eight-hundred pages, and bound the way old rare books are that commonly sit in libraries, gathering dust--not in the hands of girls at church picnics.

He offered to take the book from her, supposing it heavy, and at first thought she would not give it up. But, after a moment's consideration, she hesitantly, unconvincedly, handed it to him, then stood, and they began walking through the church gardens. It was a beautiful place with flowers of all hues, and clean walkways between them. Other young people strolled around them or stood talking in couples or bunches, and they heard the sounds of happy conversations and occasional laughter.

Miss Jennings did not try to walk familiarly with him, and the way she eyed the book caused him to wonder if she were really so distrustful of him.

"I am to understand that you are Professor Jennings' daughter," he said, trying to loosen the awkwardness he felt rising up against him.

She nodded but offered nothing further.

"I am new enough in town that I have never met your father, but I am sure he is quite learned." Inwardly, Sterling cringed at the awkwardness of the statement, knowing he must sound foolish. But Miss Jennings was not making conversation easy!

She nodded again.

"What is it he teaches? I do not believe I have heard."

"Taught."

Sterling's steps faltered for a second before he caught himself. "Excuse me?"

"Taught." She swallowed, collecting her thoughts. "He does not teach anymore."

"Well then, what did he teach in his younger days?"

"Oh, he was old then too!" She said it before she could stop herself, realizing too late that it was unnecessary and not very complimentary. Her eyes widened, and she covered her mouth with one quick movement.

Sterling chuckled and then caught himself. This was going to be harder than he had anticipated. But he was not inclined to give up.

Fortunately, Miss Jennings solved the problem after a few moments of silence by offering quietly, "He was a professor of history here at Oberlin College."

Inwardly he thanked her. "Wonderful! I teach a few classes here as well; perhaps he and I have a few things in common. Did he focus on any specific time period or continent?"

"Everything."

"Well! He must have studied a very long time!"

"Yes. We have quite a large library."

"Is that where you picked up this one?" he asked, hefting the heavy tome in his hand.

She nodded, wondering what he must think of her. But she did not know what to say. This situation was all so strange, and she had no idea how to ease the awkwardness.

He glanced down at the book's title for the first time as a clue for more conversation and was surprised to see: *The History of Faeries, 1400 A.D. to 1820 A.D.*

She watched him more closely than she meant to, to see his reaction, feeling herself color in embarrassment. Why had she chosen this book to bring today, of all she could have brought? Really, it was too cumbersome to carry anywhere. She was usually more practical.

A moment of quiet collection passed as they ambled through the gardens.

"So," he calculated quickly, "it is outdated by 81 years. What is your opinion: does it need to be updated?" He knew it was a weak attempt at sounding interested, but he smiled slightly and looked at her for an answer.

"Maybe," she replied.

He cleared his throat. "When you said your father knows all of history, you really meant 'everything'—including such...obscure...things as fairies." He cleared his throat and swallowed another chuckle. "At least, I assume this volume also came from your father's library. Are you studying to become a history teacher also?"

"Oh no." She shook her head quickly. "I study only what interests me. And only at home."

Sterling was surprised. She seemed the studious kind, and many of the town's young women were enrolled in the college, progressive school that it was. Oberlin College extolled the virtues of formal education for women and its importance in helping them in their responsibilities as wives and mothers. It also accepted students "irrespective of color," [1] which was almost unheard of these days.

"I see." A pause. "Have you ever tried your hand at writing?"

She looked at him, brows drawn together, startled by the subject's turn, then returned her gaze to the path. "No."

"That is what I teach." Another pause. "Would you like to try?" He felt abrupt, but this whole conversation was...unusual.

She shook her head. "I don't think so."

He disregarded her doubt and kept on. "Oh, but there is something about you. I think you would do well." He stopped walking to face her more directly. "Very well, actually," he amended, warming to the subject. "It would be my privilege to teach you. If your father has no objections, of course."

She said nothing. Indeed she did not know what to say! No one had ever singled her out of a crowd for anything before--let alone as a pupil. And she had always been fine with that. Mostly.

"You certainly would not be required to continue if you disliked it. I would hold you to no obligations." He spread one hand in a gesture of openness. "And we would have our lessons in a public place. It would all be quite proper, I assure you."

---

[1] https://daily.jstor.org article entitled A Progressive College's Complicated Relationship with Race.

The girl remained silent, then lifted her shoulders briefly--a gesture he took to indicate, if not agreement, at least not opposition.

"If you decided to continue under my tutelage--say, for the duration of the summer--and if at the end of our time together you felt I merit payment, we may decide on an amount that suits us both. I have my salary from the college to sustain me, but I like to teach community members whenever I can—to learn better how to teach people from all different facets of society. Could you meet at the old table behind the school once or twice a week for an hour or so? Perhaps next Wednesday morning would be to your liking."

She nodded slowly, feeling dazed. "Yes. All right." Such a sudden arrangement! Had she even quite said she was interested?

"Good. How about ten o'clock?"

A pause. "Fine."

And that was that. Much different than he had expected, but speaking with her--surprising and unexpected as the conversation had been--did nothing to sway his convictions. She would do wonderfully, and he would be successful. He really did not know exactly the best way to teach her--or at this point even what to teach her--but the ideas would come to him as he went along, just as they always did.

CHAPTER 2

BE YOUR OWN TEACHER

May 1901

Samantha only briefly mentioned the teacher of "modern writing" to her father, and only because Sterling had intimated she should do so. For the most part, she led her own life, checking in with her father when she thought it necessary, but otherwise walking through their spacious house hearing only her own thoughts and rarely hearing her voice. The housekeeper, Mrs. Dolittle, spoke to her whenever she saw Samantha's slight shadow pass the threshold of a room where she worked. But Mrs. Dolittle required few responses and seemed happy simply to have ears to talk into, whether the person attached to them responded or not. So the days passed as quietly as always, and Wednesday approached like a drifting cloud on a breeze.

Lee Sterling arrived promptly as scheduled and sat at the thick, old wooden table in the shade cast by the buckeye trees. He had a satchel of papers with him and waited, relaxed, shuffling through them as the light and shade between the branches above him sifted dappled shapes over everything beneath it. Several minutes went by before he thought to check his pocket watch. He knew she would come.

Long before Samantha reached the schoolhouse, she could see Sterling waiting there, and as she drew closer, it was as if a telescope were slowly bringing the picture into focus. Gradually she noted the gleam of his damp, newly combed, dark, wavy hair. By his clothes, she had the impression that his family was well-off. She decided he looked quite educated, startling herself with her interest and

12

perception. He seemed so very at ease, sitting there looking over the papers in front of him, an occasional breeze riffling through the papers in his hands like it did his cream-colored shirt. She felt the same breeze rising up the path to tease her hair, hat, and green cotton dress. Ducking her head, she doggedly made her way down the path that wound its way to the front of the school and through the schoolyard to the little wooden table, where he sat absorbed in his task.

She stood there silently, watching him, thinking of his given name, what a small name "Lee" was for such a tall, strong man, and how appropriate he should go by his surname: Sterling, noun, the standard of fineness, strong and polished. She hoped he was also like the adjectival definition: conforming to the highest standard of character.

"Good morning, Miss Jennings," he intoned, glancing around at her. He straightened the papers in his hands with a sharp cut against the wood. "I'm glad to see your father was not opposed to my teaching you."

She moved around the table to stand facing him. "My father? Oh." She shook her head.

He looked up again and motioned for her to sit across from him. "He was not against it, was he?"

She sat. "No."

"Good, I believed your father to be a sensible man." Then, in an effort to make more small talk, he added, "I am told your father inherited a relative's fortune shortly before your parents moved here and that a few years later, your mother died."

13

Samantha nodded, surprised by his forthrightness. "Yes. She died when I was born. My father's brother was affluent and died a few years before. Father was the only one left in his family." She wondered if she were saying more than he wanted to hear.

"I see. That must have been a challenging time for him."

"Yes, I suppose it was." She realized with a start that she hadn't thought much about it.

"I wondered how it was that a retired professor owned a mansion. I make enough of an income to live on, but I can't imagine making that much." One side of his mouth quirked up in a wry smile.

Samantha nodded again but did not know what else to add. Where was this conversation headed?

Sterling set the papers in one side of the satchel and lifted a few small, blank pages from the other. "All right, I suppose we should get started. And please, call me Sterling. I am not much for formalities, though I will continue to call you Miss Jennings for as long as you like. Here is what we will do. I will give you a topic to write on, and you just do your best and go at your own pace. I like to do this exercise at the beginning to get the mind going and the writing flowing."

He looked at her to make sure all was clear. She nodded hesitantly, unsure what was expected of her but not knowing what to ask.

"In the meantime, I will also write so that you may have a possible model for future reference. After one hour, we will trade and compare papers, and then you may take your leave. Does that suit you?"

14

She nodded, and he placed a clean sheet in front of her, then withdrew a pencil from the front of the satchel and laid it next to her hand on the table. He gave her a topic, asked again if she had any questions, then looked at his pocket watch and told her to begin.

For at least the first five minutes, she could think of nothing at all to write and realized she was more confused than she had thought, but she still did not know what to ask. Having been given such a broad topic as Freedom, she felt bewildered and almost afraid. She willed herself to remember everything she had been taught in school about writing essays, and thought hard. Finally, she put pencil to paper and slowly wrote out a few words. Carefully, she made every letter perfect and soon had a few ruler-straight lines of neatly formed sentences. Concentrating in this way, she doggedly filled two pages by the end of the hour.

Sterling raised his eyebrows when she handed her papers to him and smiled knowingly but not unkindly. He didn't say anything but handed her his paper, which made her shift uncomfortably as she noted its lengthy seven pages.

She immediately understood what she had done wrong as she read the untidy but readable essay he had written. She fell into his writing after only a moment and wondered at it until she finally emerged with the concluding sentence.

Oh, to write like this! she thought, her first interest awakened. She had never considered giving writing a serious hand, but now, even as she despaired of ever being able to write well, a desperateness to do so began to arise in her heart. Quickly she turned back and read it through again, noting the sentence arrangements, style, and vivid beauty of Lee Sterling's writing. She had been an avid reader for as long as she could remember and could easily recognize good writing from mediocre--and Sterling's writing was excellent!

When she looked up, he had completed marking her writing and was looking at her with an expression she could not read. She handed him back his essay, and he laughed outright at the wonder and amazement in her eyes. This was the first real emotion he had seen in her, and it felt good that his writing had brought it out.

"You did not believe a fellow like me had the ability, did you?"

She blushed under his laughing gaze and looked down at the rough boards of the table, folding and unfolding her hands.

When she raised her eyes, his face was arranged a little more seriously and he returned her essay. "A noble first effort," he told her kindly, and the anxious fluttering of her heart calmed slightly.

"Read through my markings, Miss Jennings, and then tell me why you think I marked what I did and what you have learned. It is important for you to see as much as possible without me pointing it all out. I do not teach you everything, you see. You must be your own teacher as well."

Sterling's words ran through Samantha's head all that week until their next meeting several days later. How could she be her own teacher? And why, throughout her years of schooling, had the teachers never allowed her to write with the abandon Sterling's essay demonstrated? It was unlike any essay she had read and did not feel regimented. Instead, it was full of emotion, the voice so strong and sure that she felt she knew him better just by reading it. Yet he wrote with a certain kind of order and control that pulled everything together. That kind of writing was so much more interesting and thought-provoking than the essays she was accustomed to, but its novelty seemed almost dangerous. The whole idea of the liberty and challenge of trying it herself--by herself--intrigued her.

During that first week, she hesitantly gave it a few tries while in the solitude of her own room. It felt risky, and she was not sure if she was doing it "right," so she was glad for her next lesson and the opportunity to ask questions and try again in the presence of her coaching teacher.

With laughter in his eyes, Sterling watched her concentrated efforts over the next couple weeks, how she bit her lower lip and gripped the pencil tightly, and he inwardly rejoiced that he had attended that picnic. He rapidly realized that not only had his impression of Miss Jennings been right on the mark but that she just might be the sort of pupil he had become a teacher for in the first place. He felt motivated to grow in his ability to be an effective tutor and teach this young woman all she wanted to learn about the writing he was passionate about.

Among other things, but most importantly, Sterling taught Samantha that facts were not enough. In school, Samantha had learned well that good marks required the recitation of good, solid facts. And so she had grown accustomed to forming her essays around facts--something she recognized now as informative but terribly boring and unemotional. Sterling's motto was "write bravely from the heart." He told her briefly of times when baring his heart through his writing had made him susceptible to others' mockery, but he firmly assured her that the courage to share, regardless, would always shine above any scorn.

"Never be satisfied with less than the best of your soul," he told her. And his normally light manner was very serious.

This proved to be harder than she expected, however. She had hidden her heart for too many years during her history of reclusiveness, and her quiet, unobtrusive personality made sharing such things difficult. She had never borne her heart to anyone, though she had sometimes longed to. Now to write of her true feelings was something she did not even know how to begin to do. She found it uncomfortable and, at times, embarrassing. But the long-buried thoughts and feelings of her heart were still very much alive, and she possessed the determination and desire to uncover what lay within. She found herself wanting to really know what she knew and felt. It seemed strange to think of things that way, to consider that by writing, she could find out what was inside her own mind, but she realized it was true that there were things she did not know about herself. And she had learned already that writing about her thoughts and feelings brought them out into the light.

Soon the Wednesday morning meetings turned into biweekly sessions. Sterling and Samantha continued to meet at the table behind the school, and Samantha began to devour the learning of writing as she had, only shortly before, devoured book learning. Their sessions gradually stretched from an hour to longer than two hours each, but neither of them noticed, so enthralled were they in the business of thinking and writing.

Gradually their discussions grew to include current trends, events, and politics. Samantha felt her mind expanding in a way she had never experienced with books alone. Explaining what she thought and felt in spoken and written words forced her to organize the intelligent clutter in her mind. She enjoyed learning about current events she had missed, and resolved to read the newspaper more often to feel that connection with the rest of the world.

Sterling caught her up on the events of the year up to this point and was not disappointed in her reactions or her written responses to both the tragedies and triumphs of the world in 1901. She was exceptionally intelligent and grasped concepts quickly, and she always had thoughtful insights into events and people.

Samantha had heard of Queen Victoria's death back in January and, like much of America, had mourned for the loss of Britain's longest-reigning monarch. Everyone said it marked the end of an era, and even here in far-off Ohio, seemingly far removed from the effects of the queen's death, Samantha had felt it. She knew all that the queen had stood for, the moral standard she had tried so hard to maintain in her family as an example to the world. And she had been touched many times throughout her life as she learned of the queen's great love for her husband, Prince Albert, who died many years ago. That love and the great grief she carried the rest of her life, demonstrated by the black clothing she wore ever after, gave the queen a human aspect that Samantha had always respected.

She had heard about the fire that destroyed the Cincinnati Opera house, also in January—indeed, the news had been everywhere for days since it was considered nearly a local event--but had somehow missed hearing that in February, an influential banker in New York named J.P. Morgan had bought multiple mines and steel mills in America and then incorporated them. Her head spun at the concept of such a billion-dollar business deal. Sterling agreed and told her, laughingly, that mathematics was not his strong suit.

Of course, she knew that in March, President William McKinley started his second term in office, and his new Vice President, Theodore Roosevelt, was sworn in. But she knew nothing at all about the devastating fire in Jacksonville, Florida that had occurred only weeks ago. Sterling explained that it spread so rapidly and destroyed buildings so completely that 10,000 residents were left homeless. There was also a rumor, Sterling told her, that many of those were blacks[2] who had lost their homes when firefighters decided to focus on saving a white neighborhood instead. Hearing this, she was incensed, which led to a discussion about the racial injustices they had seen or read about, and they felt compelled to write an essay on the topic and what they and others might do to put an end to such things. As a result of this discussion, Samantha began wondering about Mrs. Dolittle's past for the first time and what she may have experienced as a result of her color, even here in Oberlin, where most people were welcoming and accepting of blacks.

Their discussions were stimulating and thought-provoking to them both. Sterling felt a sense of satisfaction at the end of each lesson with Miss Jennings, and the excitement he had always felt in teaching returned twofold. Here was a mind he could help unlock. He himself did not hold the key, but he was getting closer in helping Miss Jennings find it for herself. She was responding and growing rapidly in her writing ability. He could see the desire in her eyes, the hunger for knowledge she'd had no access to before. After seventeen years of life locked away inside herself, seventeen years of learning about everything in the history of the world but herself, she was finally

---

[2] While I aim to be as historically accurate as possible throughout this novel, I have chosen to use the term "black" for people of African-American descent, rather than the "negro" that would have been used at the time (along with other terms) that are now considered derogatory and offensive.

being allowed a glimpse at a different way of expression and existence. She had been brought out into the sunlight and nourished with what she had thirsted for most without knowing it. Not only that, but Sterling hoped that in the process, Miss Jennings would find the door within her mind and heart that he sensed was tightly shut, its contents dusty but waiting to spring forth.

Within Samantha's heart had grown a desire that took hold of her so passionately it almost frightened her. With her whole soul, she desired to write as Sterling wrote, to know what he knew and so willingly taught her. Instead of spending long days turning pages of the great, leather-bound books, she resided in her father's library and her own room for a different purpose: to sweat and strive over blaring blank papers, pencil in hand, until her head and her wrist throbbed painfully.

Sterling found his work with Miss Jennings an exhilarating challenge, more than he had anticipated, though never in a negative sense. There were times when he thought he caught glimpses of the person in her that no one had ever seen--least of all herself. Though these instances were too fleeting and far between for him to gauge his own effectiveness, they never failed to give him new determination, for he liked what he saw. Behind that door of dormancy lay a passion that was only now beginning to be stirred, only beginning to ease around the cracks of its barricade and show itself at infrequent intervals. He liked passion in a person, for it provided strength in reaching for a goal. And determination made a person human and unique. Hadn't he found that in his own life? Without the interest passion provided, without the momentum and optimism of purpose, life was far too dull and unchallenging to interest him. He wanted to help Miss Jennings find these same qualities in her life and within herself. What he did not foresee was changes in himself.

CHAPTER 3

LESSONS AND DISCUSSIONS

June 1901

One morning in June, Sterling watched Miss Jennings as they walked through a meadow on the outskirts of town to a spot he had previously selected for their lesson that day. The sun shone brightly, giving a hint of the oppressive heat that summer would soon distill upon them. Samantha wore her straw hat as she often did, little pinpoints of white light poking through the tiny holes to dance on her shaded face. As she moved, her braids alternated between hanging down the front of her dark green dress and draping down her back, their blond-red color glimmering in the sunshine.

Samantha's eyes lit up as she caught sight of a meadowlark balancing precariously on a slim, bobbing tree branch several yards away. The bird's striking yellow breast thrust out in song, and, head back, he sang his trilling melody as if his heart were bursting with joy.

Sterling smiled at the bird and at Samantha watching it. "You like birds," he observed. They had both stopped walking to look at the pretty thing.

Samantha broke her gaze from the bird and looked at him quickly, surprised to find him still there. "Yes. Though I did not rediscover that until recently..." Her tone was a little sad as she trailed off, but then her features brightened as she looked back at the bird. "They are such precious little creatures."

Sterling nodded in agreement. "Birdsong always cheers me, no matter how tough the day." He thought a moment and then added,

23

"I think that is why God created birds: to beautify the earth and cheer the heart of man."

"And the heart of woman," Samantha added thoughtfully.

Sterling laughed with that deep rumble that never failed to make Samantha smile too. "And woman, of course," he agreed. "In fact, I think if more men would take time from their busy work to notice things like birds and flowers, as women do, maybe they would be happier. Although, I suppose that's a somewhat simplistic view of things."

Samantha nodded absently, then said thoughtfully, "I am reminded of something John Burroughs, the American essayist, wrote."

"Yes?" Sterling replied. And then, eyes twinkling, asked, "Do I feel a recitation coming on?" In the past few weeks, he had learned that she had a remarkable memory and could recite full passages verbatim.

"If I can remember it..." Samantha's head tilted to one side, and she gazed off into the distance, searching her mind for the words she knew were there. "He said something like, 'The very idea of a bird is a symbol and a suggestion to the poet. A bird seems to be at the top of the scale, so vehement and intense his life...'" She paused for a moment, willing herself to recall the rest. "Hmmm... he then says something about them being beautiful vagabonds and graceful masters... and I think he finishes with, 'how many human aspirations are realized in their free, holiday-lives—and how many suggestions to the poet in their flight and song!'" [3]

---

[3] https://www.gutenberg.org/files/5177/5177-h/5177-h.htm

"Indeed," Sterling agreed. "I have often appreciated Burroughs' way with words."

"But not all Oberlin men are poets," Samantha pointed out, beginning to walk again. "Most of them are farmers, and a bird is no more a symbol to them than is their own plow." She shrugged slightly. "Their work is being with the birds and flowers, which they probably rarely notice."

"True," Sterling returned. By now, he was accustomed to Samantha's realism and sensibility, the crucial points and parallels she drew from everyday things, but he was always curious to learn more about the workings of her mind. "Perhaps I have been too long in Cincinnati and seen too many factories and the struggle associated with that work. I guess that is what I was thinking when I said what I did about taking time for nature." He shook his head sadly. "Once one sees the haggard, hopeless faces of those factory workers—many of them mere children!--he never forgets it."

"Surely people who live and work that way have no choice," Samantha countered, her steps slowing as she considered this. And then, thinking aloud, she said, "Living in the dingy atmosphere of the city, working so many hours a day, they probably do not have opportunities to go where there are birds and flowers in abundance. And what a tragedy, Sterling!" She looked at him with eyes wide as if this were the first time she had examined the issue so closely.

"Yes," Sterling returned softly, touched by the innocence and pain in her gray eyes. "And that is one of the important things people like Samuel Gompers are fighting to change. Working fourteen hours a day is too much even for the strongest man to do day after day, six days a week. Yet women and small children are also working those hours to make ends meet. If Gompers succeeds in his efforts, a law will be put into effect prohibiting work days longer than ten hours."[4]

Samantha thought for a few moments. "Ten hours still seems too long," she observed.

"To me as well," Sterling agreed. Then with a teasing smile, he added, "But how many hours a day did you used to read those thick, old books of your father's?"

Samantha colored noticeably and started to stammer a reply, but Sterling held up a hand. "I know. I should not tease you about that. You undoubtedly learned a great deal about all kinds of history and could whip me soundly in any history match." Samantha gave a wry smile as he continued. "And I would venture to guess that nowadays, you spend at least half of that ten writing daily."

"Well..." Samantha looked at him and caught the humor and pride in his eyes. "Maybe I do some days," she admitted, "but ten would definitely be more than I could manage." She gave a sudden, brilliant smile, and Sterling felt a jolt go through him to his very center. He swallowed, speechless for a moment.

Recovering himself, he said lightly, "After ten hours, my hand would be worthless, I think." He held up his hand, flopping it around in pretended bewilderment at its lack of function, and Samantha joined in his laughter.

Sterling felt the sudden urge to throw his arms around his young pupil and embrace her, to embrace the light that shone from her. But he refrained, of course. Again. This was not the first time he

---

[4] http://www.socialstudieshelp.com/Eco_Unionization.htm

had felt such an impulse, but it surprised him every time. Instead, he bent to pluck a delicate, blue columbine from among the grasses and slid it gently into her hat band.

During her talks with Sterling, Samantha was delighted to discover that her knowledge of the world was not as limited as she thought it might be, compared with Sterling's. And Sterling was happy to recognize this as well. Samantha had never traveled outside of Oberlin, but she understood the complexities of politics and ethics as well as anyone who had seen the whole country. She realized that in her years of reading the many books in her father's library, she had developed a strong sense of history, government, and human rights that acted now as a firm foundation on which to build her own opinions and understanding of current issues.

A few weeks into their lessons, when she had arrived at their usual meeting place in front of the schoolhouse, Sterling had quoted Thoreau, saying, "How vain it is to sit down to write when you have not stood up to live."[5] He laughingly exclaimed that they must first stand up and live today before they got to their writing. She knew from experience that she could more easily discuss things while walking anyway, so she welcomed another one of their excursions.

They left the schoolyard to walk one of the country lanes on the outskirts of town, a slight breeze rippling the long grasses on either side of the road and giving slight relief to the ever-increasing heat. Soon, they found themselves engaged in an animated discussion on women's suffrage. They had broached the topic previously, but only in a roundabout way when one of Samantha's essays, entitled "If

---

[5] https://www.brainyquote.com/quotes/henry_david_thoreau_108676

I Were Samuel instead of Samantha," had touched upon it generally. But never had they actually gotten down to the meat of the subject.

Samantha tried to match Sterling's stride and looked up at him often to watch his face as he spoke. She noticed that the more excited his argument became, the faster he walked, and she smiled to herself as she lifted her skirts and stretched her own long legs to keep up. She was tall for a woman, but Sterling was a good head taller than she. Sometimes keeping up with him was challenging, but she knew he would stop periodically as he warmed to his subject and wanted to emphasize a particular point.

"I cannot get over how unjust it is that women are not allowed a say in the government of their country when, in general, they are just as qualified to vote as their husbands--or more so!" Sterling pounded the fist of one hand into the palm of the other and shook his head emphatically. "A woman keeps the household running, after all, no matter what her husband may think about who is in charge."

Samantha contemplated this, thinking of Mrs. Dolittle and how well she kept everything going at home while her father apparently did nothing. And she was "just" the housekeeper, not even the wife and mother of the household.

Continuing in a slightly different vein, Sterling added, "Women are so restrained and oppressed by society that their natural passions for living are smothered. Don't you agree, Miss Jennings?"

While Samantha formed an answer to this comment, they came upon a field beautiful with green stalks of corn in perfectly straight rows, and Sterling stepped off the road to lean against the split rail fence, distractedly, his mind focused on the topic at hand. In a calmer voice, he mused, "When girls are very young, they begin to realize the needs and possibilities of the world around them and how they might fill them with their own unique talents. It excites them so that they are filled with energy, dreams, and a desire to do great things, just like their brothers! I saw this in my early teaching and it is wonderful to see. But then, as they grow older, they lose this excitement as they come to realize that other than being a housewife, their career options outside of housekeeping are either teacher or secretary—and then only until they marry. The devastating truth is that in the pursuit of a meaningful career, gender means everything. Intelligence and ability should matter most, but unfortunately, that is not the case in today's world." Sterling shook his head and turned to Samantha. "And so girls give up and forget their dreams, reverting to their mothers' role. I suppose it is easier not to go against the grain of society."

Samantha was not sure she agreed with these comments entirely, and Sterling, noticing her expression, stopped his monologue.

"You do not agree?" he asked, his eyes probing hers. "Please share with me your thoughts; I want to know."

"Well," Samantha began, flexing both hands around the rough fence, "I agree that women are restrained and oppressed by society, as you say..." She pushed her glasses up with one finger as she thought. "And I am sure many women are frustrated by the limitations society puts upon them. But I also believe that plenty of women are naturally content with their home life and have no desire for the kind of contention that politics hold. It is undoubtedly true that many women desire to vote, but I would venture to say that their dreams never stray far beyond home boundaries because they want to create a home, have children, and care for their families. That is what they love and where their passions lie. They already have enough decisions to make and enough things to do at home and do not want or need more responsibilities added to that."

"But that's just it!" Sterling exclaimed. "If the home were not the only avenue open to them, they would have the energy and the options to make a difference in the world!"

Samantha had never been offended by anything Sterling had said before, but now she felt a little hurt by this intimation. Her blond brows knit together as she looked up at him beside her. Could it be that he did not understand women's important role and how they felt about their responsibilities? And did all men think as he did?

Samantha looked away and rested her chin on her prone arms atop the fence rail. Now that she thought about it, how did *she* know any of this? She had never known her mother (or anyone else's) personally and had never been a housewife herself, so how could she see this side of things? She had read books about mothers and their homelife, but it was more than that. She understood somewhere deep inside herself that what she felt and thought about womanhood was good. And she felt the rightness and desirability of it for herself.

While Sterling waited for a reply, suddenly aware that he may have assumed too much, she said nothing for a long moment. Then she straightened and spoke quietly and simply. "Plenty of women feel deep down inside that they are making a difference right where they are."

Sterling's steady gaze faltered, and he bit back his intended reply. For now, it seemed petty. He said nothing, looking at Samantha, the straw hat shading eyes that suddenly seemed wise and distant, as if she had pulled away from him to shield herself. He felt ashamed by what he had unintentionally insinuated in his zealous—if somewhat misled—efforts to defend women's rights.

Finally, he let out a long breath and said softly, "I'm sorry. Sometimes I speak before thinking. You are right. I was not considering all sides of the issue. Perhaps one can go too far in his thinking on either side."

Samantha was silent for what seemed a long while, during which time Sterling felt increasingly more sheepish and embarrassed. "I am sorry," he repeated. "I do realize that, even though my mother had very little to do with how I grew up, most mothers are involved in their children's lives, and they improve the world through their chil--"

He stopped abruptly. Samantha was laughing softly, amusement obvious in her expression.

"What?" he asked, his black brows drawn together. "Did I say something wrong again?"

He suddenly looked so perplexed and childlike that Samantha stopped laughing and turned fully to face him, a smile still lifting the corners of her mouth. "Maybe you should consider asking women for their thoughts and opinions," she said softly, "instead of telling them what they think and feel."

Sterling noticed how the soft breeze played with the fine hairs around her face, how her tall frame stood strong, thin, and light, yet firm in her stance. Most of all, though, he noticed how her gray eyes showed humor and insightfulness, with just a bit of lingering hurt.

He nodded humbly and conceded, "Again, you are very right."

31

Samantha turned back to watch the horses in an adjacent field and continued speaking. "And you are right that women should have more rights. My father has a book about our founding fathers that includes letters[6] written between Abigail and John Adams. I have studied that book several times and have been impressed by Abigail's wisdom and strength of character. She drew a parallel between the British government, its control over the colonists, and men's power over women. That was over one hundred and twenty years ago, and still, women do not have government representation."

Sterling nodded. "It's a crime," he agreed. "Even looking at it solely in terms of what percentage of the population women are, their non-representation is highly unjust."

"Yes," Samantha nodded, her eyes beginning to burn with feeling. "I admit that women in the past have perhaps not spoken up as often as they could have or should have. But most of them are used to being told what to do, how to look, what to say...and they do not realize that they can have a say in their own rights, instead of just internalizing what the other sex tells them should be their rights."

With barely a breath, she continued, "Abigail Adams warned her husband not to 'put such unlimited power in the hands of the husbands.' She told him, ' All men would be tyrants if they could,' and that eventually, women would rebel since they would not feel bound by laws in which they had no voice or representation. Women have not successfully completed such a rebellion, but they will someday. And that day cannot be too far away."

---

[6]Letters of Abigail Adams- http://www.thelizlibrary.org/suffrage/abigail.htm

"I heartily agree," Sterling responded, smiling at her. *She has fire, after all*, he thought. But then, he had recognized it before.

Samantha felt flustered by his look, for somehow, it was different than it had been a moment ago. She felt her face growing warm, but having started her explanation, she had to continue. "During my many historical readings, I have discovered how truly male-dominated everything is in our society, including education. I would wager you never learned of Sybil Ludington in all your years of schooling."

Sterling shook his head, marveling at how much she voiced today. He had not been able to draw this much out of her all at once before, except in her writing.

"Or Deborah Samson?"

"No," Sterling admitted.

"Sybil Ludington[7] lived during Revolutionary War times and was sixteen years old in the year 1777. She lived in Connecticut, and when the fateful day of the British invasion came, she rode through towns there and in New York, warning everyone that the Redcoats were coming. And the next day, she organized enough volunteers to fight that they actually helped beat back the British."

"Really?" Sterling was impressed. How had he missed this?

"Yes. But who do we learn about in school as the famous person who warned of the Redcoats' arrival?"

"Paul Revere."

---

[7] https://en.wikipedia.org/wiki/Sybil_Ludington

"Of course! Not to take away from anything Revere did, for he was undoubtedly a hero of the Revolution—yet Sybil's ride was twice the length of his!"

"Hmm," Sterling said, thoughtful. "I see your point. Who was that other woman you mentioned?"

"Deborah Sampson.[8] She hailed from Massachusetts and joined the army during the Revolutionary War in 1778 at eighteen."

"Joined the-- But that is impossible!" Sterling's dark brows drew together in confusion. "Women were not allowed to enlist."

"No, they were not—and are not now. She disguised herself as a man, learned to walk and talk as a man, and was known by the name of Robert Shirtleff—for three years!"

Sterling's eyes widened with amazement.

"She volunteered for a few dangerous missions and even became the general's personal aid. Her great strength and courage were legendary in her regiment. She was wounded twice, and it was only after she developed a fever later that her secret was discovered."

Sterling whistled low in appreciation. "She was not punished, was she?"

Samantha shook her head. "Fortunately, no. She had worried that she would be shot if found out, but instead, she was given an honorable discharge. And then Paul Revere wrote a letter to congress

---

[8] http://gardenofpraise.com/ibdsamp.htm and
http://www.rootsweb.com/~nwa/sampson.html

that resulted in her receiving a soldier's pension for the rest of her life."

"Perhaps that is what Paul Revere should be famous for," Sterling grinned.

Samantha returned the smile. "Perhaps. But then, my opinion counts little as a woman. After all, it is men who decide school curricula and what is printed in educational texts."

Sterling leaned back against the fence while he appraised her with a new perspective. "You should be a teacher yourself! And I had no idea you had such biting comments in you." His tone was half teasing, half impressed. "In fact," he observed, "You are sounding more and more like a feminist!"

Samantha grimaced.

"That was intended as a compliment!" he protested.

Samantha shrugged slightly and gave Sterling a wry smile. "It is merely a label given by a French socialist--who was male. I simply learn about the world and draw my own conclusions and opinions, as do you. But because I am of the female gender, if I have an opinion, I am a feminist."

Sterling was taken aback—yet again. How many times was that now today? He stared at Samantha and was relieved to see her eyes smiling at him above the serious set of her mouth. So, she was not angry with him, just making an observation. All at once, he felt a strong desire to ply the recesses of her intelligent mind more deeply and probe her soul's understanding.

Again, he felt compelled to touch her and bask in that light that was so particular to her essence. He had never imagined that the first day he saw her two months ago that the unassuming girl with the ancient book and the gray eyes could be so...fascinating. He had judged her quietness to be timidity and, yes, perhaps even shallowness--though the thought embarrassed him now. How foolish he had been to think she was an empty vessel to be filled with his brilliant philosophies and ideas. The deeper he delved into her being, the more he found to delight in while at once realizing how much remained to be discovered.

But when he looked at her, these thoughts swirling in his head, he saw something unreadable flicker in Samantha's eyes and she suddenly turned back to the road. "Care to continue our stroll?" she asked over her shoulder.

And then it was Sterling's turn to stretch his legs to catch up.

CHAPTER 4

LEARNING

June 1901

That summer of 1901 was a learning one for Samantha. Her view expanded from the world of history to the world of the present, and she learned more thoroughly to see how the two corresponded and connected. Besides historical topics, she and Sterling discussed and wrote about the issues and events presented in the weekly newspaper, the Oberlin Tribune, which Sterling frequently brought to their meetings. They were interested to note that on June 24th, Charlotte Manye, a native of Africa, had graduated from Wilberforce University as the first in her country to graduate from a United States college.[9] That led to Samantha writing an essay on "The Prejudices Faced by--Versus the Opportunities of--the Blacks." Throughout her life, blacks had always been a part of the town, and she had not given them much thought, just as she had not given whites much thought. They were all just people; many of both colors attended Oberlin College and worked at various trades. But as she wrote, she recalled what she had read about the slave trade, Abraham Lincoln's attempts to abolish slavery, and the ensuing conflicts, including the Civil War. It saddened her to consider that there were still conflicts and prejudices happening all the time around the country. She was glad Oberlin fought this prejudice, in part, by accepting students of color into its college beginning back in 1835. And she recalled the pride with which older Oberlin citizens reminisced of their participation in the Underground Railroad and how Oberlin had come to be known as

---

[9] http://www.brainyhistory.com/years/1901.html

"The Town that Started the Civil War." The long-hidden adventurous side of her enjoyed imagining what it would have been like to be a part of that, to help people to Canada and freedom. Blacks were a part of the rich history of her town and of its present make-up. She had difficulty understanding why some whites—historically and presently—found it so difficult to accept and appreciate them. She guessed it was a complicated and emotional matter, even though it should not be. Mrs. Dolittle had certainly been a mainstay in her life and her father's life! With that thought came the realization that she had always taken the woman for granted and not considered how much she relied upon her. She needed to rectify that!

At the beginning of July,[10] Sterling and Samantha read in the paper that a nineteen-year-old artist in Paris named Pablo Picasso had opened his first exhibition a few days before and seemed to have a promising career ahead of him. And on July 2nd, the bank robbers and horse thieves, Butch Cassidy and the Sundance Kid took $40,000 from a train in Montana. That made Samantha glad she did not live in the Wild West! Those two stories led to a writing session and discussion about the differences between refining a God-given talent--Picasso had apparently been a child prodigy--and taking advantage of others for personal gain, as the Wild Bunch was doing in the West.

With the arrival of the month of July came the increased temperatures that they had been holding their breath against. The sticky heat sapped everyone's energy quickly and slowed movement to a sedentary shuffle. It, therefore, became the sensible option for Sterling and Samantha not to take any more walks for a while during their lessons, and they began meeting earlier in the day when it was

---

[10] http://www.brainyhistory.com/years/1901.html

slightly cooler. Once more, Sterling and Samantha reverted to their original meeting place at the old table behind the schoolhouse. In the face of such heat, it was at times difficult for either of them to work up the usual level of excitement over the things they discussed and wrote about, but they continued to work at it as well as they could. Samantha felt herself gradually gaining ground in her quest to improve her writing skills; often, what she wrote inspired the day's discussion.

One particular morning toward the end of July, during a less-than-animated writing session, the perspiration on Sterling's and Samantha's temples tracked shiny rivulets down their faces. It was still hours from noon, but it was simply too hot to concentrate.

After a few minutes of trying to write, they looked up from their work to see if the other was as uncomfortable. Samantha felt a drop of sweat trickle down her breastbone and between her ribs, and she squirmed a little as it tickled her. "I find it difficult to think this morning," she admitted apologetically.

Sterling ran an arm over his forehead and then pulled his fingers through his wavy hair, making it more unruly than usual but somehow very attractive. The realization surprised Samantha.

"Me too," he said. "Maybe I should have called off our meeting for today."

Samantha gave him a half smile, thinking to herself that she did not mind the heat so much when she was with him. Her eyes searched his for a languid moment...so brown and warm...until she realized what she was doing, thinking that the heat of the day affected her mind's clarity. She lowered her eyes and fingered the paper in front of her. "I do not mind the heat so very much," she said, echoing her thoughts, "but I am afraid this essay is not going very quickly or intelligently."

Sterling still searched Samantha's face, wanting to know what she had just been thinking and why she looked more flushed than she had a moment before. He loved looking into those eyes behind the glasses and wished she had not lowered them. Her eyes were somehow both a mirror and a window. In them, he had caught glimpses of himself the way he wanted to be and of the pristine person Samantha was, deep and ever deeper.

When Samantha glanced up again, Sterling was still looking at her, and his eyes had turned very soft. Then he blinked, clearing his thoughts, and offered a simple proposition. "Why not write about the thing we most desire now?"

Samantha thought about that while wondering what he had seen in her that had made him look at her that way. "All right," she said.

In one minute, she had finished writing and looked up expectantly.

"Finished already?" Sterling asked, dark brows raised in surprise. He had not begun his yet and was not even sure if he should write what he was feeling.

"Yes," Samantha said with a slightly sheepish smile. "It is simple, but I don't know of anything else to add." She lifted her shoulders. "This says it all." She held up her paper, and Sterling read:

What I want most at this very moment is a long, cool rainstorm to clear the heat from my brow and the fog from my brain. That is the loveliest thing I can think of. Oh, and perhaps a nice, ice-cold drink to go with it.

Sterling could not help but laugh. He nodded his agreement. That was not at all what he had been thinking, but it was practical. And it did sound wonderful.

"What would you do if it did suddenly start raining right now?" he asked curiously. "A cool rain, unlike the warm summer storms we so frequently have."

She thought of the beginning of the summer when Sterling had talked of the importance of writing from the heart. It was not always the easiest thing to do, he had said, but doing so proved a courage that would rise above adversity. She supposed that if this were so important in the written word, it must be doubly important in verbal communication.

Her face lit up in a smile. "I think I would revert to the child I never really was and...and dance." She laughed quietly and averted her gaze for a moment.

"Dance?"

"Yes! It may sound silly or or childish..." she looked up at him again. "But you asked, and that is what I would do. Honestly."

Sterling looked at the young woman across the table from him, wondering when he would get used to the surprises he constantly found in her. "Mmm," he mused, picturing her happily frolicking through a downpour. "The thought intrigues me; it seems a very joyful thing to do, actually. Not childish."

Samantha raised her head, relieved that he understood. "Rain like that would make me happy, and dancing seems happy too. So...the two should go together." She clasped her hands and asked, "What would you do?"

He thought a moment and then asked, "Do you mind if I write it? I am not sure I can express it adequately without thinking while I write."

Now it was Samantha who was surprised. He had always seemed to be able to express whatever he wanted, whether in writing or in speech and at the drop of a hat. But she could certainly understand the desire to write out a thought before expressing it. So while he wrote, she tried to find ways to expand upon her own idea and the picture it created in her mind.

This time the writing came smoothly for both of them, and the heat, if not forgotten, was at least temporarily bearable.

When Samantha wrote all she could think of, she looked up and was glad to see that Sterling had almost finished, as well. But she was not prepared for what she read in his angular, upright hand:

If I were rain-bound
I would hope to be drenched
with someone I loved.
Then the rain would be
a happy thing.
Instead of tears,
it would seem laughter:
glorious.
So beautiful,
with her.

And if she
offered me
a kiss,
its sweetness
would thrill me,
for its purity would rival
the falling dew.
And I would be made new.
Among the laughing jewels
Of rain.

Samantha read the poem through again, slowly, and then looked up at Sterling's serious face. She blinked back the wetness in her eyes and swallowed, surprised by how tenderly the piece had touched her. She knew that writing it--and then showing it to her--had made Sterling vulnerable. And she had never seen him quite this vulnerable before. The man before her was not only a talented, effective teacher who had a wonderful way with words, but he was also human. As she was learning, he was not always humble, not always right, and not actually perfect. But to willingly open himself to allow her to see the vulnerabilities inside him raised his stature in her eyes more than anything else had.

"It-it's beautiful!" she stammered as she handed back the paper. "Thank you for writing it and for letting me read it. It...seems very personal."

Sterling nodded quietly, then shrugged and gave a half smile. "It is a rather stumbling first attempt, far from adequate. I'm sure I will realize that more fully later. But you asked me, and that is what I would do," he finished, repeating the words she had said only a short while before.

43

"Who is she?" Samantha asked, wondering why it suddenly mattered so much to her.

"I still do not know," Sterling admitted, but with something unreadable in his eyes. "I hope that one day I will know, and then...perhaps my poem will come to fruition." He looked at her, and she still read embarrassment in his posture. "It probably all sounds silly and childish—"

"No," she returned firmly. "No, it sounds wonderfully happy. And tender." She did not hear the wistfulness in her own voice, but it was there.

CHAPTER 5

THE FAIRY RING

July 1901

Early on the last Wednesday afternoon of July, as Samantha stepped out the front door to make her bi-weekly walk to the schoolyard, she heard fast hoof beats heading down the road toward her. Carrying her writing supplies over her shoulder in a leather satchel she had recently discovered in the attic, she walked down the front steps, along the long walkway, and out the gate to the road, glancing up in curiosity at the man on horseback who was drawing closer every moment. As he came into focus, Samantha could see that the horse's black coat was spotted with sweat. She expected him to dash right past her, as it appeared there must be an emergency of some sort. But instead, the horse jerked to a stop directly beside her. The excited animal snorted and shook his head in annoyance, pawing the ground impatiently.

Samantha looked up, puzzled. There, seated in the saddle, was Sterling! His hair fell in dark, untidy, waved locks over his forehead, a few beads of perspiration glistening above his eyebrows. The sleeves of his dark blue shirt were rolled up above the elbows, and his muscles showed tautly.

Samantha caught her breath at the sight of him. She had never seen him anything but impeccably dressed and well-groomed. Now his haphazard appearance took her off guard. But despite the disarray, he managed to somehow retain his usual poise, and he seemed utterly at home in the saddle. He was, undoubtedly, the most handsome man she had ever seen, and she felt the breath squeeze out of her chest at

45

the realization. She did not make it a practice of noticing, so what was different this time?

But I have noticed before, she admitted to herself for the first time. She could not have said why, but as she looked up at his grinning face and excited, piercing brown eyes, she felt her heart pick up a beat in anticipation.

"It is such a beautiful day, Miss Jennings," he cried, "and a bit cooler, thanks to last night's rain." He looked briefly at the sky, where a few grey clouds skittered across the blue. "I thought our lesson would benefit much more from being out in this"--he gestured with one expansive hand--"than at that ancient, warped table."

"But where...? We have often gone places before, but always on foot. Why? How...?"

"Just hop up behind me! You are not much more for old Champion to carry." He patted the horse affectionately, slipped one foot free of the stirrup, and offered her a hand.

Still, she hesitated, bewildered. "I-I don't understand. Where are you taking me? What—"

"Nothing to fear, Samantha Jennings. Yes, my head is on straight. I know the perfect place for our lesson and will have you home before dark." He stretched his hand toward her in a compelling gesture.

"B-before dark?" she squeaked incredulously.

Sterling laughed and the lock over his forehead bounced as he shook his head. "I am only teasing. It won't be that long! Come on! We are wasting precious daylight." Without further delay, he caught her hand and pulled her toward him, as she held onto the satchel with her other hand. She placed one foot tentatively in the stirrup and he tugged her up in one swift, strong movement, her skirts flying around her and then settling on either side. She was certain she was showing much more leg than was seemly, but she could do nothing about it.

He slapped the reins, and before she could catch her breath, they were off. She hung onto Sterling for dear life, her satchel bumping against her back.

They rode for quite a while, slowing down slightly upon reaching the woods and the cooler shade it offered. Sterling guided the energetic stallion along a barely discernible path, then slowed and turned onto another route. Samantha had never been off the regular roads and paths of the town before, always afraid she would not be able to find her way back. Anxious now about Sterling's sense of direction and confused about what was happening, she nevertheless trusted him, for he had never given her reason not to.

Carefully she relaxed her grip and leaned back from him, straightening her satchel with one hand and pushing her glasses back up her nose. Her pulse was finally beginning to drop closer to normal, but she felt extra warm in a way that was not just because of the heat of the day. And her mind still raced. She felt... She didn't know what, exactly. Embarrassment? Awkwardness? Definitely that! Sitting behind Sterling in this manner and having held to him so tightly was not exactly proper. It was certainly the closest she had ever been to a man—or to anyone, actually. And yet she could not deny how safe she felt with her arms around his trim middle and the hardness of his muscles obvious beneath the blue shirt. Even with the shock of their headlong run, she felt protected and secure and that Sterling would not allow anything to happen to her.

Unseen to her was Sterling's continual grin. He could only imagine what she must be thinking and feeling! He wanted to laugh out loud but refrained himself with difficulty, not wanting her to think he laughed at her. The expression on her face when he pulled her up behind him was one of such astonishment! He knew he had surprised her, but he was fairly certain she had caught his excitement. The fact that she had not resisted or opposed his impetuosity gratified him. And the way she clung to him now was more enjoyable than he'd imagined it might be.

After a while, they reached a small clearing among the trees where grass grew tall and fragrant, and wildflowers nodded gently. As they rode from the shade of the trees and into the clearing, the sun broke upon them, warm and radiant, and Sterling drew the horse to a stop. Samantha shivered and Sterling felt it.

Quickly he slipped out of the saddle, and his feet touched the soft undergrowth with barely a sound. He reached up, smiling, to help her down, but after handing him her satchel, she dismounted by herself without a word, needing a little space, needing to move deliberately as she regained her emotional bearings. She took a deep breath and inhaled the wild grass scent of the rain-soaked undergrowth. The smell sharpened her awareness of the woods and her physical place in it, grounding her back to reality. She watched silently as Sterling cared briefly for the beautiful black stallion.

After tying Champion's reins securely to a low-hanging branch which allowed the animal to graze, Sterling removed the saddle and placed it on the ground, then motioned to Samantha with one hand and began walking through the grass. He still held her satchel, his own draped over one shoulder, and she followed quickly after him. He led the way, parting branches before her and treading surprisingly softly for a man of his height.

After a few minutes, she felt her awkwardness dissipate as the peace of the sunlight filtering through the trees and the peacefulness of the setting began to work its magic upon her.

A few moments later, they passed a small clearing, and Samantha stopped abruptly with a stifled cry. Sterling turned immediately, alarmed.

"Look!" She pointed to the clearing. Quickly he retraced his steps, heart pounding, to find her, much to his relief and amazement, absolutely radiant with pleasure.

"Look," she repeated in a low whisper.

He looked where she pointed, then confused, turned back to her, eyebrows raised. After a moment of silence, she lowered her arm and shifted her ebullient eyes to meet his. "Don't you see?" she asked.

Sterling shook his head once, slowly, looking again at the clearing to be sure. "Toadstools...?"

"A fairy ring," she returned.

Sterling waited, without breathing, for her to continue--he had never seen her this way before. If she could get this excited over a bunch of simple mushrooms, well...now he was the one taken by surprise.

"Legend says that where a circle of toadstools grows, fairies danced the night before. According to that...this is a hallowed, magical place. It gives good luck to she who finds it."

"Oh," Sterling managed to say, clearing his throat. What else could he say? Did she really believe in fairy magic? *Absurd,* he thought. *She is such an intelligent, educated person. Why would she believe such lore? After all our conversations...* But he remembered the huge, ancient book she held when he first met her. *Perhaps she has been secluded from the world far too long after all.* He thought on this for a moment and then mused, *but then again, perhaps I am too cynical. And, as usual, I could be reading things into this that aren't even there.* After all, in the past couple months, Miss Jennings had seemed completely lucid and logical, often more down-to-earth than himself.

He became aware of her eyes on him again and looked down at her. He could tell she expected him to say something. "I am...glad you found it," he said at last, gesturing at the ring he could now clearly see in front of them.

A hint of a smile played about Miss Jennings' lips as she asked softly, "You do not believe in such fanciful things. Correct? And you think me childish for wanting to."

"I...I—no!" Sterling stammered. He hated feeling flustered. It was not a sensation he was used to (although he had felt it more frequently around her, he realized suddenly, than ever before in his life). "That is," he clarified, mind racing, "no, I do not believe in fairies and magic. But you are certainly free to believe what you will."

"Thank you for your permission," Samantha replied wryly. He missed the twinkle in her eyes.

"I didn't mean--!" *Drat, this girl!* "I just...meant..." he gestured helplessly, "who am I to tell you what to believe and what not to believe?"

She gave him a particular, long look that made him color slightly, suddenly remembering their conversation about women's rights and all he had told her she believed, without realizing he was doing it. But then she shrugged as if it were not really so important after all, and she was not offended. *She was just testing me*, Sterling realized with embarrassment.

She reached for her satchel and Sterling handed it to her wordlessly, their fingers brushing. The contact sent a spark through them both.

They started walking again, side by side this time, and Miss Jennings asked, "Sterling, haven't you ever wanted to believe in something so much that it almost did become real to you?" There was something so alive and trembling in her voice that Sterling felt as if it had reached out and grasped him by the heart. He sensed she was confiding something very personal and that he would do well to take care.

He frowned. "Like religion, you mean?"

"Well... I guess so. I had not thought of that." She shook her head. "I just wonder if I am really so different from everyone else. Because I have wished for the freedom and the...beautiful wildness...of fairies, and the assurance of the impossible that magic promises."

What a question! He had never given fairies or magic a second thought. But what she was really asking was, had he ever wanted anything that completely? Probably not; every material thing he had ever needed or wanted had been provided for him. This thought humbled him as he considered Miss Jennings' words for a moment-- and then realized suddenly what she meant.

He reached out and stopped her with a touch on the shoulder. She turned to face him and searched his face, waiting for the answer she so desperately needed to hear. And when he gave it to her, it was like a sweet, cold glass of water after a long, long thirst.

"You are not so different from everyone else, Miss Jennings. I think there are times when we all desire the impossible and want more freedom than we have. And we all hope for our most secret dreams to become a reality."

"Do you have secret dreams, then?" she asked, not as if she meant to pry into his affairs but as an honest, innocent question.

Sterling slowly lowered his hand from her shoulder and pondered this new question. Then he shook his head hesitantly, his brows furrowed in perplexity, and said, "I don't know..."

Samantha nodded as if this were the answer she had expected. "May I tell you why I think that is?" At Sterling's hesitant nod of assent, she continued. "I think it is because you have always been given what you needed and had the ability, as a man, to pursue whatever you most wanted. You wanted to become a writing teacher, so you went to university and became one."

He was a little affronted at her intimation that his schooling had been so simple and easily accomplished, but she had a point. And while she lacked significant background information, her insight into the affluent quality of his life was right on the mark, similar to what he had just been thinking himself.

"Though I have always had my physical needs met, I have been restricted socially and emotionally...and perhaps spiritually

52

too...for lack of real guidance and companionship." She lowered her eyes.

When she met his gaze again, her fair brows furrowed, and the seriousness of her expression had increased further. "Even if you were never close to your parents, at least they were a sideline to your life, people you interacted with regularly. My father has been a word, a thought, but never really a presence in my life. I cannot recall him ever giving me counsel or guidance. I have had no one but myself. Oh, Mrs. Dolittle, our housekeeper, is constant and true, but I have never confided in her. I don't know why... At any rate, I read and dreamed, living in my imagination the way I knew I could never live in real life. But I did not care. At least, I did not think I did. The dream was so much more beautiful than the reality that I clung to it and believed it with all my heart. That was my life for so many years."

"You mentioned religion," she continued. "Perhaps if I had been taught to believe in a god, things would have gone a little differently for me." She shrugged, but her eyes were shimmering with tears now, and Sterling was struck again by the realization that he had judged her both rightly and wrongly. Yet again. There was so much he did not know about her. He saw the potential in her that first day, but at the time, he had also assumed she lacked the complexity and strength of the varied emotions and passions that he now knew were a very real part of her. The passion he saw in her at this moment was something much quieter and more desperate than any he had ever displayed in his flamboyant self-assurance, but it was no less real.

Sterling wanted to apologize for his faulty judgment of her, for the community's judgment of her, and for her lack of parental guidance and connection with humanity. But that was all too large for a mere apology, and he could not get his mind around it all, much less make things better.

But still, he had to say, "I'm sorry, Miss Jennings."

She turned away and began walking again, not wishing him to see the tears falling onto her cheeks.

Sterling stepped quickly after her. "You are right! Believing in your imagination was the most powerful thing you could do at the time. That was your way of controlling your life. You did the best you could with what you knew. And you are so courageous now to be giving that up in exchange for reality with all its imperfections."

Miss Jennings wiped at her face with trembling fingers and nodded. It pained him to see the ache in her, to consider the pain she had experienced and was still going through.

"Thank you," she said simply, not knowing what else to say, wondering if she had expressed far more than she should have. After all, she had never spoken to anyone like this before. But as she searched his face, she sensed inside herself that she had done right and that her feelings were safe with him.

They walked on a few more minutes, and then, voice low, she added, "I must thank you for taking me on as your pupil. I have learned more from you than I can even express."

"Oh no," he responded, shaking his head a few times. "It is I who have learned so very much from you. I always think I have all the questions and answers, but there have been countless times these past months when you have made me rethink and reevaluate my perceptions. I think our lessons and conversations this summer have more than compensated me for anything I may have taught you."

This was a new perspective for Samantha, and she pondered it for a while. They said nothing more until they reached a larger clearing that looked suitable for their writing purposes.

Samantha settled herself among the grasses and wildflowers. Warm sun spilled through the trees and lit up her face and hair. Absently, she moved the straw hat back on her head, cinching the string ever so slightly. Then she began sketching a toadstool on a blank piece of paper.

Sterling watched her from his position beneath a tree several yards away, noting the serenity written across her face and the way the sunlight played along her braids, glinting intensely among the bright hairs. If this were a hallowed place, it was because of her, not those crazy toadstools! He watched the briskness of her hand with the pencil, how the aura of peace increased with her concentration.

Miss Jennings' question about whether or not he had any secret dreams gnawed at him. And, as he had told her, this was certainly not the first time she had really made him think. She had taken him off guard many times with her perceptive comments and questions and the way she saw right to the heart of reality. That in itself was curious, for had she not always lived outside reality in a world of her own making? Then again, maybe those gray eyes and that quick mind so easily pierced through façades because she had lived inside a façade herself and could now clearly see the difference.

Sterling set to work on his own empty paper, none too sure of himself. *A very perceptive young lady asked me today if I have any secret dreams*, he wrote. *Anything that I want so badly that I would be willing to ignore reality, if need be, and believe wholeheartedly in that dream...* Sterling's writing trailed off as he examined his thoughts and tried to touch on what was in his heart. What did he want out of life? What was really most important to him? Miss Jennings did not have an accurate perspective on his life before university, but he had never told her details about his mother, so she couldn't know. He hadn't explained how difficult his life had been at that time as he longed to break out of the privileged, elite lifestyle he'd grown up in and find out who he was and what he was really capable of. His mother wanted a life for him that was not what he wanted for himself, and she was very difficult to convince otherwise. So his early life had not been quite as rosy as Miss Jennings might assume. But she was right about one thing: at least he had a father and a brother—and friends. At least he'd made connections in society and knew people he could turn to for company and guidance.

Slowly he began to write again. *Before I left home, I knew exactly what I wanted out of life, and I reached for and grasped it. But now... What? I know I want to continue teaching, to help people, and to open minds to educational concepts, but beyond that, I don't know. What about my personal life? What about my own future? What am I missing that I should be seeking?*

Samantha sketched a few of the toadstools from memory, throwing in a couple of fairies to complete the picture. Each fairy had a pair of tiny, translucent wings and was dressed in flowing gauze-like material that tapered away to nothing just above the knees. The legs were delicate and shapely down to the daintily clad feet that barely tiptoed over the ground. Samantha had sketched often as a child but not as much in the last few years. It felt good to just let her hand go and see what it would create. She smiled at the scene she had created and touched her pencil here and there to finish the details.

Then she exhaled slowly, pulled out another sheet of paper, and began to write.

She knew instinctively, somehow, that this was the end of her fairy dream. This picture she had drawn on paper was the final scene of the act she had played in her mind for so long. Sterling was right that she had accepted reality, and even though it frightened her, she knew she had to lay down the fantasy and pursue the real thing called life. But was she really courageous enough to do it, as Sterling had said she was? She would never have described herself that way; the word felt so strange in connection to her. She felt anything but brave.

With such a tumult of emotions warring inside her head and her heart, Samantha was surprised when the writing streamed out of her so unhesitatingly. *What is courage?* she began. *It is doing something you know you must do, regardless of the terror and ignorance that pull back at you. It is forging ahead into the unknown, even though Comfort calls its siren song and makes you dizzy with its heady promises. I know this because today I decided to sever ties with my past fantasies once and for all and chose to reach for more fruitful dreams--though I have, as yet, to find what, exactly, those are.*

The words seemed to spill right from her heart through the pencil without snagging on doubt or worry along the way. Neatness discarded, she wrote with the passion the fairy ring had inspired within her, though she knew she no longer believed in its magic. Sterling, glancing up now and again, could see the emotion and determination as it burned within her thin frame. Her posture, her expression, her manner proclaimed something new, and her hand seemed to gather up the proclamation to fling it joyfully and recklessly across the page.

For nearly two hours, she wrote in this way, utterly lost in words and ideas, gradually losing momentum but gaining in surety and confidence. When at last she leaned back with a sigh, her intense emotion nearly spent, her hand throbbed, and four entirely dull pencils lay beside her. Without even looking over what she had written, she laid the papers aside--including the drawing—and lay back on the grasses in a fit of contentment. She could not believe how glorious and radiant she felt! It was as if she had fully discarded her old life and started anew, and this different person that was somehow still herself was lighter, freer and purer. It overwhelmed her that she could feel such a powerful feeling and thought she must not be wholly connected to the earth. *I have never been closer to heaven,* she thought. *Maybe there really is a God, for I have read that God is our Maker and that 'God is good.' If He is my Maker, He must be good...or these feelings within me would not be possible.*

Sterling saw that she had finished, saw her spent exuberance, and understood the look of infinite contentment he saw in every part of her slight form. Slowly he tucked his pages of musings into his own satchel and rose, shaking the stiffness from his limbs, and made his way to her, the long grasses swishing with every step.

Her eyes were closed, mouth turned up peacefully. She breathed in the simultaneously sharp and muted scents of the grasses and flowers around her while her fingers trembled with fatigue. Sterling smiled at a large, dark smudge on her calloused index finger.

Softly, so as not to alarm her, he sat near her and asked, "May I read it?"

Immediately her eyes flew open, and she sat up, an expression of intensity suddenly flaring into her face. She handed him the papers and moved away a little in order to study him in unbroken concentration. Desperateness took over the contentment--desperateness for her writing to be fully accepted, to be more than good. Her every muscle tensed while he read and re-read. Heart pounding, she was still entirely unprepared for his reaction.

Without a word, Sterling leaned across the long grass, placed gentle fingers under her chin, bent his head, and touched his lips to hers. A shock ran through them both and the papers dropped from his hand. The moment—a jewel of time--thrilled Samantha to the core yet also frightened her. She did not know what these feelings meant or how to contain or explain them.

They pulled back at the same moment, both breathless. Samantha looked at him wide-eyed and uncertain.

Unsure himself, Sterling watched her expression and felt instantly sorry for his impulsiveness. He should not have done that! Miss Jennings did not understand, and now he had frightened her. He should have controlled himself! But how? Her writing...! Such passion, such fervor! She had carried him along on a fantastic journey through her mind and the workings of her spirit, away on wings he had never flown with before. It had done something to him deep inside his being, and by her concluding sentence, he had felt transcended beyond the world's grasp.

He really had not known any other way to tell her, to express his appreciation for every perfect word. And yes, he had felt a longing for her too.

He longed to understand her more, to comprehend the feelings of her heart. He had wanted to touch her, to feel the magic that surely flowed from her. If she had wanted to persuade him of the reality of fairies and their rings, he would have believed her now. She amazed him and he realized suddenly that this feeling had been coming on all summer. It was like nothing he had ever experienced.

His impetuous plan to spur them both into new and better writing had maybe worked a little too well!

She drew back, reminding him of a scared rabbit he had once seen in these very woods. But the intensity still lingered, and he could not tell if her trembling was born of excitement or fear.

"Miss Jennings... I-I'm sorry." Even as he said this, he realized how inadequate it sounded. Lately, it seemed that he had said these words to her often—and he had always meant them--but this time more than ever. "I did not mean to... It's just that..." He picked up the papers he had dropped and clumsily dusted them off. After a moment, he raised his eyes, mentally willing her to speak, to save him.

She remained silent. She saw the conflict in him, but words were beyond her just now.

"It's..." He lifted his shoulders helplessly and shook his head. "I have never read anything like this!" Gingerly he set the papers near her. He lowered his head again, trying to summon words that would be adequate.

"Th-then it's good?"

Sterling looked up to see the papers shaking in her hands as she retrieved them, the intensity like fire in her eyes. Expectancy showed in every line of her posture.

He let out something like a laugh, looking at her incredulously. "Oh, Miss Jennings, it's...*you* are...incredible! I can't describe..."

Samantha relaxed, and her expression took on his disbelief.

They said nothing more for many moments, Sterling still trying to gain a hold on reality, Samantha made entirely speechless by the revelation that her writing could affect this man--himself such a talented writer--so deeply. Both wondered wordlessly what the kiss had meant.

Eventually, Sterling arose, somewhat shakily, to gather his things, and Samantha watched him go. Then she stood, prepared to leave, and followed him out of the dense undergrowth to where Champion lazily grazed.

Sterling sent her off on the energetic young horse, then began the long walk home alone. He figured she would be more comfortable riding the huge stallion by herself than with him, the man who had intruded on her personal space. The man who had taken her off into the woods, far from any chaperone or public place, and who had kissed her without so much as a by your leave. That had not been part of his plan, of course, but he should have known better than to give into so much impulsivity in one afternoon! What was wrong with him?! He had been schooled in all of society's conventions since boyhood; he knew better! Fortunately, he also knew that Miss Jennings was knowledgeable enough about riding to be safe, and Champion knew his way back to town.

Sterling realized now that his rash dash to her house and headlong run to the forest had not been an appropriate way to behave with a young lady, no way for a gentleman to act. Not only had he dragged her away into the woods without pretext and undoubtedly frightened her out of her wits, but he had managed to do it all without taking into consideration her own desires or any protocol she wished to uphold. And it had not even been necessary to come out here at all. He had only thought so. *She came to trust me,* he lamented, *she communicated with me in a way she never has to anyone, in a way no other has to me, and I betrayed that trust.*

Passion was a good thing, a wonderful thing, yes, but only in its place! He trudged gravely along the many miles of country road, his guilt stabbing at him with every step. Could she ever trust him again? He felt like such a foolish, foolish boy.

Hot, sticky, and tired, Sterling arrived at the Jennings' mansion a couple of hours later. All was quiet, and he could see that no one was about. Champion stood at the gate, waiting for him, munching a mouthful of weeds and grasses, looking perfectly content. Sterling reached out and rubbed a hand over the horse's black mane. Champ showed every indication of having been cared for, his coat, clean and dry, with no hint of dried sweat, and his mane brushed through. Sterling was grateful for that.

"How are you, old boy?" he intoned softly, caressing the horse's muzzle. Champion stood still a moment, tolerating Sterling's touch, then lowered his head to tear off another mouthful.

Sterling sighed. "I suppose we should head home." He glanced at the mighty residence set far back from the road, willing a curtain to move--anything! But the mansion sat silent.

With a slow, disappointed sigh, Sterling turned back to his horse and began to prepare the saddle to mount. Then his hand touched something on the other side, where he had not seen. He walked around the horse and saw it: a slip of paper. Quickly he unfastened the string that held it in place and read two simple words: *Thank You.*

CHAPTER 6

MOVING ON

August 1901

During the following week, Samantha went about in a frenzy. Her energy spilled forth in abundance. There were not enough daylight hours to accomplish all she wished! She was compelled by an inner force that had not been present in her before, a momentum that pushed and pulled and demanded her attention. She had to write, that was all: no other questions or answers. And this time, nothing suppressed or restrained her. This time the clean pages in her notebook did not stare up at her blankly but seemed to smile in comradery. There was no end of things to write! It was as if, after so many years of silence, she had been given a voice. Now if her head ached, it was from writing too much instead of from trying so hard to figure out what to write. "Night owl Samantha" now found herself skipping down the massive staircase well before dawn to go for an early walk to "get the juices flowing," as Sterling would have said.

And Sterling was in her thoughts much of the time. When he sent her off on his own horse, leaving himself to walk, she had still been so stunned and unsteady by what had transpired that she made no protest. Indeed, she had ultimately appreciated the ride and enjoyed taking control of the big horse herself. It had helped to clear her head and have some space from Sterling to start processing what had just happened. She was unsure of why he sent her off on his horse alone, and she still didn't know what his kiss meant. Yet she fully expected him to keep their regular Wednesday appointment and looked forward to it, hoping answers would be forthcoming.

When Wednesday came, and she arrived at the schoolhouse, however, he wasn't there. This concerned her a little and she wondered why he did not come. She tried not to dwell on this particular worry and to remember, instead, all the good that had transpired over the past few months as she went about the rest of her week. This was not difficult, for what she had felt and experienced throughout the summer were not things she had ever known before, and the novelty was still heady. She wanted to remember the companionship they now shared, the sense of excitement that had arisen with their varied discussions. She remembered their need to communicate thoughts, opinions, and ideas and to find out what the other person thought in return. And at night, just before drifting into a dream-filled sleep, her fingers gently touched her lips where Sterling's own had pressed.

This same week of Samantha's great energy and direction, Sterling found himself unable to rid his spirit of its melancholy. His former confidence was replaced by self-degradation. He went about his teaching duties at the college in as much seclusion as he could manage. After a week of this, he suddenly realized that perhaps he knew now a tiny part of how Samantha had felt in the midst of her long Jennings' mansion silence. But thoughts of Samantha only drove him deeper into his melancholia.

Finally, he decided all he could do--the only way to push his life forward and continue--was to leave Oberlin. *Besides,* he tried to reason *I never meant to plant permanent roots. My role as a teacher is not thus. I teach and then move on. The quarter is at its end, and Samantha has, indeed, learned. My, how she has learned!* He shook his head in amazement as he recalled again what she had written in the woods.

So he made arrangements for departure, buying a train ticket for Columbus on a whim.

This sudden sense of purpose succeeded in alleviating his mood for a couple of days. But then, thoughts of leaving his favorite pupil threatened to return him to his previous mood. At the same time, the prospect of seeing her again frightened him—and nothing had frightened him for a long time. His writing no longer consoled him; his mind was too much in turmoil to allow concentration, even for reading. He found no pleasure in things he always had before and could hardly be prevailed upon to smile. His associates noted a change but could not quite lay a finger on what it might be or what could have caused it. And they did not know him well enough to find out.

***

The day Sterling left town was slightly overcast, the sun coming through the clouds hazy and tinted, the humidity almost visible in the shimmering air. The horse that pulled the cab shook his mane against the heat and snorted in discomfort. Sterling found himself in sympathy with the fellow.

"We're almost there, sir," the driver called, urging the horse on through the crowded streets. Turning to Sterling for reconfirmation, he asked, "Directly to the train station?"

Sterling nodded absently, scanning the town one last time as they rocked over the dirt streets. Oberlin was a mid-sized town, he supposed, but small according to his standards. He guessed there could not be more than 4,000 people here and probably less. It lacked some of the luxuries of the bigger cities, of course, but all in all, one could live fairly comfortably.

Things were different here, yes, but the rustic quality of it all held an innocence and charm for him that he had found nowhere else. He did not want to leave after all, he realized. Was he making a mistake? The buggy began to slow as they neared the train station, and the road grew more congested.

Suddenly, from the corner of his eye, he saw a familiar movement and turned instinctively to look. From across the road, Samantha was gazing up at him, wide straw hat firmly in place, braids shining, glasses glinting. She clasped a leather portfolio in one hand, a coin purse in the other, and seemed to have just emerged from Sorensen Hardware. Her eyes behind the wire rims were large and surprised--as surprised as his own, no doubt. He wanted to look away, to urge the driver on quickly, but an ambling line of cattle inconveniently moved across their path at that moment, forcing the buggy to halt.

He shifted uncomfortably under Samantha's gaze and his mind rushed to think of something to say.

"Sterling!" Her voice had a new quality about it that he didn't remember hearing before. Her expression was sober, though questioning, and held a depth of feeling he could not begin to interpret. She looked at him, her earnestness evident, and he felt captured by her gaze. He wanted to speak, to tell her anything to break free from that look!

But then the horse took up again, and they left her behind, her gaze compelling, a shimmering vibrance between them that was more than sunlight and humidity.

***

Samantha did not know for certain of Sterling's departure from Oberlin until several days after he left. She wondered where he was going that day she saw him, recognizing that he was heading toward the train station but hoping hard enough to convince herself that he was not really leaving for good. The news drifted slowly but steadily: some were disappointed (especially several of the young ladies), some relieved (his ideas had been altogether too liberal for their tastes), but most had had little or no association with him and treated the information nonchalantly.

To Samantha, the news hit like a blow and temporarily numbed her senses. For days she thought up possible reasons for his leaving. Had someone in town offended him? Had she offended him? But no, he was not the type to take offense easily or to pick up and leave over some perceived slight. Had he engaged in unsavory dealings...gambling perhaps?... and fled to avoid confrontation? No, that could not be it either, for Sterling was not a man with such vices and had always been a perfect gentleman, though he was a bit impulsive at times. She realized she had not even arranged payment for him—and after all he had done for her! The thought brought chagrin and regret, as she knew he deserved compensation for all the time and effort he had spent with her, despite his words to the contrary.

Then she thought, with a smile, of their frantic ride to the woods and the ensuing experience. Had he never taken her out there, she would perhaps have never learned the missing ingredient, the opening key, to her writing. She should have better expressed her gratitude to him while she had the chance. Surely he was not leaving because of what had happened between them that day...? The idea seemed too far-fetched. Strong, confident, and in control, Sterling would not run away after an unexpected kiss in the woods, would he? She was the one who had acted afraid and unsure! How confusing that their roles had reversed so completely; she wasn't sure what to make of it.

Finally, she came to the conclusion that Sterling was simply needed elsewhere. Perhaps his family had called him home to Kentucky, or more likely, he was just moving on to find others to teach. He had helped her progress to the point she needed to be and had therefore fulfilled his obligation as her teacher. But...why had he not informed her? It seemed strange he would not come and say his farewells, would not have mentioned his impending departure at their last meeting--or at the very least, said something to indicate his plans when they met in town.

At least I thanked him the last time, she remembered gratefully, recalling her verbal expression in the woods and her small note left on Champion's saddle. It was not enough, but at least it was something. *He did what he came here to do, and now he must move on. That is all.* And the idea satisfied her. At least, she told herself it did.

CHAPTER 7

AUCTION

September 1901

Sterling sat in his room, looking out the window in frustration. On the desk in front of him, crumpled and smudged papers lay in chaotic disarray. The mess looked exactly the way his mind felt! He sighed, short and brusque, angry with himself. Why could he not collect his thoughts?

Upon arriving in Columbus, he had discovered that he no longer thrived on city life and longed for somewhere slower-paced and quiet. And so, his inquiries into teaching positions had led him to Worthington. It was a small town only about twelve miles from Columbus, but it afforded him the space and peace he sought. Tomorrow he would begin teaching a class of seventh-year students at the Worthington Boys' School[11]--which he had so far had a difficult time working up any excitement over. He had spent two hours today trying to outline a lesson plan for one lousy subject, to no avail. He hoped his difficulty was only because this was the beginning, that it would get easier as time went on.

Impatiently, he set pencil to paper once again and wrote a few short lines. But each line said the same thing--and what it did say was dispassionate and completely uninteresting. The last thing he wanted to do was bore the poor children, but that was exactly the direction he was headed.

---

[11]Fictional

Adding to his inability to concentrate were four lines from a poem by Ben Jonson called "Song to Celia"[12] that he had come across in his preparations. The words kept running through his mind, and refused to be ignored. The poem was not one he would teach these boys, for they were still too young to appreciate or enjoy it, but in his search through his favorite book of collected poems, his eye had happened to fall upon this one whose language he had always enjoyed but which now meant something for the first time:

Drink to me only with thine eyes,
And I will pledge with mine;
Or leave a kiss but in the cup,
And I'll not look for wine.

Now the words seemed to apply directly to him and his time with Samantha. He knew what it was to drink to her with his eyes, to feel that his soul would always be thirsty for her presence. No pledge had been exchanged between them, yet instead of leaving "a kiss but in the cup," he had dared to leave one on her lips in that spontaneous, brazen way he must conquer. He wished he had not done it, oh how he wished it! But at the same time, he could not forget it or the way it had felt, for he had been looking for wine, and he had tasted the headiest, most delicious drop of it imaginable.

But memories, whether painful or joyful, would not prepare him for his first week of teaching.

Angrily, he threw the pencil across the room, its tip breaking against the wall, and stood up so abruptly that the chair fell backward with a bang. In a few quick sweeps, he left the room, suitcoat in hand,

---

[12] https://www.poetryfoundation.org/poems/44464/song-to-celia-drink-to-me-only-with-thine-eyes

and hurtled down the boardinghouse steps into bright outdoor sunlight.

A few moments later, he strode along tree-lined High Street and made his steady way to Stanton Avenue, a strong breeze teasing through his dark hair and ruffling his shirt. His long legs took a harsh pace, the muscles of his broad shoulders rippling beneath his shirt as his arms swung with momentum. Gradually the peace of the afternoon began to soothe his tumult. His fists relaxed, the taut line of his forehead smoothed, and after a time, even his pace slowed.

Walking along Stanton Avenue, he soon reached the fence marking the property of Walnut Grove Cemetery and slipped through a wide, wooden fence marking the property. He strode out across the great expanse of green, the well-kept tombstones protected by high, graceful trees. He knew he could find serenity here among the history of old pioneers.

***

Samantha studied the sign, contemplative. It read, in large block letters: ANNUAL AUCTION TO BE HELD NEXT THURSDAY AT NOON. PROCEEDS DONATED TO THE LATE EDWIN SMITH FAMILY. She knew she would have nothing better to do that day other than her writing, and she had never been to the auction before, though she was aware that it happened every year for different causes. These days she seemed to "get out" more and desired to socialize a little--something she had never wanted to do before. Yes, she supposed an auction would be interesting, even exciting. And she would bring money along just in case something happened to catch her fancy. She had never really bought anything just for the pleasure of it, and she felt daring even to think of it. Besides, it was for a very good cause.

In fact, when the day came, and she stood there looking at what was being offered, listening to the auctioneer's quick, lilting call, she felt so daring that she made a bid on Sterling's horse. She had not known he left his horse behind or that it would be up for bid at the auction, but the competition was more exhilarating than Samantha would have guessed, and winning felt even better.

"She looks like the old professor's daughter," she heard someone say afterward. "I guess she can afford a horse like that."

Samantha blushed a little to hear this, for she knew she had spent an awful lot of money, which to her seemed almost scandalous. But she knew enough about horses to recognize quality horse flesh when she saw it. Purely from an investment point of view, of course. That was what she told herself, but she knew there were other, more personal reasons why she wanted Champion, and so ultimately, the victory greatly exceeded the cost. She and Champion would get along well, she knew, and though he may have thrown many a rider, he would never throw her.

***

Sterling's walk through the cemetery had renewed him, started his thoughts flowing again, and lifted much of his depression. On returning to the desk, he finished his lesson plan in an hour. With that completed, however, his spirits plummeted again, dropping him once more into dissatisfaction and discontent. Why could he not shake off these feelings? It was all starting to wear him down.

After the first week of teaching, Sterling felt a little more in control and a little less nervous about his new job. Teaching children was so different from teaching young adults! But the days passed smoothly, and his students seemed to be learning. However, where a day of teaching had always left him feeling satisfied and complete before, now he felt an absence of both. He felt disconnected, disjointed, and at odds with his spirit. The question Miss Jennings asked of him in the woods still pricked at his brain, needling him for an answer. Yet he still did know what dream he had—or should have—that meant everything to him. What did he want out of life? What was the point?

His students seemed somewhat aware of his inner chaos. At times he caught the boys looking at each other, eyebrows raised, questioning, and sometimes laughing at each other behind their hands. Though this grated on Sterling, he ignored it the best he could. He knew he had to reign himself in and immerse himself in his work and his students. If he could only devote himself to them, he'd be more than successful--peace of mind might finally take hold of him again!

CHAPTER 8

CHANGES

September 1901

There were a lot of things Samantha wanted to learn—and many she needed to learn. Now with a beautiful stallion on her hands, she realized more fully how little she really knew about horses. She almost wished she had not been so impulsive in buying him at the auction, for it was all a little frightening, but she did still want him and was determined to put her fears and ignorance behind her.

The first logical person for her to talk to about the matter was the live-in handyman who looked after Professor Jennings's cow, mule, and two old horses and who had been with the family almost as long as Mrs. Dolittle. Samantha had never had a real conversation with Martin before, but she was determined to start and approached him early one morning. She called his name as she saw him walk into the stables, a little bent now in his later years. He turned and lifted a hand, surprised to see her there. The sunrise filtering through the trees highlighted each leaf of the aspens, each needle of the pines in a warm, golden-pink glow that thrilled Samantha. She longed to walk out among the trees and write what she felt but reminded herself that there was a time for everything. *And now is the time to learn how best to care for my beast.*

Samantha joined the old man in the doorway, and they entered the large stable together. She explained her predicament to him and watched his eyes grow round as he heard her story. He gazed appreciatively at the mighty horse whose presence seemed to fill the

75

entire stable and, walking with her to his stall, ran a reverent hand along Champion's flank.

"You surely have a good eye for horse flesh, Miss." He whistled low between his teeth, and Champion's ears swiveled toward the sound. "I saw him weeks ago, that day you brought him home, and I've never forgotten. I brushed him down for you while he waited for his master."

"Yes, thank you for that."

"I couldn't believe my good luck at being able to care for such a horse." Martin smoothed his grizzled beard in thought. "Then he came back, and I wondered where he came from." He turned to Samantha. "But then," he admitted, "I heard all about it from my old friend who works at the Hampton place." He smiled at her with a twinkle in his eyes that told her he could not quite believe she had done such an impetuous, marvelous thing. He turned his attention back to Champion. "What a horse. What a horse," he kept saying, shaking his head. "It will be an honor to tend to him, Miss."

"Thank you, Martin, but I really must learn to do it myself. I would greatly appreciate it if you would teach me how to be a good horsewoman. I am fond of the creature and want to do right by him."

"Oh, right you are. Right you are," Martin responded, a little absently, as he continued to stroke the horse.

Samantha spent the better part of the morning learning the particulars of horse care. Perhaps she could have learned everything more quickly, but Martin was a very thorough teacher and had had so many experiences with horses that he easily took tangents that required Samantha's careful steering to direct him back on course.

She enjoyed the time with both the horse and the old stable hand and was sincerely grateful for Martin's willingness to share his expertise.

When Martin seemed to be running out of things to teach and stories to tell her, Samantha expressed her gratitude to him, brushing hay from her dress and preparing to return to the house. "You have taught me so much—all of it valuable—that I am afraid I will not remember it all when I am doing it on my own!"

Martin returned her laugh with a slow grin of his own and shook his gray head. "No matter, Miss. It does this old heart good to reminisce a bit. Apologize for my ramblings. Anytime you have a question, just let me know. I'd be pleased to run it by you again."

Samantha thanked him once more, patted Champion's flank, and returned to the house to wash up and gather a picnic lunch for herself.

Plump Mrs. Dolittle visibly started when Samantha entered the kitchen, then shook her head. "I just can't get used to the changes in you, Samantha girl! Your...energy...is so unusual."

Samantha smiled absently and pushed her head farther in the cupboard to see if they still had that box of biscuits she remembered seeing the other day.

Realizing what the girl was up to, Mrs. Dolittle lined a covered basket with a large blue and white checkered napkin and began loading into it the items Samantha placed on the counter.

"The Samantha of a couple of months ago would never have poked through the icebox and cupboards nor hummed to herself as you do." She wondered what had happened to create this new, radiant girl. She practically flitted, butterfly-like, from one place to the next, whereas not three months ago, she had been a mole, sitting holed up in the study day after day. It was a puzzle. Indeed it was. But a delightful change! If she, herself, were young and energetic, she would want to join Samantha on a nice little picnic, as well. But at least she could see her on her way, well stocked, and hope to hear about the outing later. It really was a beautiful day, despite the heat.

A few days later, Samantha succeeded without too much difficulty in securing Champion's saddle, bridle, bit, and reins. She felt a bit sweaty and dirty afterward but triumphant in the success of her first attempts with the huge horse. She had not only retained the information Martin had imparted to her so far but had completed the task herself! She caressed the coarse, black hair of Champion's mane and thanked him for his relative patience. She could tell he was excited at the prospect of exercise but held himself in check for her sake.

As they set off, Samantha could not help but grin. Though she felt a little awkward and more than a little frightened, it was delicious, riding high on the great Champion, to feel such barely-controlled power beneath her. When she had ridden him home from the woods that day, she had not quite appreciated this feeling, but now she couldn't ignore it if she tried. She leaned forward and told him quietly, "I will let you run, I promise—but not yet." Once they had trotted up the road to where it became two worn wheel-rut tracks with a strip of lumpy grass growing in between, Samantha turned the stallion's head and guided him carefully through the trees. The day was growing uncomfortably warm and both horse and rider were already dampened with perspiration, but Samantha did not notice as she intently focused on riding and taking in the scenery about her.

Eventually, the trees thinned into a meadow with tall, flowing grasses and a few scattered groups of tall wild sunflowers with small, cheerful heads. Sprinkled liberally throughout the meadow were many charming Flowering Spurge with their little white five-petaled faces spread to the sun. Champion, sensing his moment, broke into a run. Samantha sucked in a gulp of air in surprise and clutched the reins tightly. She guessed she had a lot more to learn about horses than one morning with Martin would allow. But perhaps this horse was also more unpredictable than most...like his previous owner. Had Champion made Sterling impulsive, or had Sterling's natural flair for the spontaneous rubbed off on his stallion? Or had they both come naturally and independently from these traits?

Other inconsequential questions flashed through Samantha's mind as she worked to maintain her balance on the galloping horse, to learn his rhythm and mold her body to it. Champion picked up speed as they descended a rolling hill, and Samantha felt her hair coming ever more free of its plaits, flowing wildly behind her. She loosened her panicked grip on the reins and bent forward, relaxing into the stallion's motion. This was more glorious than she had remembered! She laughed out loud--she couldn't help herself.

The moment brought a certain memory sharply into the focus of Sterling seated in front of her and the feel of her arms around his firm middle, her cheek pressed against his warm back. She could still remember the hardness of his muscles and how it felt to feel his breathing and heartbeat through his back. She remembered that her panic had melted into surprise and then, by the end of the ride, into wonder. The whole sensory experience had been a defining moment for her, she realized suddenly. She did not know why, but that ride had provided the impetus to write in a way she would have never

79

thought possible—as if that dash through the forest had added the remaining ingredient that magically broke the spell holding back her creativity.

As long as she was thinking about these things, she might as well include something else. She had not even known the doubt was there, but when Sterling kissed her, she had suddenly felt the incredibleness of someone—anyone—wanting her that way. She knew now that she had not fully recovered from the novelty of Sterling's interest in her: First as a pupil, then as an intelligent person for whom he desired success, then as someone more. It was all so new to her. Without knowing it, she had subconsciously decided years ago that she would be an old maid forever, content to read her books in the dusty, shadowed library all her days. Well, now that unintentional decision had dissolved, she knew she could never again convince herself that such a colorless picture of the future would satisfy her.

In addition to imagining her future, she had recently tried contemplating her past. But nothing much came to mind besides her seventeen years of self-isolation and buried heartaches. What was there between her father and herself that had never allowed her to know him very well? And why did she know next to nothing about her mother? In all her ruminations about the matter, it was becoming apparent to Samantha that knowing herself would require a better knowledge of who her parents were and where she came from. But how could she gain that knowledge? Her father had never been one to encourage conversation, so Samantha hadn't learned to talk with him. But there had to be a way to learn what she needed to know... Learning, at least, was something she had always been good at.

Samantha allowed Champion to run to his heart's content and exulted in his joy until, at last, she began to feel a little sore with the unaccustomed riding. She slowed his gait, then, and directed him to a shady place beneath a tree at the edge of the meadow. There, while her horse grazed nearby, Samantha released the thoughts of her heart until her wrist ached.

In an effort to make good on her resolve to stay abreast of current events and the state of the world (and for reasons reminiscent of Sterling), Samantha began buying a copy of the Oberlin Tribune almost every week. She poured over each page until she knew everything in it almost by heart. This exercise brought her a measure of satisfaction and confidence that she was really aware of her world and could intelligently converse about it. Though she knew Oberlin was just a small northern corner of Ohio and she was only one insignificant person in it, reading the newspaper made her feel part of something bigger. And the connection she felt to the present world was so different from her link to the history found in her father's library. She felt as if it grounded her geographically and within humanity, a more whole connection than she had felt before.

But on the sixth of September, Samantha, along with the rest of the nation, was shocked and shaken by the news that native Ohioan, President William McKinley, had been shot down in an assassination attempt at the Pan-American Exposition in Buffalo, New York.[13] The President survived a few more days while the nation held its breath, but died in the wee hours of the morning on September 14th. It was reported that 100,000 mourners paid their last respects while his body lay in state in the Buffalo City Hall. Only the day before, Theodore Roosevelt had been sworn in as the twenty-sixth president of the United States. She remembered with sadness her discussion with

---

[13] https://en.wikipedia.org/wiki/Assassination_of_William_McKinley

Sterling about the President and his new Vice President. Little had they known that Pres. Mckinley's second term would be so short!

In a little over one week, the country's leadership had undergone a sudden, unexpected change, and Samantha could not help but recognize the parallel to her own changing life. What would the future bring for both her and her country? It seemed that whenever she felt content and that things were going well and predictably, the proverbial wrench was thrown into the wheel. It appeared that, indeed, nothing was ever certain except change. Into her mind came the wise words of Benjamin Franklin: "When you're finished changing, you're finished." She supposed that must be true—and she wasn't finished yet!

CHAPTER 9

FACE THE CAUSE

September 1901

Sterling sat in the empty classroom staring at scuff marks on the wooden floor between the desks, trying to think of something more to add to his lesson plan for the next day. That seemed to be what he was forever trying to do: more!

A fortnight had passed since school began, and still, he found himself reaching and running after ideas that barely eluded his grasp. It was so frustrating not being able to achieve the level of performance he had always met before with the kind of teaching he was used to. When he had finally decided to accept this position that was so graciously offered him, he had vowed once and for all to give up his "modern" ideas and just stick to good, old, traditional teaching. He would hammer away at "readin,' writin,' and 'rithmetic" like most teachers he knew and try to make the best of it. Those newfangled ideas he had learned at the University of Cincinnati had gotten him nowhere but trouble in the end.

He felt he was going nowhere at all—the students were going nowhere--yet the school's superintendent had found time to personally congratulate Sterling on his "excellent work with the boys" and the "commendable progress" they were making. Sterling found it difficult to appreciate this, despite the superintendent's good intentions, for he felt he deserved none of it, and he had not personally recognized much progress in his students yet. But maybe he was expecting too much from the young boys.

His eyes shifted to the streaked chalkboard across the room with its yet un-erased rows of numbers. How boring they looked! True, arithmetic had never appealed to him like language, literature, and writing, but it could be made interesting if one worked at it long enough. Yet he had spent more than twice as long on his lesson plans the last few days, and they still had not evolved into anything particularly interesting.

The thing of greatest interest to him all day was a writing prompt he had written on the blackboard at the front of the room and the ensuing short discussion it generated. The quote still looked out at him from its place on the blackboard as if to reprove his melancholy:

"Thy fate is the common fate of all;
Into each life, some rain must fall."
-Henry Wadsworth Longfellow

As Sterling read the words again, his mind unwittingly returned to his discussion with Miss Jennings about rain. *But the rain Longfellow speaks of is not that kind of rain*, he thought ruefully. *This rain has no joy in it. It is cold and unfriendly, and heartless. It is rain that no one wants to fall upon his life, but which is a part of life. So why can I not accept that, dry myself off, and remember to carry an umbrella next time?*

He caught himself wishing that he could be back in Oberlin with Samantha, philosophizing on the subject and hearing her insights.

"What is wrong with me?" he angrily asked himself with a slam of his fist against the desk.

"What was that my young friend?" a man returned, poking his head around the doorframe. He had a pleasant, intelligent face and looked at Sterling expectantly.

Sterling straightened quickly and raised his head to the door. He smiled ruefully at the superintendent and said apologetically, "I am only frustrated with myself, sir. Nothing more."

"Nothing less, no doubt," came the reply as the man entered the room.

Sterling nodded and leaned back against the chair again. "Actually, you are exactly right," he admitted.

"Is there anything I can do?" the superintendent asked, taking a seat at one of the desks. He was a slight man and looked younger than his years, despite the shiny crown fringed with graying hair.

"I wish there were! I honestly don't know what the problem is." Sterling shook his head and shrugged in a gesture of exasperation. "But," he waved a dismissive hand, "I don't want to take up your time. I know you are a busy man...."

The superintendent shrugged easily and smiled at Sterling, pushing his glasses up slightly with one finger. "This is part of my job, my boy. I am here to help."

Sterling lowered his head to the sheaf of papers and attempted to straighten them. "I really doubt you can help me—begging your pardon, sir."

"Try me, my friend. Perhaps you are right, but I think the trying would help you feel better."

The papers in Sterling's hands stilled as he reflected. Finally, he looked up and nodded. "I suppose it would." He laid down the papers and clasped his hands together on the desk. "Well, make yourself comfortable. This may take a while."

Sterling told him everything he thought necessary about his teaching predicament, appreciative of the murmured agreements, and nodded understanding. He felt comfortable with the superintendent and even forgot for a while that this man had the power to release him should he find it necessary. Then he asked his advice on the matter. "I don't know how much of this is just my perspective and how much is reality." He shook his head unhappily. "I just don't know, sir! I want to do right by these boys, and I keep trying, but I'm honestly not sure if I am cut out for this kind of teaching." He sighed once more and gave the superintendent an imploring glance, then sat back, relaxed, and laughed at himself with another shake of the head.

"Well, Mr. Sterling, I do not believe you are a hopeless case, not by a long shot—and please, call me Mr. Grover; I am not much fond of formality."

Sterling nodded. "And just plain 'Sterling' will do for me."

"All right, 'just plain Sterling,'" Mr. Grover said, his eyes twinkling. "Here is what I think. Your predicament is a little different from our typical teacher here, I must admit. However, plenty of teachers struggle with many of the same things with which you are wrestling. Sometimes those of us on the administration end of education see a teacher who tries less than his best. It is always gratifying to meet teachers like yourself who worry over the possibility of not being the best of their very best. I think perhaps I may be able to offer some suggestions after all. I do not pride myself on wisdom, but age can have its advantages." Mr. Grover's face was alight with good humor, and Sterling felt himself relaxing more, allowing part of his burden to be shared for once.

"...I would encourage you, my friend, to involve yourself more thoroughly in the lives of your young pupils. Perhaps keep yourself abreast of their after-school activities and attend a few. I do not want you to feel restrained by the requirements and regulations of what the system expects you to teach, but to go to work *working with* the students, *learning* with them."

Sterling frowned and nodded thoughtfully. "That makes sense."

Mr. Grover's eyes rose to the ceiling as he considered his next words, then continued. "Try to be less of the removed, dictatorial teacher and more of the knowledgeable adult who is open to more learning, and you may find the boys opening up to you and becoming more teachable. But mind you, don't let them take control, for they are liable to do that if given the chance." He chuckled. "There is a fine line there, and it takes practice learning the balance.

He looked hard at Sterling and then nodded knowingly. "I think what you need is to feel the small, more immediate rewards that make teaching enjoyable and help you keep going. How about more rewards and fewer batters over the head with self-reproach...." Mr. Grover's bushy eyebrows rose in question as he waited for Sterling's response, but seeing his serious expression, Mr. Grover began to laugh. "Ease up, man! I am not worried about you letting things slide and failing to teach the curriculum. You will find the right balance between academic learning and real-world learning. I have no doubt. Relax a little and let the boys teach you something. Find humor in what amuses them and recognize what interests them. You may be surprised at what you find."

Sterling was silent a moment. He nodded contemplatively as if tasting the idea for a moment. Finding it good, he nodded decisively, then firmly answered, "I shall do my best."

"But not over and above that, mind you," Mr. Grover returned, pointing at him with a commanding finger and a smile as he rose to leave.

"Yes, sir—I-I mean, yes, Mr. Grover."

"And you need not always be the epitome of all seriousness," the superintendent added with a laugh.

"I'm sorry, Mr. Grover. I have not always been this way, believe me."

"Oh, I believe you." Mr. Grover's face still creased with a faint smile.

Sterling rose and walked around the desk to meet Mr. Grover. They shook hands warmly, and Sterling thanked him gratefully for his time and advice. Mr. Grover waved a hand in dismissal. "Any time, my young friend. Whenever I can do anything more for you, just give me a holler."

Sterling nodded his assent, and Mr. Grover paused at the door. "Oh. One other thing. If you truly want this whole problem resolved, I would advise you to face the cause of it, whatever it—or she—is. Good luck to you!" And he was gone, with a cheery whistle and a light step.

Sterling could only blink.

He took another walk through the cemetery that evening and contemplated what Mr. Grover had told him. He could see the wisdom in his advice and decided to do as he suggested. Soon he was attending such events as his pupils' baseball games and piano recitals. Seeing his students involved in activities outside of school helped him to understand them better and know where they were coming from. For the students, having their teacher support them in their extra-curricular interests broke down barriers and made them feel comfortable enough, at times, to confide in him when they had academic difficulties they needed help with. And they began to make more of a concerted effort to learn the things he tried to teach them in school. Parents began inviting him into their homes for supper, and he started becoming involved in important local events.

Sterling noticed one boy in particular: a freckled, lanky redhead named Jerome Tomlinson, who struggled in nearly every subject. Into the fourth week of school, it became apparent to Sterling that Jerome was falling behind and seemed to have stored up quite a bit of resentment as well. Sterling kept an eye on him and deliberated on a course of action. Most of the other boys only spoke to Jerome if it were unavoidable. Jerome didn't seem to have many friends but carried an attitude of indifference. Sterling wondered what his home life was like and if he were getting the positive attention he needed. Since the boys wore uniforms, Jerome's appearance looked the same as all the others and gave no indication of his economic standing. Sterling tried to find out what Jerome was involved in outside of school, but either the boy really was not involved in anything, or he just did not want to talk about it, for Sterling got nowhere with his questioning.

Jerome did not seem to want to talk about many things, Sterling noted, so he determined to pay close attention and observe what kinds of things might interest him. If he could find a clue, an angle to work from, he would perhaps have some way to reach the boy.

At the end of the fifth week of school, Jerome had a particularly bad day during which he answered very few questions correctly and spoke derisively to anyone who talked to him, managing to retain only a modicum of respect for the teacher. At lunchtime, as the boys headed outside, Sterling placed a hand on Jerome's shoulder.

Jerome stiffened and turned to look at Sterling. The momentary fear in his eyes was instantly covered by defiance, and he drew himself up as tall as he could manage. "Yes, sir?" he asked tightly.

"Jerome," Sterling said quietly so the other boys still in the room would be less likely to hear him, "would you mind staying behind a moment? I would like to ask your advice on something."

Jerome's light red brows furrowed, and his attitude softened a little. Sterling could tell he was surprised and curious.

Sterling returned to his desk to busy himself until everyone had filed out and the loud stomping across the floorboards ceased. Then one pair of feet clomped slowly across the room, and Jerome stood before him, expectant. "Yes, Mr. Sterling, sir?" His voice was still hard, and he sounded as if he were trying not to sound too interested.

Sterling looked up at him and smiled. "Thank you for taking time out of your lunch to help me," he said. "You see, I have this problem with my desk. It's given me grief since I arrived, and I have never been one for carpentry."

The freckled face relaxed, but Jerome asked, still a little suspicious, "How did you know I fix things?"

"Oh," Sterling said lightly, inwardly relieved he had guessed correctly, "I didn't know. You just seemed the type. I've talked to Mr. Grover about my desk, but he has been so busy with more important things that he hasn't gotten around to it yet. I thought maybe if you could help me, we would not have to bother him again. And...perhaps you could teach me what my father could never get me to figure out when I was younger."

"Teach you?" Jerome asked, his shoulders relaxing even more, but a confused expression troubling his features.

"Yes... You know: how things fit together, and what to use to fix them, that kind of thing. I was never interested in anything of that nature as a boy, and so, in the end, my father could not teach me. But now I wish I had learned," he said ruefully.

He waited a moment while Jerome stood uncertainly before him. "What do you think?"

"Well," Jerome said finally, "I fix everything at home—I'm the man of the house, you know--so I could probably help you out." Sterling thought he detected a little pride in the boy's voice at this pronouncement.

"That would be very much appreciated," he replied, honestly grateful. "Let me show you. Come around to this side and look at this drawer." He stood up and bent to pull on the stubborn drawer. "See. It sticks."

91

Jerome felt the drawer and tried it himself, then nodded thoughtfully. "I've fixed one like this before. It wasn't too difficult. My tools are at home, though. Could I bring them tomorrow and work on it after school?"

Sterling smiled and nodded. "Of course. Whatever works best for you. I always stay after for a while. And...well, maybe while you're at it, you could fix that desk two rows back on the left, as well. It has a leg that does not quite reach the floor, and I've noticed how it rocks and jiggles whenever the student sits in it."

Jerome trudged across the room to examine the other desk and seemed to understand immediately what needed to be done. "That will be easy to fix, too," he declared confidently, straightening up.

"Thank you, Jerome. I'd be much obliged to you."

Jerome nodded once, quickly, retrieved his lunch pail from the shelf at the back of the room, and clomped down the steps outside without another word.

Sterling smiled to himself and rubbed his slightly stubbled chin. He had a feeling this was going to be a good thing for both of them.

CHAPTER 10

STRUGGLING TO EMULATE

September 1901

After a morning of writing and contemplation, partially in preparation for an essay contest, she was thinking of entering. Samantha headed to the kitchen for something to eat. Somehow, writing always made her hungry, but that was not the only reason she wanted to go to the kitchen. After weeks of deliberation and formulating questions, she had decided that her best hope for filling in the gaps of her past was to pose her questions to Mrs. Dolittle. She actually knew very little about the housekeeper's personal life and background, but she did know that she had come to work for the Jenningses before Samantha was born and, therefore, ought to know something. Even if she had no close connections with Samantha's parents, hired help sometimes knew more about their employers than the employers themselves, so this seemed like a feasible plan. Didn't it? Samantha sure hoped so.

She walked into the sunlit kitchen and was relieved to see Mrs. Dolittle at the wood stove, where a small teapot gently steamed as it steeped the herbal tea she loved so well. The large windows above the sink and at the side door were open, and a languid breeze washed through the room, almost from one end to the other.

The round, gray-haired woman turned and, seeing Samantha in the doorway, smiled easily. "Hello, Samantha! I thought you might soon be hungry. I made a few sandwiches and sliced some of that cake left over from yesterday. Would you like some?"

93

"Yes. Please." Suddenly, at the prospect of what she was about to do, Samantha did not feel hungry anymore. But she placed a couple of plates, utensils, and napkins on the table and then took a seat.

Too anxious to sit long or to wait for Mrs. Dolittle to sit across from her, Samantha took a deep breath and plunged into the question she had wanted to ask for so long. "Mrs. Dolittle, I need to ask you a question."

The woman looked up in surprise from the cake and sandwiches she was piling on a plate, and then her face slowly softened into a smile, the laugh lines at the corners of her eyes deepening. "Ask away, child."

All of a sudden, Samantha did not feel ready for what she was about to ask. She did not know how to word it, but after a moment's pause, she plunged ahead anyway. "What...what can you tell me about my mother?" She sounded terribly abrupt, even to herself.

Mrs. Dolittle looked at her with large dark eyes, momentarily stunned, and for a long moment, seemed to have forgotten the food entirely, but she quickly recovered and nodded. "I suppose it is about time you asked such a question. I thought you would never ask, but I can see you are ready now." She thought a moment and added, "You've changed so much in the last while, my dear. I would hardly know you if I hadn't seen it coming on gradually."

Samantha was gratified to hear those words and the tone with which they were spoken, but she would not be distracted. "Please, I am ready to learn about my mother now. Father has hardly spoken two words together about her my whole life, and I want...I *need* to know why."

Mrs. Dolittle looked at her fondly, then turned back to the stove where the sweet, earthy smell of the herbal tea beckoned. With a corner of her apron, she removed the lid and poured two teacups full. Samantha carried the cups to the little table and set them in front of the two chairs while Mrs. Dolittle set the sandwich plate in the middle. After placing a small pot of honey with a spoon between the two place settings, she settled into the chair opposite Samantha and gingerly raised the warm cup with two surprisingly slender brown fingers.

"I've waited a long time to tell you these things, my dear," she began. She took a sip of her steaming tea and then set it down, looking very serious. "The professor—your father—has never liked me to speak of her."

Samantha felt a flood of anxiety rise up within her at these words and tensed herself, ready to defend her position and stubbornly persist if need be.

But the woman continued, and Samantha relaxed again as she said, "But he isn't here with us, and you do need to know. I can see that. You have a right to know. And your father should understand that much." She wagged a finger at Samantha. "He told me long ago that if you ever asked, I could tell you, but only then."

Relief washed over Samantha.

Mrs. Dolittle looked down into her tea for a long moment as if it would tell her how best to proceed. "Oh, child," she said finally. "Your mother was such a fine, dear woman, and your father doted on her so." She raised her head, and Samantha could see the misty, harking-back look in those dark eyes. "She was the best thing that ever happened to him. That was why her...passing...almost ended him.

95

I've never seen a man so distraught and...distracted by grief as he was. If it had not been for his need to care for you, his new girl-child—the way you demanded that he give of himself--" Mrs. Dolittle smiled wryly for a moment and then grew serious again, "he would easily have followed Lovenia to the grave."

This simple revelation affected Samantha to the core as she thought of the distant, infinitely closed man she knew. That he could feel so deeply about the gentle phantom who was her mother made her thoughts of him stumble in confusion. Suddenly, she felt as if a long, cold finger had wound its way through her chest and around her heart. An even more powerful longing rose up, warm, to push the coldness out, a longing to know the woman who had so captivated her father in life and all but taken his spirit with her in death.

Samantha looked at Mrs. Dolittle intently, her blond brows knitted together hard. "I know she died when I was born," she began slowly, "but please tell me why it happened... How...? I know next to nothing..."

Mrs. Dolittle shook her head sadly, setting the cup down after taking a sip. "Only the dear Lord knows why, but I can tell you how. I did not know your parents until a couple of years before your mother's death when they moved here and hired me. But over the years, because of my contact with your father and the facts that I pieced together, I think I have a pretty accurate picture of what happened. I know they met in Worthington, where they both lived at the time, and that Lovenia never had a strong constitution. Perhaps her delicateness and dependency were part of what endeared her to your father, for it seems that he felt a strong desire to protect and strengthen her. Of course, the difference in their ages could have accounted for this too, since he was seventeen years her senior."

Samantha nodded. She did remember that about her parents.

"Lovenia was so trusting, so loving, that Basil's stiff, aching heart finally began to mend after a lifetime of heartache. They were married after a sufficiently long courtship when she was twenty-one, and he was thirty-eight years of age. I would venture to say that the professor has ever been a quiet and solitary man, but with Lovenia in his life, he was no longer lonely in his quietness. He cared for her and tried to make her strong and whole the way she had made him feel, but a year later, when she bore a baby boy, it nearly killed her. As it was, the baby died, poor little mite. And Lovenia wavered between life and death for weeks, then remained very weak for months after that."

Mrs. Dolittle looked at Samantha through the memories and noticed that the girl's gray eyes were wide as if all this overwhelming information and the emotion it contained were filling her brain beyond capacity.

"I'm sorry, Samantha," Mrs. Dolittle patted her hand across the table and looked at her in concern. "Perhaps hearing all this at once is too much for you. I suppose I ought to go more slowly."

Samantha shook her head dumbly, then shook it again, more vigorously. "No," she answered firmly. "No. It is a lot to take in, but it is also...well...it is also good to hear, to finally know details. Please continue." And then softly and dazedly, as if she were the only one in the room, "I had a brother? Father had a son? Why have I never known?"

97

Mrs. Dolittle's brown cheeks rose in a sad, gentle smile. "The death of that baby nearly broke your father's heart too, but as he still had your mother, he could bear it. The doctor told Lovenia that trying to have another child would kill her, that she was too small-boned and weak to ever make childbearing possible. And that, though not entirely unexpected, was another blow to your mother that grieved her deeply."

Mrs. Dolittle sat quietly for a moment, and Samantha wondered what she was thinking. Then she blinked as if to clear her mind of too-close memories and continued. "As I recall, she was part of a fairly large family—she had a few sisters and a brother—and she had always dreamt of having enough children to 'fill a house with.' Your father, in a real fear for her life, insisted that they obey the doctor's orders to the letter and, in addition, did everything he could think of to bolster Lovenia's strength. With his kindness and concern, he tried to make her forget the baby she lost and the little ones she would never have." Mrs. Dolittle's dark eyes filled with tears, and she used her napkin to dab at them.

Samantha swallowed the huge lump that had suddenly risen in her throat. The food was all but forgotten. How had Mrs. Dolittle learned so much about the past that she, Samantha, should have known but was completely ignorant of? Hearing from the housekeeper about her own family's history gave her a strange sensation. The woman was a greater wealth of information than she had even hoped. And she had been here all the time, but Samantha had never asked. Why had she never asked? Why had she never really tried to talk to her?

Mrs. Dolittle cleared her throat and gave a watery smile. "I always get weepy thinking of the difficult times that sweet young woman had to pass through. And your father too."

In all the years Samantha had known Mrs. Dolittle—her entire life—she had never realized the woman cared so deeply for her parents. For the first time, it struck her how ironic the name Dolittle was, too, considering how very much the housekeeper did to keep the Jennings household running. And then a surprising thought struck her. If Mrs. Dolittle still felt so strongly about Lovenia Lewis Jennings, who had been dead for seventeen years, how might she feel about Samantha, whom she had watched after (in a removed sort of way) ever since? Samantha realized again that her complete absorption in the lives of book characters and historical events had previously blinded her to Mrs. Dolittle's real care for her and her father. She had honestly always just seemed part of the woodwork as if she belonged with the house, Samantha recognized with chagrin. Mrs. Dolittle had always chattered on and never seemed to mind when Samantha paid her little notice. But could it be that she had hoped for someone to listen to her with an open heart and accept the love she desired to give? For she could see that love now, obvious in Mrs. Dolittle's eyes. Now the lump rose again in Samantha's throat, and her eyes filled with tears.

"Thank you for telling me all this, Mrs. Dolittle. I... I feel I must apologize for not paying much notice to you in the past. I am certain you were a comfort to Mother. And you do so much for Father and me, but we take it all for granted, and I—"

Mrs. Dolittle waved a dismissing hand and shook her head. "No matter, my dear, no matter. I have been as happy here as I could hope to be anywhere. And talking with you like this does my old heart good." Then in the brief silence that fell upon the two women, Mrs. Dolittle finished her tea quickly as if to give herself something to do to keep more tears from appearing.

"More tea?" she asked Samantha, who started slightly, realizing she had not yet touched it, and declined.

"I hope you do not mind, but I still have so many questions—more, actually, than before."

Mrs. Dolittle chuckled and patted the napkin to her mouth. "I don't mind. I am glad--very glad!--to answer any questions I can."

"Well, then... How long after the baby boy—my brother—died did my parents move here from Worthington?"

"Well, if I remember right, another three or four years passed before your father dared to make the trip. By that time, Lovenia seemed strong enough and had urged him for some time to pursue his desire to teach at Oberlin College. She was eager for him to have that opportunity, especially since she couldn't fulfill her own dream."

Instantly Samantha's conversation about dreams with Sterling came back to her, and she wondered what that must have meant for her mother to take up her father's dream in place of her own. "My mother...was quite an unselfish woman, wasn't she." It was a statement, not a question, and was the only thing Samantha could think to say to express the tenderness and compassion that rose up inside of her.

Mrs. Dolittle looked at the girl's thin, flushed face, the bright braids that framed it, and the clear gray eyes behind glasses. She could tell Samantha was feeling one flood of emotion after another, and she took her hand firmly in an effort to create an anchor for her. "That she was. Unselfish to the very last. And someone I am still struggling to emulate after all these years."

That is what I should have been doing, Samantha thought with pain. *Dear, dear Mrs. Dolittle, I owe you so much.* She gripped the woman's rough, gentle hand and was suddenly very grateful to be young and to gain this knowledge with time to improve herself, time to learn more.

After a few silent moments of reflection, Samantha, at last, asked the question that had been eating at her from the beginning of their conversation. "Why, if the doctor told her it would kill her, did my mother have me?" She thought she knew the answer, but it was at once too terrible and too wonderful to say aloud.

"Ah." Mrs. Dolittle's black brows raised, and she released Samantha's hand. "Lovenia wanted children more than anything in the world. She... Well, it's hard for anyone to give up their dreams, no matter how large or small. And to Lovenia, being a mother was all she had ever wanted. She yearned for motherhood because she loved children and loved caring for them. She wanted one of her own."

Samantha nodded and realized she did know the answer to her question. Her stomach clenched in dread and anticipation.

"As you know, your father received his older brother's inheritance upon his death, which allowed him to buy this spacious...empty...house shortly after your parents arrived in town. I believe it was your father's attempt to help Lovenia fulfill her dream in a different way. He thought perhaps if she started a school or something of that sort, she would have a house bustling with children after all, and it would ease her heart. She was caught up with the idea and eager to begin, but the trip to get here so exhausted her that for weeks the most she could do was draw up plans while sitting in bed." That far-off look came back into Mrs. Dolittle's eyes as she added, "She would often tell me about those plans and what a grand school it would be someday, with so many beautiful children in it, learning and growing together."

Then Mrs. Dolittle's eyes focused sharply on Samantha again. "But you see, that dream never fully replaced the old one, and after they had lived here two years, your mother somehow convinced your father that she was fit to try for a baby once more—though, I must add, she still did not feel up to starting her school."

"But she knew it was too dangerous to have a baby!" Samantha exclaimed. "How could she take the chance when it would mean her life?" Samantha's insides twisted as she thought of the gamble her mother had taken. If only she could have been satisfied with her lot in life, she would still be here! *But...I...would not*, she recognized with a sickening jolt.

Shaken, she looked at Mrs. Dolittle, and their eyes locked for a long moment. She saw that the dear housekeeper recognized the connection Samantha had just made in her own mind about the impossible decision and risk Lovenia had made. She understood what Lovenia had done for her daughter, and Samantha wanted her to know that she understood now too. "So," she said slowly. "It was either my mother or myself. And she chose to give herself that I might have a chance at life."

The power of such a decision, such a sacrifice, hit Samantha with far greater force than anything ever had in her young life. Though she was not exactly sure why, into her mind came the picture she had seen in her father's beautifully decorated Bible of Jesus nailed to the cross. The realization that the one who had given her birth had valued her more than she had her own life was too incredible an idea to capture all at once. Samantha had never known such love within herself, and her mind did not grasp how it was possible. But her heart swelled to embrace the wonder of it, and before she knew what was happening, she was weeping and Mrs. Dolittle moved beside her to take her in her arms.

CHAPTER 11

THE PROPOSITION

September 1901

A week later, on a Friday, Sterling talked to Jerome after school about the prompt and complete repairs he had made. He sat on the front of his desk while Jerome stood before him, silent. The boy's gaze shifted from the floor to the window as if to say he didn't expect much from this conversation.

"I just wanted to thank you again for the fine work you did for me."

Jerome shrugged.

"And I would also like to make a proposition."

Jerome looked up, curiosity lighting his eyes for a split second. "A proposition, sir?" he asked, looking away again.

"Last week, I told you that years ago my father tried to teach me the art of repairing things, and I just never quite grasped it."

Jerome nodded, looking at the wall.

"I was wondering if you really would consider taking me on as your pupil. Now that I want to learn, you might have more luck with me than my father did." It was both a question and a humorous jab at himself.

The boy glanced at him, and Sterling couldn't read his expression.

"All I can offer you in return, to complete our bargain, is any extra assistance outside of school that you may need in the subjects of your choice. You could choose the subjects, the focus, and when you wanted direction, and I'd just be along to guide you a bit." He paused for a long moment while he watched the wheels turning in the boy's head. "What do you say?"

Jerome looked a little doubtful, and Sterling was afraid for a moment that he had said it all wrong and this was not going to work after all. Quickly he tried another angle. "Since you fixed the desks, I have realized how many other things in this place are not in the condition they should be—and could be with your help. I have been thinking about how beneficial it would be for me to know how to fix those things myself. Maybe that way, if someday I am head of a household, my home will not fall into complete disrepair..." He grimaced, then grinned at Jerome.

The corners of Jerome's mouth twitched in spite of himself, and then his forehead furrowed slightly, the freckles running into a small, brown line. "All right... I think so," he said slowly. "But give me a few days. I need to check with my mother."

Sterling checked himself from breathing an audible sigh of relief. "Definitely. Take all weekend or longer; just let me know what you decide. And," he added, "I do not want you to feel pushed into anything either, so I'll understand if you would rather not or if you have too many other things to do." As he said it, Sterling knew he would be disappointed if the boy decided not to agree to his bargain, but he also knew there must be other ways to reach him and that he would figure out what to do instead if it came to that.

"I do have things to do," Jerome said shortly, "at home, you know... Just let me think about it, and I'll tell you later."

Sterling nodded and watched him leave, wondering what conflicts were going on inside the boy's head and heart.

***

Monday morning, Jerome entered the classroom a few minutes before the other boys arrived. Sterling, busily writing last-minute instructions on the blackboard, turned when he heard Jerome's footsteps. He nodded to him and finished the sentence he was writing, then put down the chalk and wiped his hands on a nearby rag to rid them of chalk dust.

"How are you, Jerome?" he asked.

"Fine," the boy replied, nodding, a tone of genuine courtesy brightening his voice.

Sterling waited for whatever Jerome wanted to tell him, giving him time.

"Sir, uh, I've thought about your proposition...and I...uh...I think I could do that." He shuffled his feet nervously and ran a hand under his nose.

Sterling smiled slowly, gladly. He had felt sure the boy would accept, but not until this moment did he feel at ease about it.

Just before the bell rang, he and Jerome agreed on a couple of mutually agreeable days every week for them to work together after school, and then Jerome tromped over to his desk and took a seat. Watching him, Sterling could almost swear his shoulders pushed back with more confidence than usual.

Jerome seemed, in fact, to welcome the work, though after talking to him briefly about his home life, Sterling knew that the boy had more than his share of the load at home out of necessity. After Jerome fixed the creaky, splintery steps outside the classroom, Sterling took copious notes. Mr. Grover happened to pop his head in while Jerome was in the middle of showing Sterling how to build a much-needed cupboard for the classroom.

"Well, what have we here?" he called out cheerily from the doorway. "Do you never cease working, Mr. Sterling? Such industry!"

Sterling stopped hammering and looked up. "Not at all, Mr. Grover. Jerome, here, is the industrious one. Quite a genius, really. He is teaching me how to be more useful."

Jerome looked up from his work and nodded at Mr. Grover. "Sir."

Mr. Grover walked into the room to take a closer look at their work. He placed a hand lightly on Jerome's shoulder. "I always knew you were hiding important talents, my boy. Teaching Mr. Sterling the art of being useful is quite a noble pastime. I hope it will be worth the effort." He winked.

Jerome's mouth twitched at one corner, and he gave a small smile. "Sure," he shrugged. "He's doing fine. It's nothing, really."

"When you finish in here, I can think of several other projects that keep getting put off around the school...if you are interested."

The boy hesitated, unsure of what response to give. Sterling could tell he was weighing his options, calculating the missed time at home, wondering what would be the best thing to do.

"I would pay you for your services, of course," Mr. Grover added. "We lost our handyman last year and I haven't had a chance to replace him yet. I hoped we could manage without one, but the school is becoming shabbier by the week, and I could truly use your help."

Jerome was sincerely interested, Sterling could see, but he said only that he would let Mr. Grover know in a few days. "I need to talk things over with my mother," he told him. "She needs me at home, you know, and I don't want to—"

"—Oh, by all means." Mr. Grover nodded understandingly. "Obligations at home definitely outweigh any needs here. See what she thinks and give me your answer later. Either way, I'm gratified to see such fine, intelligent work coming from one of our own students. Keep up the good work, lad."

"Mr. Sterling," he nodded formally at Sterling and shook his hand with a hint of a smile in his eyes, as if to say, *it looks like you're being successful in your endeavors.* "Good day to you both."

When Mr. Grover had gone, Jerome picked up a nail and positioned it, but as he raised the hammer, he paused for a moment in thought. "Mr. Sterling, do you think... I mean, does Mr. Grover...." He lowered the hammer and looked at the floor. "Um, is Mr. Grover serious? He really needs my help? And he'll pay me?"

"Yes," Sterling answered, and Jerome looked up at him. "I told you that you were good, Jerome. This sounds like the perfect arrangement—for the school, at least. I know your mother counts on you to do a lot of things at home, but maybe she wouldn't object to you bringing in a little extra money as well."

Jerome shook his thatch of red hair quickly a few times. "No, she wouldn't object to that. She would be grateful for some extra money, for sure. I'll just have to see if Alfred—he's the hired help at home—can take over a couple of my jobs when I'm not around."

Sterling patted the boy's back. "Do what you need to do, Jerome. Mr. Grover will understand."

Sterling held a nail gingerly between his fingers and, with the other hand, tapped it in with the hammer. The nail cut straight and true, perfectly in place after only two taps. "Would you look at that!" he crowed. "I've never done that before. Almost as well as you!"

Jerome hit his nail in with only one stroke and grinned at Sterling's excitement. "Well," he shrugged, "you have a good teacher."

Sterling laughed, tickled by the boy's first show of humor. "That I do. The best."

CHAPTER 12

KATHERINE BODEEN

October 1901

Samantha sat on her bed and lightly bit the tip of her new fountain pen as she looked at the new, leather-bound journal spread on her lap and thought of what she should write. Some mornings she was happier than others and some days were not great, but this was going to be a wonderful morning—she could feel it! She decided last week that she needed to start a record of her changed life, to document the things that mattered to her now and the improved person she was becoming. Now she held the journal, she just needed to decide how to begin.

Ah well, she thought after a few more minutes of contemplation. *Perhaps it does not really matter how I begin so long as I do.* Finally, she put pen to paper.

October 16, 1901

Life is so fascinating, fresh, and brand new. I feel like a baby chick who just hatched out of an egg and looked about at the bright world, blinking with wonder.

For one thing, I never imagined I would be the proud owner of a magnificent black stallion—and capably care for him myself! Champion and I are very accustomed to one another now and go for a run a few times a week. Learning how to handle, control, and care for him fills me with a certain confidence and power.

She looked at what she had written and thought how it had already been over two months since Sterling's mysterious departure. Her teacher was gone, but she remembered how he had taught her to be her own teacher, so she tried to continue her morning writing exercises as often as possible. Journal writing could be included in that, she supposed.

The most important thing that has happened to me lately is what I learned from Mrs. Dolittle about my mother. I feel an intense desire to know my mother as well as I can. She gave me life, and my birth brought fulfillment to her most cherished dream. But she did not live long enough to enjoy that. In her death, I lost not only my mother but also a portion of myself; and somehow, I think that if I learn who she was, I will learn who I am as well. I have never given much thought to what kind of a woman I want to be, but now I know that what I become is my choice. And I choose to be the kind of woman my mother was...

The terrible heat and humidity of the summer had finally dissipated, much to everyone's relief, and so far, October was very pleasant indeed. Some mornings Samantha felt like taking a walk rather than riding Champion, and she would meander down the road through town and past the places she and Sterling had visited, or walk to the school to write reminiscently at the sturdy, warped table in the yard, hearing children's voices from inside the school house. Other times, like today, she wandered around the beautiful grounds of the First Congregational Church of Christ[14] at the corner of Main and Lorain Streets,[15] admiring the summer flowers and their varied scents. In addition to the contained clumps of jaunty, yellow black-eyed

---

[14] http://www.oberlin.edu/external/EOG/HousesofWorship/FFirstChurch.html
[15] http://www.oberlin.edu/external/EOG/HistoricPreservation/HPFirstChurch.html

Susans, Samantha especially delighted in the gorgeous, purple asters, each one so small but plucky. But it was the multicolored snapdragons that never failed to make her smile. She loved to pinch their cheeks and make their little jaws drop open--a feature that always cheered her.

She settled beneath one of the huge sycamore trees to gather her thoughts in preparation for her daily writing exercise. More often lately, in addition to regular writing, she would sometimes just sit and think. All that she had learned from her conversation with Mrs. Dolittle still clung to her like a delicious, bittersweet dream. She found herself thinking about her mother almost constantly, wondering what she would have done in this situation or what she would have thought or said in another. And, at times, as she was carried away in her imaginings, physical pain would rise up within her, an ache that she had no mother to confide in or from whom to receive direction. It was as if, having been much too young to mourn seventeen years ago, she was now belatedly swept into her own private grieving period.

It was in this frame of mind that Samantha met someone who added an element of depth to her life that she could only describe later as "light." It was as if her whole life, she had walked under cloudy skies, and then suddenly, the clouds parted and sunshine flooded over her.

She sat well-engrossed in her writing when a group of young people began arriving for some kind of gathering on the church lawn. Their appearance disturbed her concentration, and she could not help but take quick glances at them while she wrote. After a while, a dark-haired young woman in a blue, flowing dress left the crowd and began walking towards her. Samantha looked up from her paper and watched the young woman approach, noting her small build and happy countenance that, even from a distance, was strikingly beautiful. The girl saw Samantha watching and smiled as she drew closer, then sat across from her on the grass and tucked her feet beneath her.

"Hello," she said. "I'm Katherine Bodeen. What is your name?"

With one finger, Samantha pushed her glasses up snugly against her nose and looked at the girl curiously, feeling that she was somehow familiar. "My name is Samantha Jennings." An uncertain pause. "Do I know you?"

"I don't know." Katherine returned her searching look and, after a moment of reflection, brightened. "I think I remember you from school. Have you lived here all your life?"

Samantha nodded.

"So have I. Is your father Professor Jennings, who taught at the University of Ohio before coming here to the college?"

"Yes." Samantha was not surprised. The town was not big enough for anyone to not know who her father was, even if it was only by hearsay.

"My uncle attended school there in Columbus and was very impressed by your father's knowledge and his 'method of delivery,' as he termed it."

Samantha was startled. Very few people she had ever talked to had known her father personally in that capacity. "I... Thank you." She struggled to think of something else to say before adding, "I think he enjoyed teaching very much."

"Yes, I think so, too," Katherine responded, nodding. "And how about you, Samantha? I have not seen you around for quite a while." She said it as if Samantha had only recently quit the social circle.

"Well, I..." Samantha did not know what to say, realizing anything she did say would mark her more as a recluse than ever. But when she looked back into Katherine's agreeable face with its blue eyes framed by long, dark lashes, her nerves calmed. "I did go to a church picnic last spring," she offered weakly.

Katherine's slender brows furrowed in thought. "So did I, but I didn't see you there."

Samantha looked at her for a long moment, wondering what the girl was thinking, and then averted her gaze. "I didn't see you either," she softly returned.

"Oh! I know," Katherine laughed suddenly, its tinkling quality reminding Samantha of a merry stream rushing over pebbles. "You must have gone to the Methodist social. I always go to the one hosted by First Church. So many of my friends are members of this one that I sometimes forget there is another church in town. My apologies."

Samantha shook her head, and a small smile turned the corners of her mouth up again. "No need... I understand."

"Since you are here, why not join us for the lecture?" Katherine asked, gesturing toward the small crowd of young people now beginning to take their places on the semicircle of chairs. "They are always interesting...if not always thoroughly entertaining." Katherine smiled but added the last part in a low, confidential tone.

Samantha could not help but smile back, could not help but like this friendly girl, and did not resist as Katherine got to her feet and helped her gather her things, then linked an arm through Samantha's and pulled her toward the ring of chairs. It felt good to be included. Better, even, than she had thought it would.

Over the ensuing weeks, Katherine persuaded Samantha to join her group each time there was a lecture at the church and helped her to become acquainted with several of the other young people. Samantha noticed how much everyone seemed to like Katherine and how many of the young men vied for her attention and looked at her with longing when they thought no one was watching. She also came to realize that she had never heard Katherine say an unkind word about anyone, unlike some of the young women who seemed to thrive on gossip. She had sometimes wondered what it would be like to be beautiful, and now she told herself that if she were in Katherine's place, she would be just as gracious and accepting of everyone as she was. At least, she hoped she would—although that was a moot point.

Samantha began to enjoy her time with the young people more and more and felt grateful for Katherine taking a personal interest in her. She had wanted some kind of social interaction like this but had not known how to initiate it, so Katherine's appearance in her life was fortuitous, to say the least.

CHAPTER 13

A BALM TO HIS SOUL

October 1901

The week after the school officially employed Jerome, Sterling received an invitation from the lad's mother to join them for supper that Friday evening. By this time, Sterling had received several invitations from various families, which he always accepted graciously and gratefully, but this time he felt genuine anticipation at the prospect of meeting Jerome's mother and seeing the boy in his own environment.

Sterling had had a few opportunities to tutor Jerome after school, in between the boy's repair duties. He discovered that Jerome actually excelled in mathematics once he focused on it, and was privately relieved about that, as he did not know in how much detail he could have assisted the boy on that subject. When it came to penmanship, all Jerome lacked was practice and, in reading, patience. What he really struggled with was expository writing. Besides simply needing to work on spelling, Jerome seemed bored with the whole affair. Sterling tried to make it as interesting as he could while still staying within the bounds of the school curriculum, but he felt so limited! He would not do anything to jeopardize his contract, for he had signed it and committed himself to follow through. This was what he had wanted, after all, to abandon his newfangled teaching practices and settle down in a conventional teaching community. But in times like this, when he struggled against his lack of freedom for someone else's sake, he felt his resolve weaken. Could he really commit himself to this kind of teaching indefinitely?

116

At any rate, he would have supper with the Tomlinsons and see where that led him and what more he could do to help Jerome.

As Jerome had work to do at school that Friday after classes, he and Sterling would walk together to his home. For the first time this school year, Sterling finished all necessary corrections and lesson planning before he left the school, which meant that his weekend would be free. He was simultaneously grateful and anxious about the prospect of rest, but pushed the anxiety to the back of his mind when Jerome entered the classroom at the end of his duties.

The boy had donned a cap and overalls over his uniform, and Sterling noted that he looked dusty and a bit smudged. A thin film of dirt on his face added to the chaos of the freckles, which bunched together in groups when he smiled and asked, "Are you ready to go, Mr. Sterling?" He gestured with a broom in hand. "I just have to put this away and pull off my dusty overclothes."

Sterling looked up from the papers he was organizing and nodded. "I just need five more minutes."

Once they were on the road, Jerome did not say much, as usual, but this time the silence was companionable instead of awkward. Sterling felt himself relaxing, felt his muscles loosening as they strode along, and was doubly grateful for the opportunity to escape from his routine and to be heading in this direction instead of toward his lifeless little room. The long, brown grasses beside the road rippled in the slight breeze, making a pleasant sound that Sterling found soothing. A few late fall flowers peeked their heads out from the grass here and there, still bravely clinging on, despite the cooling temperatures. Their innocence and simple attractiveness suddenly made Sterling think of Samantha. The image caught him off guard and made him falter a step or two before he pushed it away, relegating it once more to the furthest recesses of his mind.

About half an hour into their walk, the Tomlinson land came into view. It was a modest-sized piece of property, not more than forty acres. But Sterling could tell that it was definitely plenty to manage for a widow, her young son, and the hired man. Cattle grazed here and there in the fields, and the remains of a large summer garden took up a sizeable section near the house. A spacious orchard flanked the opposite side, and Sterling could see that many of the trees were still laden with ripe apples of varying colors and shades. It was a charming place that caught his interest immediately, somehow reminding him of his own childhood growing up on a large plantation that grew hemp and raised thoroughbred horses.

Sterling sensed Jerome looking at him and glanced over to see the lad eyeing him for an opinion. "This is a great place you have here," he told him enthusiastically. "It seems peaceful and orderly...and those apples look delicious!"

Jerome nodded. "We always sell lots of them, but Ma also bakes and bottles a whole bunch. So, we have plenty of them to get us through the winter."

"I think apples like those would get me through the winter, too," Sterling chuckled.

One corner of Jerome's mouth lifted in a slight smile. "I'll bet Ma made one of her famous Dutch apple pies for dessert."

Sterling rubbed his growling stomach and closed his eyes briefly. "I haven't had Dutch apple pie since I lived at home, where our cook, Nancy, made them every now and then. Coming home from school to a warm slice of pie and a glass of cold milk... Now that was a piece of heaven."

"I'll bet my ma makes 'em better than your Nancy," Jerome challenged, humor in his eyes.

Sterling caught the banter in his tone and quickly returned it, grinning. "You may be right, but I'll have to try a few slices myself, to judge."

Jerome just grinned back.

As they walked down the path toward the neat little cottage, the front door opened, and Mrs. Tomlinson stood watching them approach. She wore a white ruffled apron over a simple green dress that contrasted with auburn hair beginning to silver at the temples. She was of average height and looked sturdy and strong. When they walked up the steps, she bent to kiss Jerome on the cheek. "Welcome home, son. And welcome to our humble abode, Mr. Sterling." She shook his hand firmly. "We are so pleased you could join us for supper."

"I thank you for the invitation, Mrs. Tomlinson. You have a good boy here, and I've wanted to meet his mother for some time now. It's a pleasure to finally meet you."

"Come in, come in." She waved him inside after Jerome and motioned toward a chair. The furnishings were simple but well-made, spotless, and well-cared for. "Jerome has told me about you for weeks now, and I have to say how grateful I am for what you have done for him already." She put an arm around Jerome's shoulders, and the boy looked at the floor, scratching the back of his leg with the shoe of the other foot.

Sterling didn't want to sit while his two hosts were still standing, but at Mrs. Tomlinson's urging, he sat. "Oh, the gratitude is definitely mutual, ma'am. Jerome has a real hand for working wood and fixing things, and we are getting to the point at the school where we don't know what we did without him."

"I often tell him he is talented, but he has always struggled with school, and no teacher has found his way to recognize what Jerome is capable of until now." She patted Jerome's shoulder and looked at Sterling, her brown eyes clear and intelligent.

"Well, any service I can be to him—or to you—will not be enough to make things even." He chuckled. "Not only do I have the best-looking room in the school now, but I can hammer a nail straight! For me, that is quite a feat. And Mr. Grover told me the other day that he would have hired the boy long ago had he known--and I quote-'the wonders he can work on this old school.'"

Mrs. Tomlinson laughed quietly and nodded, pleased. "I admit, his extra time at the school makes things tight here for Alfred and me, but we can sure use the money he brings in. Besides that, I feel it is important for him to be involved in something he loves that allows him to develop his abilities."

Sterling looked from Mrs. Tomlinson to Jerome and smiled, noting the boy's simultaneous embarrassment and pleasure at being the focus of their talk.

"I can see you have a wonderful mother, Jerome," he told the boy.

"She is good to me," Jerome simply acknowledged.

Mrs. Tomlinson patted his shoulder again. "All right, well, I am sure you two are famished after a long day at school, so how about some supper? Jerome will show you where the pump is out back, Mr. Sterling, and then we will sit down for some food."

Sterling thoroughly enjoyed himself that evening. There was a peacefulness to the Tomlinson's home that felt like a balm to his soul. Afterward, he sensed an ease and a calm within himself that he did not remember ever feeling before. The food was delicious, and he was quick to admit, to Jerome's satisfaction, that the apple pie after dinner did exceed the deliciousness of Nancy's after all.

He felt accepted and appreciated here in a way he had never felt while growing up in his own home. He had thought then that he had everything required to make one happy: good food in abundance, fine clothing, horses, and land to ride them in, his every need met by loyal servants. He grew up knowing his family was well off, that they had a good name and were considered one of the best families in the area (hadn't his mother told him that, time and time again?), and that his father carried quite a bit of political clout in the community. But at home, he had never felt as comfortable in his own skin as he did in the Tomlinson's home. That was a curious thought to ponder.

When he went off to university, Sterling was aware enough of his privileged station to be briefly grateful for the opportunity to attend at his parent's expense. That he be allowed to pursue a profession at all was cause for gratitude. As heir to the family estate, he should have been required, like most young men of his acquaintance, to focus all his attention and energies on learning how to one day take over. He was relieved when his parents had finally seen the futility of forcing him into a role he did not want and was not suited for, particularly since his younger brother had a natural aptitude for seeing to the affairs of the family businesses. Sterling knew he was privileged in so many ways, but it was difficult to fully appreciate what he had always had.

Yet amid all the comfort and ease he grew up with on that huge, rambling Kentucky estate, he had never truly felt as at ease as he did now with the Tomlinsons. They obviously respected him, yet at once treated him as part of the family. They also welcomed any help he was willing and able to give, and he liked feeling needed. That was certainly one feeling he had never experienced at home. At least once a week, he accompanied Jerome home for a meal and would then spend the rest of the evening working on the land or in the barn until the sweat ran in rivulets down his face. His father would have been proud, he thought ruefully, to know he hadn't forgotten how to do hard physical labor, even though it was not what he had chosen as a profession.

Some Saturdays, he spent all day at the farm, harvesting winter squash, digging up onions and potatoes for winter storage, picking the remaining apple crop, and rounding up cattle for Alfred. It felt good to work with his body instead of just with his mind and to work for someone else, without pay, per se. In actuality, he felt that he was more than paid for his efforts because he felt really appreciated for the first time in his life and as if he were making a difference. True, there were times in his short teaching career thus far when he had felt that he made a difference in the life of his students, but this was something else again.

He came to think of the Tomlinsons as the closest friends he had ever had, friends with whom he could truly communicate, who were willing to listen and discuss things with him.

Often, Sterling worked alone while Jerome was off hammering or sawing away at some farm project or other, and Mrs. Tomlinson bottled and baked in the kitchen. But at other times, she and Sterling worked together, and it was during these times that Sterling came to know her and the hard times she had been through that had made her the strong, wise woman she was today.

She was almost old enough to be Sterling's mother, but how different! Her husband had died ten years earlier, so Jerome was barely two when his father passed. Mrs. Tomlinson still wore her wedding band and spoke of her husband fondly.

"He was good to me," she said, "and good to the boy. He doted on the little tike all the more because of the baby girl we lost a few years before. Losing my husband, too, was difficult--very difficult-- but we have managed. Alfred was a godsend and helps us to no end, and sometimes the neighbors come by to lend a hand as well. Jerome has a good life, I think, even though he has to work hard. At least he knows he has a mother who loves him."

Sterling was surprised to feel tears prickling in the corners of his eyes and blinked them away. "Yes, indeed. That is definitely something to come home to. And perhaps his life is all the better because he has to work so hard."

Mrs. Tomlinson agreed. "There is real value in work: it is good for the body and the soul. We surely appreciate all the help you have given us these last few weeks, Sterling."

"It is my pleasure, ma'am," he replied, meaning it.

***

Before long, Samantha absented herself from the Jennings' mansion not only one night of every week (besides Sunday) for church functions with Katherine, but she also attended a few women suffragette meetings, joined the Ladies' Quilting Society of Oberlin, and even became a member of the Oberlin Woman's Club, which had just formed that year. Katherine joined the club also, and as they walked to their monthly meetings, arm in arm, they would quote the club's motto together with solemn faces, then dissolve into laughter because it seemed "so prim and overly serious": "To bring together women interested in literary, artistic, scientific and philanthropic pursuits, with a view of rendering them helpful to each other and useful to society."[16] Still, they did believe in the importance of each of these things and learned much each time they attended.

The books on Samantha's personal shelf grew dusty (Mrs. Dolittle had never set foot inside Samantha's room), but her spirits brightened, and her soul moved from its previous systematic plodding to a blithe skipping. Life was suddenly *life* in the complete, broad, wonderful, true sense of the word. After the euphoric state of self- and world recognition, Samantha had moved into a calmer, more constant state of general happiness. It was not that she no longer had difficult days or that she did not still grieve for her mother, but overall, she felt more content with life than she ever had before.

Establishing herself in her new social routine made Samantha's days fully busy and fulfilling for the first time. She reveled in her involvement and began to develop friendships among the youth of the town.

---

[16] http://oberlinarchives.libraryhost.com/?p=collections/controlcard&id=132

Those who had known Samantha before counted the change as extraordinary, and admittedly, it took some getting used to. The older folks who noticed simply accounted the change to growing up. Once established, Samantha was generally accepted and integrated into town, no longer living on the outskirts of society in her own secluded world. Of course, there were those who still could not forget the way she used to be "so unfriendly" and "acted as if she were the whole world," but this attitude was kept by those who were not well-loved themselves due to their proficiency in criticism.

Samantha was not exempt from life's disappointments, disillusions, and painful reminders. There were times when she was tempted to retreat back into the safety and comfort of her previous existence, where she did not have to work so hard to learn how to act and how to talk to others. But she refrained from succumbing to that temptation and tried to learn from each disappointment and difficulty.

October 21, 1901

I feel I have graduated in my views of the world. People are a part of me now. Whereas I used to notice only the nature of animals and trees, (fairy rings), now much of that interest has shifted to my fellow beings. I am fascinated with behavior: gestures, voice inflections, facial expressions, and the like—-things I never noticed before. I am learning what is acceptable, hospitable, and gracious and how to effectively express myself to others. My thoughts, I have discovered, are not completely foreign or strange to the other young women and men I associate with, as I had always supposed. They, in fact, share some of their own parallel ideas and concerns or laugh heartily at my naïve assumptions and quickly prove their points in words that are both non-threatening and convincing. I find myself liking them! I never thought I would seek this kind of knowledge or connection, but now I find it a relief.

More even than <u>that</u> kind of relief, though, is the peace and solace I am finding in God. Because of Katherine and her kind invitation to join her church group, I have begun to contemplate more fully who God is. I want to know what connection I have to Him and what, exactly, Jesus Christ's sacrifice means for me. I have started reading the Bible, and the other day when I came across Exodus 14:2[17], I knew that is what I want to be able to say someday for myself: "The Lord is my strength and song, and he is become my salvation: he is my God...."

All I know so far is that He is there somewhere listening to me when I pray—for I have begun to do that too. And what a wonder it is to be comforted during the darkest nights when I think I am all alone.

Sometimes I feel overwhelmed by all the wasted years of my life without God (and without a purpose), and I wonder if Sterling knows Him. We never discussed religion, except in passing, during our varied discussions, so I do not know. I do remember that last day we were together, just after I found the fairy ring when I asked him if he had ever wanted to believe in something so strongly that it almost became real to him. He asked if I meant religion, which I did not. But now that I do have religion, I don't think it is at all like that: that the power of believing in it is what makes it true. I think that only those whose hearts have been touched and changed as mine can understand how it really is. God is not some obscure idea that people thought of once upon a time to satisfy their own need to explain what they could

---

[17] All Bible verses quoted from the King James version.

not understand. He is an actual, loving Being, and I feel privileged to be acquainting myself with Him.

I hope Sterling finds Him too.

CHAPTER 14

THIS DESPAIR, THIS BLISS

October 1901

Sterling awoke in a sweat and sat up. Why did these dreams have to haunt him? He generally kept himself so busy during the day that thoughts of Samantha were almost completely crowded out. And yes, in his mind, he now thought of her by her given name, though he had only ever called her "Miss Jennings," as was appropriate. At night all the repressed thoughts and emotions flooded into his dreams, set free at last.

He shook his head to clear it and opened his eyes against the darkness in an attempt to black out the image indelibly printed in his mind. In his dreams, just as in reality, the girl became lovelier every time he saw her. He had once thought her looks average, but delving into her soul as he had during the summer had brought her to life before him. And now his night dreams reflected that depth and strength of character that only increased her attractiveness to him.

But his dreams were also full of hopelessness: Samantha, forever reclusive and untrusting of men—because of him. Her hair growing wild about her face, her eyes haunted behind the glasses, pained and searching. Samantha, riding Champion (riding Champion?!) across a never-ending plain that he somehow knew would end nowhere and at nothing, yet both horse and rider pursued relentlessly as if possessed. He, reaching across a misty gulf, straining to reach Samantha's hand, calling out to her to see him, to forgive him, to tell him what to do to redeem himself, but hearing a roaring in his ears as the wind threw back his words.

Sterling forced himself to breathe in deeply, to concentrate on slowing the rough beating of his heart. He gripped the bedsheets and shoved his face into them. He wanted to weep and could not. He did not know how to find relief from this anxiety, this bottomless aching.

He got out of bed and felt around on his desk for a match. He needed light! Once the candle was throbbing in its cheery, comfortable way, he felt a little better, but he still had to do something to rid himself of the emotional burden he felt, if only momentarily. From the desk drawer, he withdrew a sheet of paper, picked up a pencil, and began to write. The words came to him with a sudden rightness, as if he had had them in his head all along. He wrote quickly, digging into the paper in his desire to shed the weight he felt, as if each letter weighed a pound:

> *This despair that fills me,*
> *That crushes all my little pleasures,*
> *Remains forever by my side,*
> *My companion in sleep,*
> *My haunt by day.*
> *Its damp darkness has become me,*
> *This despair: Remorse.*

It was short but heavy with the weight of his emotions. When he lifted the pencil from the paper, the instrument felt light, as if it would spring from the page. He looked over his work briefly, noting how appropriate were the flickers and shadows the candle cast over the page, augmenting the ominous words. He did feel considerably better, but still, a burden lingered over him. He sat, head down, feeling weary.

After a few moments, another image came to his mind that brought some light and hope into his soul, as it always did. The image of a small, folded paper bearing those two simple words: *thank you.* He did not know what they meant (thank you for what, exactly?), but somehow he always felt infused with gratitude and a sense of relief when he remembered them, as he did now.

He took another deep breath and let it out slowly, then blew out the candle and lay down again, trying to fill his head with images of anything but Samantha before he finally fell back into a fitful sleep.

***

Samantha looked down at the pages she had just written and read them over again to herself, liking the picture she saw...

I enjoy being out of doors in a way I never have before and especially love to write in such a setting. Writing!--such a passion for it possesses me that I often wonder if I can ever get enough of it. I feel as if I shall never be satiated. I hope, at least, that all this practice is improving my abilities, though I have not yet determined in what direction to channel them.

Recently I began trying my hand at poetry and have found, to my astonishment, that the results are not actually too poor. As long as I do not have to rhyme and can write in free verse, as Walt Whitman and Sterling do, I manage well enough.

I shall copy here one that I wrote yesterday:

This bliss that fills me,
That swells to increase my joy,
Now remains beside me always,
My lover, my friend, my companion.

130

It brings new life to my soul,
Brushes back the cobwebs,
This bliss I call revelation.

I wonder how my teacher would like it... I think of him often still—perhaps even more than before—and wish I could show him all that I have written since he left. I want to watch his eyes as they read over my work and see the way his mouth lifts when he is surprised and pleased. I want to hear that low, mellow voice tell me what he is thinking and how I could improve or clarify my writing. I wonder where he is and if I'll ever see him again, now that I understand.

Now that I know I need him.

Subdued, Samantha shut her composition book and looked down at her hands resting on its fragrant, new cover. She rubbed at the shiny callus on her index finger, trying half-heartedly to remove the pen smudge there and thinking about Sterling once again. He had been not only her teacher but also her friend, for he had really listened to her, and it had seemed that he honestly cared about and wanted her to be the best she could be. Katherine was that way, too: a true, devoted friend for whom she felt most grateful. When she really contemplated her blessings, it almost brought her to tears. How empty her life had been without Katherine and Sterling! They had helped her find the meaning of living.

She continued trying to focus on gratitude and thinking about all her blessings, as she had recently read in 1 Thessalonians chapter 5: "In everything give thanks." She supposed that meant during hard times, too, which would undoubtedly be difficult, but she decided to start with the day-to-day. She wanted to learn how to exercise her ability to see everything around her through a gratitude lens. It wasn't too difficult, she found, because she was naturally optimistic, but she still found the intentional effort worth the reward, for she was happier for recognizing her blessings. It would soon be the month of Thanksgiving, and she wanted to be ready for it!

As she considered all she had to be grateful for, her thoughts often settled on Mrs. Dolittle, with whom she now spoke regularly and of whom she asked many questions. The older woman was proving to be a willing listener, an able source of information, and an affectionate confidante. How had Samantha missed these things about her for so long? She felt a sense of regret about all the wasted years when she could have had a friend right here in her own home but had done little more than co-exist with the efficient housekeeper. Samantha was grateful Mrs. Dolittle harbored no resentment about that and was now happy to supply her with friendship and any answers she could.

One morning while helping Mrs. Dolittle bottle their recent apple harvest, Samantha felt it was the right time to ask her about her life history. She sat at the table, cutting and peeling apples by the dozens, while Mrs. Dolittle stood at the stove, pouring boiled syrup over the hot jars filled with fruit. When they ran out of space in the kitchen to set the finished jars, they pulled the large dining room table into the hallway just outside the kitchen to use as well. Bottling was a long, taxing chore and a hot one, but not unpleasant, and Samantha felt a sense of fulfillment as she watched the jars slowly adding up. They would enjoy apples all winter at this rate!

"Mrs. Dolittle," she said thoughtfully, "you have told me so much about my family history and filled in details that I would never have known without you. But what about your own family? I would love to hear about your history! I feel remiss in never having asked you before."

"Oh my!" the older woman exclaimed with a chuckle. She finished with the last jar in the batch, wiped around the rim, and placed the zinc lid with a firm twist. "I guess I haven't talked about my history much, have I... It's kind of you to be interested." She glanced up at Samantha, smiling.

"I *am* interested. I want to know all about you, what and who made you into the strong, wonderful person that you are. Have you always lived in Oberlin?"

Mrs. Dolittle nodded. "I have. That was the first of the gifts my mother gave me--before I was even born." She hefted a new bucket of clean water to the large pot on the stove and poured it in to begin making the next batch of canning syrup.

"Before you were born?" Samantha asked. "You mean she came here to give birth?"

"Yes. She was born and raised a slave in Richmond, Virginia, and she refused to bear a child into slavery too. She had experienced how slavery ripped apart families--only her sister had remained with her by then. All other family members were sold away to other plantations throughout the slave states--and she did not want history repeating itself if she could avoid it. To that end, she avoided long-term relationships with any of the slave boys and would not marry. But, as you know, no slave had rights of any kind." Mrs. Dolittle sighed and shook her head. She measured sugar into the big pot and began to stir again while she thought.

In her intense interest to hear the rest of the story, Samantha forgot all about the apples in front of her and sat, transfixed, watching Mrs. Dolittle with dread.

Finally, she continued. "One of the master's sons took an interest in her and could not be dissuaded. So when she found herself with child at the age of 21, she determined that she had to escape slavery and bear her child somewhere that would allow it opportunities that she never had."

"Wow." Samantha shook her head in sorrow and wonder.

"Yes. She wanted more for my life than working on a tobacco plantation from sunup to sundown, and she felt that obtaining an education was key to making a different life for herself and her baby. Of course, she would never get that where she was."

"Education, yes!" Samantha exclaimed. "Your mother was an intelligent woman!"

"She certainly was," Mrs. Dolittle agreed. "And so very brave. I really don't know how she did it. She traveled about 500 miles on the Underground Railroad, mostly alone, sometimes with small groups. I don't know how she survived, pregnant and on the run, but she was determined and stubborn. In the end, I think those two qualities are what made it possible for her to do what she did. And her reliance on God. She had a firm belief in Him and that He would guide her, and He did. He surely did. There were several very close calls, but also many kind and sacrificing people, and she always felt that miracles occurred along the way."

"Do you mind sharing with me about those miracles?" Samantha asked, her face bright with interest.

"Well, let me see..." Mrs. Dolittle gave one more stir to the pot and then joined Samantha at the table, groaning involuntarily as she sat. She looked into the distance for a moment, thinking, then picked up an apple and began peeling and speaking at the same time. "Just getting out of the slave quarters, unseen and unheard at night, was a difficult and crucial step. So her success in doing that might be considered miraculous. But she related to me that she felt the first miracle that occurred was when she was about 20 miles out of Richmond. She would, of course, walk all night and then hide in the woods all day so as not to be seen. The second or third night of walking, the master's tracking hounds came close, and she thought for sure she was done for. She did the only things she could think to do: climb a tree and stay there, and pray as if her life depended on it– for it did."

Samantha looked at her wide-eyed. "What happened?"

"When she had climbed as high in the tree as she safely could, she wrapped her arms around it, squeezed her eyes shut, and prayed for all she was worth. The hounds came mighty close, sniffing and barking, passing by her tree more than once, and she was terrified they were going to "tree" her as if she were a raccoon. But each time, after a pause, they passed right on by, baying as if they were hot on her trail. Somehow, Her pursuers never caught even a glimpse of her."

"Incredible! What a terribly frightening situation, Mrs. Dolittle! I can only imagine... She gave you an amazing legacy, didn't she?"

"That she did." Mrs. Dolittle nodded emphatically.

"Both our mothers did so much to ensure our good life. In different ways and completely different circumstances, to be sure, but both were courageous women who cared more about us than about themselves." She looked up at the older woman, eyes glistening with a film of tears.

"They did, indeed."

"Was Oberlin your mother's destination?"

"Oh, no. I am not sure she even knew about Oberlin until she arrived. Like most slaves, she was on her way to Canada."

Samantha nodded. "Because Canada abolished slavery in 1834."

"Exactly."

"Did she stay in Oberlin because she liked it here and felt safe, as so many others did?"

"Yes. She received such a warm reception and was so thoughtfully cared for in those first few weeks after she arrived that she hoped living in Ohio, a free state, would protect her."

"I am so glad she felt safe here!" Samantha said. "I remember reading that 3,000 runaway slaves sheltered in Oberlin between the 1830s and 1850s, on their way through on the Underground Railway. And that by the 1850s, out of the 2,000 Oberlin residents, about 400 of them were escaped, slaves."

"That sounds about right," Mrs. Dolittle agreed. "My mother was one of them. She lived with friends for a few months, working at whatever odd jobs she could to earn her keep. She had only ever worked in the tobacco fields, so she needed to learn many new skills. But she was always willing to learn whatever she needed to support herself and me. After I was born in 1841, she would strap me to her back and take me with her to whatever labor she performed."

"Is that how you learned so many housekeeping skills?" Samantha asked.

Mrs. Dolittle chuckled. "I guess that was how it started. Mama said when I got a bit older, I would peek over her shoulder and watch while she cleaned or cooked, or planted the garden. And when I grew too big to be carried, I would tag along on foot and help with small chores. Apparently, I would sometimes exasperate her with all my questions," she laughed. "But as soon as I was old enough for school, she enrolled me at the Little Red Schoolhouse."

Samantha clapped her hands in delight. "I never knew you attended school there! Do you remember it?"

"I do have a few memories of it," Mrs. Dolittle smiled. "As you know, it closed in 1851 and we moved to a bigger building. I would have been ten by then. I immensely enjoyed learning, and after chores every evening, I would teach my mother what I had learned at school. In that way, my mother was finally able to learn how to read and write, as she had always wanted."

"So," Samantha said contemplatively, "she saved you from slavery first, and then you saved her from ignorance!"

Mrs. Dolittle nodded slowly and thoughtfully. "I haven't considered it in quite that way before, but you are right. All I knew at the time was how much enjoyment I experienced acting the role of teacher. Mama was a quick learner and insisted I not be easy on her, so in no time, she knew as much as I did."

"Did she ever attend Oberlin College?"

"No, she never did," Mrs. Dolittle said a little regretfully. "In her spare time, she read every book she could get her hands on, but mostly she worked. She worked hard to support me and put me through school. She felt that her mission in life was to make sure I received a good education. And I surely did. Not everyone at the college felt that colored people like me should attend with all the white folks, but I felt accepted, overall, and challenged in good ways."

Samantha watched her in surprise. "I don't know why I never knew you attended college! Why, you are more educated than I am!"

Mrs. Dolittle smiled a little bashfully and waved a sticky hand as if to dismiss Samantha's praise. "I enjoyed my time there and graduated after I finished the women's two-year course of study. It was a bit disappointing not to receive a degree, but I did feel fortunate to have the opportunity to attend college at all, considering where I came from. Perhaps if I had been a bit more tenacious and determined, like my mother, I could have insisted on taking the 'gentleman's course'--even though it was not recommended–like Mary Jane Patterson did."

"Oh, yes!" Samantha exclaimed, thinking back to what she had read about the woman. "Wasn't she the first black woman in the country to receive a bachelor's degree?"

"Yes. She and I attended Oberlin during some of the same time, but I was always a little intimidated by her. She was so intelligent and so determined. And very pretty, as well. Some described her as 'vivacious' and 'forceful.' She accomplished a lot of good in her life for the poor and needy, and also as a teacher and principal out east. She died a few years ago, you know."

"Now that you mention it, I think I did hear she died. It sounds as if she left a great legacy, too."

"For my people, yes. Though she never married or had children of her own."

"But you did! When were you married?"

"Well, that was part of the reason I was satisfied with only two years at the College." Her face lit up with joy, and she laughed at the memory. "I met Mr. Dolittle, he swept me off my feet, and we wanted to get married and start a family."

Samantha grinned. "That is so sweet!"

"Well, I thought so, but my mother wasn't too keen on him for a while. He had to really work his way into her good graces before she would accept a different future than she had envisioned for me."

"Hmm." Samantha tilted her head to one side as she thought about this. "What future had she planned for you?"

"She always wanted more education for me and hoped I would be a professional woman. Never having had much in the way of a family life herself when she was growing up, she didn't see the attraction or understand why I would want to settle down like that."

"She never married, then?" Samantha asked.

"No, she never did." Mrs. Dolittle shook her head. "I think she was too scarred from her experience with the master's son and too independent. She didn't trust most men. She would always say, 'My only Master is the one in heaven, and I don't aim to let anyone else have my heart.'"

Samantha nodded. "She suffered through very hard things."

"She did. And she was a very good mother. Once she recognized the real love that Ambrose and I had for each other, she came around. She didn't want to stand in the way of my happiness, and she could see that we did make each other happy, so eventually, she gave us her blessing."

"Wonderful!" Samantha clasped her hands together and smiled. "I just love happy endings."

Mrs. Dolittle chuckled. "Not everything went easy for us, of course, but we struggled through the hard times together and always held fast to our marriage vows. We taught our children to be hard workers and center their lives on God, and we made a good life. All the children grew up to respect and love us and be upstanding citizens of the community. Some pursued higher education, and all are successful in their chosen areas. I feel blessed."

Samantha nodded. "I wish for the blessings of a family like that one day, myself. And *you* have been a blessing in our lives for so long!" She smiled fondly at Mrs. Dolittle. "I have just one more question—for now."

Mrs. Dolittle chuckled.

"Why did you start working for my mother?"

"Well, now, that was one of the hardest times in my life, and I don't mind saying it. Ambrose passed away shortly before your parents arrived here, and I was looking for regular work to support my family. My youngest child was only seven years old, and with Ambrose gone, it was up to me to support my children. Being hired by your mother was a great blessing to my family and me, and I have stayed on ever since–though now I only support myself. I have saved up enough that I know that when I am too feeble to work anymore, I will have enough to live on for the rest of my life."

"Oh, when that time does come–in many, many years–I hope you will live here with us still! I will take care of you!" Samantha exclaimed.

Mrs. Dolittle patted Samantha's sticky hand with her own sticky hand, and her eyes filled with tears. "Thank you, my dear. That does my heart good. My two daughters have said the same thing, so when the time comes, I will have a difficult decision to make."

"Oh, of course, your daughters would want that honor. I didn't think–"

Mrs. Dolittle smiled. "It is always good to have options, isn't it?"

CHAPTER 15

A POSSIBILITY

November 1901

One Saturday at the beginning of winter, Sterling chose to spend the day at the Tomlinson's farm. A couple of short snowstorms had come already this year and melted away shortly thereafter, but now in this third week of November, one could feel the bite of winter approaching in earnest.

Mrs. Tomlinson had asked Sterling if he would mind giving her a hand in the kitchen. He knew nothing about the workings of a kitchen and told her as much, but she laughingly dismissed the notion that men did not belong in kitchens and assured him he would be as busy as ever helping her there. Feeling up to a new challenge, he helped her carry in from the cellar several large, orange pumpkins, then washed them off and set them on the table, ready to be scraped out and made into all sorts of tasty goodies. These baked goods would sell for a fair price at the bakery in town, with only a small portion of the money going to the shop owner. The man was not only a kind soul but also a shrewd businessman who knew from experience that Mrs. Tomlinson's pies and pastries brought more holiday business to his shop.

Sterling busied himself with cutting and gutting the pumpkins, setting aside the seeds with their stringy pulp to be cleaned and roasted later. He was so involved in the work that it startled him when Mrs. Tomlinson began to speak quietly as she finished mixing pastry dough.

"I do not mind telling you, Sterling, that you are like a son to me now." She added a little more flour to the dough and began kneading it in with her strong, able hands. "I always wanted several children, and the fact that the Lord only allowed me to keep one has been a great sorrow to me over the years, though I am certainly grateful for Jerome. She paused a moment and pushed a lock of auburn hair out of her eyes with the back of one hand. "But now I feel as if He has finally granted me one more in you." She spoke gently but with a sureness that suggested she had contemplated this matter before. How was it that he and the Tomlinsons had known each other for only a couple of months? He had felt so welcome and at ease here right from the beginning.

Sterling felt his face warm with pleasure at her open, motherly affection, and a little lump rose in his throat. He swallowed and smiled. "Thank you, Mrs. Tomlinson. I feel that too. Knowing you has made me realize what I missed in my own mother without knowing it at the time. I truly feel at home here, and I appreciate how you have welcomed and befriended me--you and Jerome both."

"Tell me about your mother," Mrs. Tomlinson offered, as she began to flatten the dough with a rolling pin. "You have never said much about her."

"Well," Sterling grimaced, "she is a difficult woman to live with. She has very strong ideas about our family's role in high society and what we owe or do not owe the lower classes. She wanted to hear nothing of my desire to be a teacher." He scraped the last of the seeds and strings from the first pumpkin and cut into another. "Generally, the most I saw of her was during meals. She would get carried away talking about the latest gossip from the ladies' club and whose charity picnic she planned to attend next. She didn't care to hear much about what I had recently learned in my studies." He stopped cutting for a moment and looked at Mrs. Tomlinson. "I guess we never really communicated, now that I think about it."

Mrs. Tomlinson pondered this while she finished rolling out the dough and laid down the pin. "How unfortunate."

"Yes," Sterling agreed. "But at least I knew no different, so I felt no loss. I thought all mothers were aloof like mine, that the way of sons and mothers was to lead completely different lives." He delved into the belly of the pumpkin with a large spoon and pulled out the insides with strong, hard strokes. His shirtsleeves were rolled up high, his right arm slimy with pumpkin guts all the way up to the elbow.

Mrs. Tomlinson placed a pie plate gently upside down over the newly smoothed dough and cut around it, knowing just how much bigger to make it so that the dough would fit inside the plate. "And yet, as a teacher years later, somehow you knew that aloofness was not the most effective method for teaching children." She removed the plate and began folding the dough over itself into fourths in order to transport it safely to the plate.

"Well, actually," Sterling chuckled softly, remembering his talk with Mr. Grover at the beginning of the school year, "I would not say I necessarily came by that naturally. Perhaps if you asked Jerome, he would tell you I was a bit distant, myself, at first. Maybe I still am. I did not attend the university to learn how to teach children. I actually never intended to teach them."

"Really?" Mrs. Tomlinson sounded surprised.

"I had a naive and unrealistic view of my future career. But I have learned more in these first couple months of teaching at the Boys' School than I ever expected. More, in many ways, than I learned while sitting in classes at the university."

Mrs. Tomlinson looked up. "How is that?"

"Oh, the school I attended taught wonderful ideas. Concepts that..." he stopped scraping for a moment, spoon in midair, searching for the right words to explain. "...Concepts that made my head expand while my brain did somersaults."

Mrs. Tomlinson chuckled. "My, that must have been quite an experience!"

He lowered the spoon and continued scraping. "I thought about things—everything—the world!--in ways I never had before. It was exciting and very intellectual. I could not get enough of learning: all the latest styles, methods, and subjects—it all fascinated me. I lived and breathed ideas. Of course, writing has always been my passion, so I determined to become a personal writing teacher—a tutor, if you will—to all the rich young people who, like me, had had no particular guidance in that pursuit but who yearned to. I would be their guide, their light in the dark." He said the words loftily, in self-derision. "I figured I was set for life! And my professors encouraged such grand plans. I suppose they have worked at the university so long that they have forgotten what the real world can be like!" Sterling laughed, and Mrs. Tomlinson smiled at his flow of thought and words, his self-recrimination.

"But your plans did not work out, I take it."

Sterling shook his head. "Let me just say, I may well have been the only rich boy with a passion for writing who desired a mentor."

"Surely not the only one?"

Sterling set the second clean pumpkin next to the first, both of whose internal bellies now gleamed naked and golden. Then he reached for another. "Well, not quite the only one," he conceded. "After graduation, I tutored a couple of students there in Cincinnati for a year or so, but they grew bored with it after a while and did not find my 'innovative' ideas and 'modern' techniques as exciting as I did—as the professors had."

"So you gave up those ideas?"

"No, not yet. I told myself I just was not in the right place, that I needed to move to more 'fertile' ground, so to speak. Somewhere more countrified, where they would welcome modern ideas instead of taking them for granted. You see, I had a very simplified view of things and did not realize at the time that open-minded people are to be found in all walks of life, in all economical groups, and in varied geographical areas—or not."

"Was that change successful?"

Sterling paused, suddenly feeling that familiar sorrow that always crept over him when he remembered the things he kept trying not to remember. "Successful? I don't know..."

Mrs. Tomlinson sensed the sudden change in mood and watched Sterling struggling within himself. She cut a second round of dough and formed it into another pie plate before venturing quietly,

"I do not mean to pry, Sterling. You have no obligation to relate your life to me."

He shook his head. "I know. But I want to, I...I think I need to, Mrs. Tomlinson. I haven't discussed this with anyone, and suddenly I feel as if you are the only person in the world who might understand and give me the counsel I need." He put the spoon down and stood still, both orange-slimed hands resting firmly on the table.

Mrs. Tomlinson looked over at him, and he raised his head to meet her eyes.

"I would be honored," she answered simply.

Slowly Sterling chose another pumpkin and began cutting once again while he gathered his thoughts. It was painful to make himself think of these things; he had refused to look at them in the daylight for so long that he was not sure what he would find. And yet, there was a faint sense of impending relief as well.

"There may have been some success," he conceded finally. "I like to think there was. But I was there for such a short time... I planned to live in Oberlin for a couple of years at least; I liked it there, and folks were accepting of me. I was fortunate to find that it actually is a place where new ideas are welcomed, even encouraged. I even bought a horse to be sure I would have transportation and recreation. I grew up on a horse farm, and from the time I was very young, I have rarely been without a mount."

"Bought a horse? Just for the time you would be there?" Mrs. Tomlinson repeated, obviously grasping the true affluence of Sterling's position for the first time with that one comment.

"I admit it may have been a bit impulsive, but it seemed the right thing to do at the time, and I had the money. I figured it would be more reliable than an automobile, and cheaper." [18]

Mrs. Tomlinson nodded and gave a wry smile. "I am still not certain what I think of the 'horseless carriage.' I am glad there are very few in Worthington as yet."

He began scooping again, continuing to talk as he worked. "Automobiles are certainly something to get used to. At any rate, I was in Oberlin no more than two weeks when I attended a church picnic with an associate, and that was where I met her."

"Your pupil?"

Sterling nodded, but the title sounded so foreign and inadequate now. Samantha had become so much more to him than a pupil that it almost startled him to remember how things had started.

"Yes, she became my...pupil, but I was the one who sought her out. I cajoled her into trying one lesson, and she reluctantly agreed. She must have thought me crazy! But true to her word, she arrived on time for the lesson."

"What did she think?" Mrs. Tomlinson asked, caught up in the narrative.

"By the end of the lesson, she seemed truly interested for the first time, and I thought I sensed a desire in her to learn the things I had to teach about writing. The way her attitude and demeanor changed gratified and inspired me. It gave me high hopes that things

---

[18] https://en.wikipedia.org/wiki/Category:Cars_introduced_in_1901

would proceed as I wanted them to, that I had a star pupil on my hands."

He remained lost in thought for several moments, and the kitchen was quiet but for the scraping and patting sounds of their individual domestic efforts.

Finally, he began again: "I have never seen anyone progress so rapidly at anything before in my life! It was fulfilling to know that I had seen in her what I thought I saw, that I did have something exciting to offer the world after all.

"I learned that her father was an old college professor who inherited quite a large sum of money and generally stayed to himself in his large estate, spending little of it. I, therefore, knew that I could be paid for my services to his daughter, which meant that in another aspect, I had chosen well also. But soon, the experience was so rewarding that I completely forgot about any payment incurred. Working with Samantha was a reward in itself. Her excitement to learn and to improve her abilities made me remember why I had wanted to teach in the first place. And her eagerness to develop her writing reminded me of my own passion for it."

"I can see how such an experience would be very fulfilling," Mrs. Tomlinson nodded. And then, after a pause, "But you speak of it unhappily. Surely it did not end there?"

"It all began in May...and ended in August."

"So short a time?"

"Yes, and yet how wonderful while it lasted."

Mrs. Tomlinson now began to guess at something she had not felt she had a right to wonder before.

"The experience with Samantha was so rejuvenating to my drooping soul after the disappointments I experienced. And I ruined it all."

"You?" Mrs. Tomlinson couldn't imagine how that could be the case. All she had learned of his character thus far denied that he could have done such a thing. Sterling's bereft expression tugged at her heart, and she wanted to comfort him. Finished with the pie crusts, she moved to the table where Sterling still scraped away, and she began to separate the seeds from their sticky strings, placing the slippery white discs onto a greased, flat baking pan.

When, after several long moments, Sterling still had not offered an explanation, she began to talk, hoping to make things easier for him. "I am afraid I don't understand, Sterling. I have never seen you as anything but the perfect gentleman, nor have I ever heard anything but good about your teaching. How could you have ruined such a marvelous teaching opportunity with such a promising and talented pupil?"

Sterling took a deep breath, held it, and let it out slowly. "I guess you could say I took advantage of my position and...well...became too caught up in the emotion of the moment."

"We all make mistakes," Mrs. Tomlinson intoned quietly. "Surely whatever you feel you did was not really so terrible..."

"Perhaps not..." Sterling conceded reluctantly, "but to me, afterward, it was quite terrible. It represented a breach of trust, a lack of consideration and respect, and particularly a lack of self-restraint. I refuse to explain it away or to excuse myself."

Mrs. Tomlinson felt a smile rising within her as her suspicions were confirmed. *Poor dear*, she thought.

Neither of them spoke for another long moment. Sterling could not speak, for he was once again racked with the memory of what he had done. Mrs. Tomlinson did not speak, for she was concentrating on suppressing her amusement and gathering the right words to help him. When she felt composed enough to speak, she turned to him, placing her sticky hand on his sticky hand, forcing him to stop and look at her. "I do not know what you claim to have done, Sterling. But the young man I see before me is one who is gentle and kind and desires the best for those around him. Falling in love with a girl who shares your interests and needs you as no one has needed you before is not a crime." She moved away to give him space to think about her words and watched him with concern and motherly affection.

Sterling was visibly affected by what she had said and searched her eyes for further enlightenment. He seemed to relax a bit after a moment, but then turned away. "I did fall in love with her, Mrs. Tomlinson, didn't I? I had not realized that until now..." His voice was soft and bewildered. He looked stunned and sure all at once. "You are right. But if I truly loved her, why did I violate her trust? Why did I compromise her position? I had no right to do that."

The room was silent again, and Mrs. Tomlinson sent a prayer to heaven, asking for wisdom.

Then slowly and laboredly, as if it cost him everything to say it out loud, Sterling concluded, "I...kissed...her. Without asking. And it frightened her."

Mrs. Tomlinson was silent for only a moment. "You had no chaperone, then?"

Sterling shook his head mournfully. "No, and that is a part of my guilt also. We were not courting, I was merely her teacher. I had not thought through things enough to realize that I, a young man, should not take her, a young woman, alone into the woods. I was so focused on the brilliant lesson I would give my student that the thought of a chaperone did not even enter my mind! But even so, we should not have been alone like that, far from any other person."

The pain in his eyes was evident. *The poor boy needs comfort and reassurance*, she thought. *He is so good at heart and doesn't even realize it.* "You meant no harm, Sterling. A kiss is a natural reaction of being in love. What is so wrong with a small kiss now and then, though no one speaks of it?" She looked with compassion at his downcast face, wishing she could relieve the regret she saw there.

"You forget how brief my relationship with her was!" he responded, his voice louder. "And I do not know if my feelings were reciprocated: she seemed to still look upon me as her teacher." He looked up from the table. "A teacher does not behave that way with his student." He gained momentum as he spoke, and the pumpkins were forgotten as he forged ahead. "I am sure that you, who are so kind to overlook my faults, cannot fail to see that I was in the wrong in that."

"Perhaps. However," Mrs. Tomlinson paused and proceeded carefully, "what if the young woman did feel as you felt and had progressed into thinking of you romantically also? What then? Would that not lessen your guilt and change the picture somewhat?"

Sterling was taken aback. "I... I don't know! I do not see how that could have been possible."

After a moment, Mrs. Tomlinson laughed softly, the tension in the room easing, then began picking through the mess for pumpkin seeds once more. "Do you find it so hard to believe that a young woman—any young woman—would find you attractive and enjoy being with you?"

Once again, she had caught Sterling by surprise, and he colored a little for the second time that day.

"You could not possibly mean that she...that she might have..." Sterling shook his head as if to dismiss the thought.

"And why not? Perhaps the possibility will give you something different to consider—for I do think it possible."

Sterling suddenly remembered the little note Samantha had left him, the memory of which had been his salvation several times over the last few months. At once, Mrs. Tomlinson's impossible words took on a hint of validity, and he found himself considering them after all...

CHAPTER 16

RUPERT WINTON and H.D.T.

December 1901

When Katherine told Samantha about the town's annual Christmas Ball to be held the first Saturday of December, she decided she ought to attend, though doing so went against the person she had always been. Just the thought of being around all those people made her nervous, and she had no idea what she would do when she arrived, but it seemed like a proper venue to continue to meet others her own age and to learn the skills she had never concerned herself with before. Accordingly, she accepted Katherine's offer to come by for her. But thinking about attending the dance without any knowledge of how to dance or dress or behave almost paralyzed Samantha. Katherine, as always, could tell that something troubled her, and when she pressed, and Samantha reluctantly told her of her concerns, Katherine did not laugh nor even seem surprised. Instead, she promised to help by giving her "lessons" twice a week until the night of the dance.

These lessons succeeded in teaching Samantha a few of the more basic dance steps, and she began to feel more confident in her ability to keep a conversation going, as well. She was also very grateful for the tips and instructions Katherine offered (at Samantha's urgings) on how to look her best through her manner of dress and grooming. Simply through her contact with Katherine over the last couple of months, watching her interactions with others, Samantha had learned a great deal also.

In fact, she had learned such a variety of new things over the last few months that it was difficult to remember where one stopped and the other began. They were all part of the making of the better person she wanted to be--someone who was more socially capable and who had meaningful relationships with others.

She found herself glad for the frightening decision she had made to go to the ball, for her social life did take a step forward with her attendance. Many young men asked her for a dance that night, and though she had never danced in her life—except in Katherine's dining room as she tried to keep up with her friend's deft feet—she caught on to the steps quickly. And incredibly, her ignorance and openness to learning, instead of discouraging the young men, gave her an attractive naivete that made them eager to teach her. Though nervous, she had never been self-conscious and was not that night either. She had taken great care to do all she could to make herself presentable, but there ended her concern with how she looked. Her nervousness gradually gave way to excitement, and she felt herself flushing as she watched all the beautiful dancing young people and tried to follow what they did.

No one would have referred to her later as the "belle" of the ball, and none of the other young women felt threatened by her presence. Some of them did wonder where the "new girl" had come from, and a few tittered to each other behind their hands as they watched her sometimes stumble in her dancing. But the positive attention Samantha received and the enjoyment she found there that night were more than enough to make her discard her timidity and step from the shadows of her reclusive, solitary life a little more each week.

Every time she found herself without a partner that night, she made her way to a chair by the refreshment table for a rest and to give herself a chance to simply watch. Seeing so many attractive people, their movements, their associations with each other, their expressions, their train of conversation, fascinated her. One of the young men whom she met that night asked for a few dances, though Samantha wondered why, since she had stepped on his toes numerous times. But often, when she sat on the side, Rupert Winton would make his way to her again to offer her a drink or a sweet or to enter into light conversation with her until she was ready to dance again.

Rupert looked clean and pressed, and the gentle expression in his eyes made Samantha feel comfortable. His broad, simple face was browned from working out in the elements year-round, and his light brown hair swept neatly over his brow. He was not a big man, but the broadness of his shoulders and the brawn of a body accustomed to hard labor made him appear so. He was pleasant to talk to and danced, if not gracefully, quite capably (though, who was she to judge, after all?).

When the musicians played the last reel, ending in uproarious applause by all in attendance, and began to pack away their instruments, Samantha felt a touch on her shoulder and turned to see Rupert standing there once again, offering his arm. "May I escort you home, Miss Jennings?" he asked. Samantha noticed the little beads of perspiration just below his hairline and rimming his top lip and realized for the first time how warm she felt too.

She looked up at him, her cheeks still flushed from the exercise and excitement of the evening and her damp hair curling at the temples. She liked the way he looked at her, how like a little boy he seemed in his eagerness to help. "Well, I... I came with someone..." she started to explain, but seeing the instant disappointment in his eyes added quickly, "so I need to let her know that I have another way home."

Without seeing the relief relax Rupert's expression, Samantha glanced across the floor to where Katherine stood, a young man on either side of her, and after a moment, caught her eye. Katherine smiled at her and gave an encouraging, approving wave, and Samantha took Rupert's offered arm. "All right, we may go now. And thank you."

"That's it?" he asked, looking from Katherine to Samantha and back again. "Do you need to talk to her?"

Samantha laughed and shook her head. "I already told her."

Rupert shrugged. "All right, then." He began working his way through the crowd toward the coat room, where stood a group of people Samantha had not yet met. Rupert introduced his friends to her and helped Samantha with her coat as they all prepared to leave together. Falling snow added to that already on the ground, and the cold air nipped their faces, but the drive in the horse-drawn sleigh seemed almost magical to Samantha. They were all bundled up warmly and packed tightly together, singing carols as they rode along, stopping every little while to let someone else off. Samantha felt so alive and full of vitality that her face wore a perpetual smile, and watching her, Rupert's slow smile appeared again and again.

***

Sterling sat at the desk in his room, as tired as he could ever remember being. He closed his eyes and rubbed a hand over his face, letting out a long sigh. His stomach rumbled, reminding him that he was overdue for supper. Being a "real" teacher was harder work than he had ever anticipated and in ways he had not expected. It was not without its rewards, to be sure, and he was growing to know and understand the boys better all the time. But all the planning and preparation beforehand, and then the corrections and grading afterward, left very little time for anything else in Sterling's life at this point. He supposed it would become easier with time as he grew better at doing it all.

At times like these, thoughts of his family's wealth crept into his mind, tempting him with the reminder that he did not, after all, have to work like this. But the idea of being a professional gentleman repelled him. His mother saw nothing wrong with it, of course. If a person were privileged to be born into a high level of society, it was his duty to fill that role well--and then, of course (with an attitude of condescension), to help those less fortunate. Even with all his wealth, Sterling's father had always been a working man. But his labors as overseer of his own land were considered in keeping with his gentleman status, so doing so was not stepping below his rank. And while Sterling could tolerate that kind of work, he took no enjoyment from it, as his younger brother did.

Sterling felt the same drive to work, to contribute to--if not make--his own keep, as his father and brother did, but his views were somewhat different. He saw no logical reason why a wealthy man of supposed aristocratic lines should not contribute to the whole society in which he lived, as well as any other man. He had had nothing whatever to do with his birth into such a station, but he did have a great deal of control over what he did with it and what he became. And Sterling did not feel he could do much of either if he lived on his parents' estate, polishing his riding and hunting skills all day or helping his father oversee the land, and attending every function of high society imaginable each evening in an attempt to find and woo a rich heiress. Considering the inanity of such a life sickened him.

There were few things now that annoyed him more than facades and pettiness.

So, he would be a teacher, and he would work, and he would not give up just because he was tired.

He opened his eyes and surveyed the room that could have been described as "austere." His bed, a washstand and basin, a towel on a hook, a tiny mirror, and this desk and chair were the only furnishings. His mother would have been appalled, but he found no reason to add anything to what was already here. He had the necessities, why should he concern himself with more than that? He spent most of his time at school anyway. And after all, his favorite historical figure and author, Henry David Thoreau, had lived willingly with fewer amenities than these and learned a great deal from the experience. That, to Sterling, was one of the measures of a great man.

Without thinking about it, his gaze fell upon the strips of paper posted above his desk, sayings he had picked up from his readings of Thoreau's works over the years. He read slowly over them again, though he had long known each by heart:

"Go confidently in the direction of your dreams! Live the life you've imagined. As you simplify your life, the laws of the universe will be simpler."[19]

Well, Sterling thought to himself dubiously, *my life is pretty simple right now: I plan, I teach, I make corrections, and I start the*

---

[19] https://www.goodreads.com/quotes/8105541-go-confidently-in-the-direction-of-your-dreams-live-the

process all over again each day. It's simple, but I wouldn't say that as a result I am living the life I imagined. Far from it, in fact...

"If you have built castles in the air, your work need not be lost; that is where they should be. Now put the foundations under them."[20]

Is that what he had done with all his teaching ideas up until now, built castles in the air? Is that what he had done with Samantha? Was that his problem, that he was overly adept at creating pretty pictures in the air but overtly lacking in the ability to ground them in reality?

He paused in his thoughts and considered these questions. He knew he was an idealist--always had been. But Samantha was very much grounded in reality. It seemed to him that any castle he may have built that had anything to do with her could not be lost because even during the years she had lived in her dream-books, she had somehow built a foundation under her that gave her sure footing no matter what happened. She was practical and down-to-earth, much more so than himself, he admitted. And yet she had had the irresistibly charming quality of still being able to imagine and to dream—and to do so passionately. Perhaps successful castle-building required the perfect balance of all of these things that Samantha seemed to have in order.

What was it she had asked him that fateful morning? "Sterling, haven't you ever wanted to believe in something so much that it almost did become real to you? Do you have secret dreams?"

For the first time, the answer came with paralyzing swiftness, and it was *yes*. He sat, stunned by the novelty of this revelation.

---

[20] https://www.brainyquote.com/quotes/henry_david_thoreau_105332

The only secret he had was Samantha. Not her as a person necessarily, but the way he felt about her, the way she had opened his eyes and heart when he was trying to open hers. And the thing he wanted most in the world was to see her again, to be near her and feel that...*light* he had experienced with no one else.

But did he believe this need--this *want*--enough to make it a reality? He did not even know yet what it meant to believe in and desire something that strongly. A few years ago, he would have said that he did, for his desire to attend college and make a life for himself had been strong and insistent and propelled him forward for a long time. But now? Compared to what he felt for Samantha, even that former desire seemed trivial.

He read from the fourth slip of paper: "Man is the artificer of his own happiness."[21]

Sterling shook his head. "You have told me that so many times, H.D.T.," he said aloud, "and I have always believed it and pursued my life accordingly. But as of late, I have learned that things don't always turn out in the nice little packages one intends. I did what I thought was right, and I was happy at the time. Happier than I have ever been, in fact, though I did not realize it then.

"But a woman is the artificer of her own happiness too! And I am not so sure that the happiness she is creating would include me. Without her, my happiness is not complete, but what of hers? I am not as convinced as I once was of the truthfulness of your statement, Thoreau."

---

[21] https://cartereducation.medium.com/quotes-in-context-thoreau-that-if-one-advances-confidently-80ca9b987fa8

He turned to the fifth and last quote. "Success usually comes to those who are too busy to be looking for it."[22]

"Now *that* I still believe," Sterling said emphatically. "At least the part about staying busy. So, I will go back to my corrections and forget I ever had this monologue with myself." He swiped at the air with one hand as if to brush away all his musings, and chuckled wryly, then thought a moment and sighed. "At this point, whether success comes or not is irrelevant anyway."

With that, he turned back to the stack of student papers and tried to believe his own words. After a while, when he found himself still unable to concentrate, he decided to get a quick bite to eat and then, perhaps, take yet another walk through the cemetery. The place was beginning to feel a part of him; it was a closer refuge than the Tomlinson's home and did not require any intelligent conversation. For times when he needed fresh air and solitude, he could go there and find both.

***

After their initial meeting at the Christmas Ball, Rupert Winton invited Samantha to the town orchestra's Christmas concert with his friends. And another time, she joined them as they attended the college's play adaptation of Charles Dickens' book *A Christmas Carol.*

Another evening, he arrived at her door with a basket on his arm to ask if she cared to join him for a picnic, which he had packed himself. Samantha laughed in delight (a picnic in the winter!) and, as she did so, watched the apprehension on his face smooth away and

---

[22] https://www.azquotes.com/quote/294079

the tension in his eyes ease. She invited him into the parlor, where he immediately set to work building a fire in the fireplace, and she spread out the blanket and food he had brought. Mrs. Dolittle quietly added two steaming mugs of spiced, hot cider and some bottled pears and then silently left again, taking care to stay nearby but out of sight. Samantha and Rupert situated themselves on either side of the food, and what started out a little awkwardly ended in a wonderful evening. The crackling warmth of the fire relaxed any awkwardness while their fingers and mouths grew greasy from fried chicken and biscuits. Mrs. Dolittle hummed at her work and smiled contentedly to herself as she heard Samantha's laughter from down the other room.

Samantha enjoyed talking with Rupert, the comfortable way he made her feel, and how she could talk about almost anything with him. Rupert liked to watch her, and the animated way her eyes expressed everything she felt as she talked. Miss Jennings had such interesting things to talk about, and for those times when it grew quiet, he wished he could think of clever topics in return. But he did not feel backward with her the way he sometimes did with other girls. He was not sure how she did it, but Miss Jennings had a way of calming and delighting him all at the same time.

CHAPTER 17

THE LETTER and CHRISTMAS VISITING

December 1901

The following few weeks passed in a blur for Sterling. He managed his classes adequately but found himself constantly redirecting his thoughts to focus them on the tasks at hand, instead of on the new knowledge that he did have a secret dream after all. The realization had taken hold of him with surprising force and the power of it filled him almost beyond his capacity to hold. How he wished he could go back in time, back to the woods and the fairy ring, when Samantha had asked him with such innocence, "Do you have secret dreams, then?" He would have taken her hand and told her that yes, he did, that *she* was his dream, and one he fervently hoped never to lose, for now she meant more to him than anything else ever had.

But no, that sort of thing could only happen in hindsight and only in his mind. If, at the time, he had known the real answer to her question, would he really have told Samantha? Would that timing really have been right--for either of them?

His last conversation with Mrs. Tomlinson and the counsel she gave him had had a powerful effect upon him, particularly those words which had forced him to ponder the impossible. He did not know what to make of that: of the possibility that Samantha had felt anything for him besides the feelings of a student for her teacher. As a woman, Mrs. Tomlinson might have an insight into Samantha's heart, but the prospect still seemed too incredible. After vacillating back and forth on the matter all week long, Sterling finally came to the conclusion that maybe that was not the important issue after all.

First of all, whether or not Samantha had any special feelings towards him, he had still crossed a boundary he should not have, and he continued to feel guilt for that violation. Secondly, it had happened nearly six months ago, twice as long as their actual acquaintance, and there was no telling what Samantha felt toward him now. For all he knew, she had forgotten him—and perhaps she had found some other young man who really was a gentleman, not just in word alone. Thirdly, and above all, regardless of any other considerations, she deserved an apology. He owed her that much as a human being and especially as one whom he now knew he loved with all the strength of his heart.

But neither could he shirk his teaching duties to take time off to ease his conscience on this matter, so it would have to be postponed. He yearned to go during his Christmas holiday, but he had already committed to spending the time with his parents. Though, if truth be told, he would much rather go back to Oberlin than to Lexington.

He wanted to make this apology right and he needed to fulfill his obligation to the school as well—and he could not do both at once. Yet, this waiting was no longer tenable. Unable to tolerate the infinite-seeming silence between them, he determined to write a letter to let Samantha know some of what he was feeling and that he intended to visit her to express his apologies in person.

As he wrote the letter, he found himself wanting to write far more than was prudent and had to stop himself several times from making admissions to her that he knew would be much too forward. How he longed to write *I am forever thinking of you*, or *How I long to see you again*, but he was afraid that would be too strong and would perhaps even push her farther away. After many stops and starts and five or six new tries on fresh paper, he finally finished a short letter that he felt was adequate, if not very demonstrative of the depth of his true feelings:

December 14, 1901

Dear Miss Jennings,

I write to you with a heavy heart for any dishonor I have brought upon you by my conduct, this July last. It is with strong feelings of regret that I offer you my sincerest apologies and profoundest wish that I can in some way atone for my imprudent actions. I am presently employed as a teacher at the Worthington Boy's School and can therefore do no traveling until the end of the term, at which point I hope to meet you to express my heartfelt apologies in person.

Wishing you the best of a beautiful life and the blessings of your bounteous talents,

I am yours sincerely,

Lee Sterling

He sealed the letter, feeling lighter than he had in months, and took it to the post office that very day. He hoped Samantha's reaction to it would be favorable, that she would receive it in the manner in which it was given. Having made the decision to find her when school ended made Sterling feel better. Just having a goal in sight eased his anxiety. Though he often still had trouble concentrating during the day and the night dreams continued, his spirit calmed with this plan of action, and before long his uneventful twenty-fourth birthday had come and gone, and Christmas was upon him.

Christmas was always a lovely affair at Sterling's home growing up, at least as far as the outward show of things went. His mother lavished every room with festive decorations of pine boughs, holly, mistletoe; bows of green, red, and white; and candles of all sizes in ornate holders. She also drew up menus for the most sumptuous foods for their table. When Sterling grew old enough to see beyond the surface celebrations, he recognized that, to his mother, the season was the perfect excuse to host parties that showed off her beautiful mansion and décor for the ladies of the community to ogle over. Never was she so happy as when she was busily engaged in the midst of an important social event. So, Christmas was a happy time at the Sterling residence.

Sterling's father was not half so inclined to indulge in frivolities and would rather have remained in his study with the newspaper or out in the stables with his horses, but he dutifully traipsed into the woods every year for the perfect Christmas trees for his wife. She always insisted that there be three and that they stand tall and straight with branches evenly distributed all around. One— the tallest—was placed in the front yard near the steps to the front veranda and was artfully sprinkled with colorful plaster birds and their twine nests, with red velvet bows scattered throughout. Another was stationed in the high-ceilinged front entryway and looped with the traditional popcorn and cranberry strands, with a few paper gift boxes in red and gold interspersed among the branches and a shining gold star on top. The third was the "masterpiece" tree, carefully placed in a prominent corner of the impressively large ballroom where the polished shine of the dark wood floor reflected the lights from the tiny electric bulbs that had been installed in very recent years. Sterling's mother spent days decorating these trees every year and meticulously directed a servant or two to help her, for they had to be done just so.

All of these memories came back to him as Sterling dismounted from the train in Lexington, Kentucky after an all-day journey and hailed a horse-drawn sleigh to take him the rest of the way to his parents' home. Though the driver was not personally acquainted with Sterling, he knew well enough where the Sterling estate was located and soon made his way through the maze of city center and beyond to where the houses spread farther and farther apart and the snow on the road was less traversed.

Besides feeling weary after all-day travel, Sterling felt a sense, if not of excitement, to be going "home," at least a feeling of familiarity and anticipation to see if anything had changed in the two years since he had last visited.

Wilson opened the door as Sterling walked up the steps and ushered him in, expressing his gladness at seeing "the young master." Sterling was very glad to see the elderly, gray-haired man, as well, whom he had known all his life. Wilson took his coat and hat and led the way into the sitting room where Mrs. Sterling sat, calmly putting the finishing touches on her latest guest list. When she saw who had arrived, she arose, smiling, and put out a gloved hand. "Lee, my dear. How good to see you." The modulated tone of her voice was deep, strong, and aristocratic, and just hearing it brought back a rush of memories.

"And you, Mother." Sterling took the offered hand and then drew her into a brief embrace. It had been so long since anyone had called him by his given name that it sounded very strange in his ears. He thought she looked a little older than the last time he had seen her, though her white hair was just as perfectly done up as ever in its poofed pompadour, and the few wrinkles around her eyes and mouth seemed not to have multiplied. But there was something in her face, a loosening perhaps, that seemed to indicate she had given up a few more years of life.

Mrs. Sterling ordered tea and ushered her son closer to the fire blazing cheerily in the grate. "You must be cold and hungry after such a long ride," she said, her brown eyes taking him in casually but with a faint air of scrutiny just under the surface.

"Yes," he admitted, "it was longer than I expected, but so much preferable to riding horse and buggy the entire way, as in your day."

Mrs. Sterling raised her eyebrows and nodded in affirmation. "It most certainly is an improvement. The modern age has produced a number of conveniences that make one wonder what we ever did without them."

They settled themselves into plush chairs, and after a brief pause, Sterling asked gently, "How have you been, Mother? I am afraid I have not kept up a correspondence with you and Father very well."

"Oh," she waved a slow, graceful hand as if to dismiss the question. "I am well enough. No more than the usual small troubles. Your father has felt a bit more of his rheumatism coming on these last few months. But he has all the help he needs with the hemp during the growing season and with the horses year-round, and he never complains. You know how he is."

Sterling nodded. "Yes."

"And how are things progressing for you at that boys' school?" She asked the question as if it left a bad taste in her mouth.

He ignored the insinuation and crossed one leg over the other as if he felt at ease. "I cannot complain. They are really very good boys and seem to be advancing in their studies."

Mrs. Sterling nodded slightly and raised one manicured eyebrow. "Of course, they would progress more quickly if they each had a tutor at home, as you and your brother did. But...I suppose not everyone is as fortunate as we are and can afford to hire them."

"No, that is true." Sterling smiled wanly to himself, remembering all the little speeches his mother had made over the years about how "fortunate" their family was in comparison with others and that they must think kindly of others, regardless of their lower positions in life. "Perhaps they cannot *all* help the circumstances they are in, so we must encourage them to persevere," she was fond of saying. But other than monetarily, Sterling could not recall ever seeing her help them do so.

"You know we have more than adequate money to support you, should you decide to shrug off the workingman's lot." Mrs. Sterling gave her son an appraising look and, after a pause, added, "I still find it difficult to understand why you would choose to work when you have the choice to be a gentleman. And to work for such low wages! A common teacher, of all things. Of course, not that you are common, my dear, but what an occupation!"

Sterling breathed slowly for a moment, willing himself not to be drawn into the old argument. "I rather enjoy it, actually. And I believe I have learned more than my students; it is really quite fulfilling."

His mother gave him a dubious look.

"Anyway, I know I do not have to rely solely on my teacher's salary, thanks to the large inheritance you and Father have made available to me. I do appreciate that."

Sterling could tell he had said the right thing when his mother looked momentarily pleased. "I am only glad you have allowed us to give it," she said. "Though I've noticed you haven't used much..." she looked at him shrewdly for a moment but did not demand an explanation. "What a pity it would be to have to permit one of our own flesh and blood to live in poverty!"

Then changing the subject, she asked, "And how is Society in that town you live in?" Now she had arrived at the topic he had known she inevitably would: Society with a capital "S." "Have you met any young ladies of merit recently?"

The image of a girl in a straw hat and plain cotton dress, with bright hair and deep, gray eyes behind wire-rimmed spectacles, came to his mind, but he shook his head. Samantha was not the kind of girl his mother referred to. Feeling like he was giving a speech he said, "I have chosen to involve myself as much as possible in the lives of my students and have honestly been too busy to seek out the society circles of Worthington." *Too busy and too uninterested*, he added to himself. "My closest friends are the Tomlinsons, to whom I frequently offer my services, as they have a large farm to maintain without much outside help."

Mrs. Sterling shook her head regretfully. "But how will you ever meet the right kind of girl if you never attend Society functions? Probably no one out there even knows who you are." Her voice sounded almost pouty, as if she were scolding him for a great lack of judgment, like he was depriving Worthington citizens of a great honor.

With effort, he refrained from snorting at the idea, choking down a laugh.

"You know you do not want to marry a country girl," she continued. "You were brought up for better."

Sterling felt himself growing more and more irritated but tried to keep his voice light. "Who said I was planning to marry yet, Mother?"

"Oh. Well," she waved her hand again, "you know, eventually." She looked at him sternly. "You are only growing older, son. You will not want to remain a bachelor indefinitely."

"Perhaps not," Sterling consented, "but I am still only twenty-four years old--and that only recently. And I am just beginning my career." He suddenly remembered why talking with his mother made him tired.

He was grateful the tea things arrived then, and shortly thereafter, his father entered to greet him. He seemed genuinely pleased to see Sterling, his gray mustache turning up at the corners. But, as always, he had very little to say and quickly grew restless in their company. After a brief visit, he excused himself, shook Sterling's hand, and returned to the stables.

CHAPTER 18

DISCOURAGEMENT

December 1901

Samantha returned home late from the town's Christmas Eve celebration, tired enough to sleep for an age. She reviewed the evening in her mind as she walked slowly up the long staircase to her bedroom, long gown gathered up in one hand, lighted lamp in the other. She acknowledged to herself that it had gone well. And honestly, this was the best Christmas Eve she had ever experienced: Martin and Mrs. Dolittle had accompanied her and Rupert, and the reading of the Holy Birth had definitely been the highlight of the evening for her, along with the warm feeling of peace and the comfortable sense of community. But the event had left her wanting, somehow.

She did not regret going, but she felt a lack of...she paused in her ascent, trying to grasp what she felt, but the words eluded her. *Well, something was missing*, she thought as she continued her climb. As on other occasions, she was aware of a difference between herself and the other young people that she could not quite lay a finger on. There were a few dances, most of which she danced with Rupert, but her heart was not in it, and it had all seemed a game to her, pointless. She was not sure why. For no reason, some moments she felt very alone, even amid such a crowd of people, and that was the worst kind of loneliness she knew.

Sometimes it's just like this, she told herself firmly; she always recovered and this would be no different. She reached the landing and turned left, holding the lamp high to light her way down the dark hallway.

I guess inside I am still the same girl, regardless of all that has changed in me. Often I still prefer my own company to that of a crowd, and quiet to the buzz of talk and laughter. There is nothing wrong in that, is there? She shook her head and shrugged. *I have never been ashamed or embarrassed to be Samantha and I do not intend to be so now.*

She opened the door to her room and stepped inside, shutting it softly behind her. Setting the lamp on top of the small table by the door, she used its light to help her see another lamp, which she lit and placed on the bedside table. The added light brightened her spirits slightly and she proceeded to prepare herself for bed with a lighter heart, feeling a bit better just by being back in her comfortable room that was her safe refuge. But several minutes later, chilled with her face washed, hair in a braid, and nightgown donned, she knew she would not be able to sleep without first trying to figure out what she really felt. Sometimes she still had to write whatever came to her mind in order to discover what she was thinking and feeling. She would never forget that lesson from Sterling.

She wrapped herself in an extra blanket and carried the bedside lamp to her desk. As she pulled out a sheet of paper, another poem began to form itself in her mind. Half an hour and a few editings later, she copied the finished product into her journal to contemplate later, when she was not so exhausted:

UNSOCIAL BUTTERFLIES

Uncomfortable in the claustrophobic masses

of lost freedom and lowered mobility

Wary, disdainful of suppression to the mold

of "free-thinking individuality"

and cookie cutter sociality

Weary of sameness—

different in their sameness.

Content to know a few whose colors and patterns

yield designs of perfect symmetry

that only deepen as time progresses:

yellow to gold, orange to flame,

blue to ocean...bottomless.

Content to flit among themselves,

absorbed in determining the course

of the world

and the order of their personal chaos,

to flutter close to home,

unassuming,

happy in their identity.

And they're the labeled unsocials.

Aren't we all butterflies,

attracted to our own

and entertained by the rest?

The exercise of writing the poem had fulfilled its purpose and Samantha felt considerably better. She didn't have any answers, but at least she did not feel so alone now, somehow. Fatigue broke over her in a wave that was so all-consuming she barely remembered to blow out the lamps after a short prayer before falling gratefully into bed.

***

All in all, Sterling's visit to his parents' home was tolerable, but by the end of his fortnight stay (which seemed much longer than that), he was more than ready to return to his own little room on the second floor of the boarding house. That realization surprised him, for he had never thought he would look upon the lifeless little room with any degree of anticipation. Before returning to Kentucky, he had felt that after such a long absence from his parents, he ought to visit them--his brother was still away on business for their father and had not made it home for Christmas. Now, duty fulfilled, he was glad to have a place to return to and a job to take up his time and attention. He had missed that autonomy and purpose while at home. He would not miss his mother's constant concern with social events and local gossip, and it would be a relief to escape from her meaningful introductions to the "most important and beautiful young women of the county."

At his mother's insistence, he had attended a few Christmas balls and parties, but every time he came away with the impression that beneath all the beautiful faces, fancy gowns, and glittering jewelry, these women were uninteresting and shallow (like his mother, he painfully admitted). They seemed to have no individual ideas or firm convictions apart from what their social position had spoon-fed them since babyhood. He was aware of the fact that he was considered one of the most eligible bachelors in the region and that every one of these young women was very interested in how comfortable his family's money could make her.

Perhaps he was too cynical—surely not every young woman was like his mother!--but every question asked of him felt like it was loaded with insinuations about his bachelorhood and imminent need to find a wife whose status would complement his own.

He felt a strange and acute sense of distinction and disconnection from these people now, though he had always considered himself one of them growing up. Everything seemed like a shiny, suffocating veneer. Very few of his dance partners made anything but a half-hearted attempt to become acquainted with him as a person or to find out what made him of value besides the inheritance that was his through no effort or talent of his own. He refused to raise any false hopes or to start the gossip wheel spinning, so he spread himself around as much as possible, never dancing more than once with the same young woman, never seeming too interested in the conversations.

Girls of this sort used to interest him, he realized, but at that time, they were the only kind he had ever associated with. Until he met Samantha, he had not known there were young women with unique interests about the world and with burning desires to learn and improve themselves. The main woman in his life had been his mother, and the young ladies he met at social events seemed very much like her. Knowing Samantha had changed his entire perspective. After her, how could he be expected to take an interest in the façade-dripping women of his mother's persuasion? He realized he should not assume that all of them were exactly alike and with ulterior motives, but they all came up short compared to Samantha, no matter how much he gave them the benefit of the doubt. He had met someone real and seen into her soul, and he had no desire to find out if any other girl could be as interesting to him. He sincerely doubted that was even a remote possibility.

Of course, these realizations did not make his life any easier, whether while at the balls in Lexington or back in unassuming Worthington, so he pushed the thoughts away and tried to fill his days once more with the students with whom he had been entrusted.

Sterling continued to make frequent visits to the Tomlinson farm, helping with chores and anything that could be done during the winter. Generally, however, the time was spent in front of the fire talking with Mrs. Tomlinson while she knit stockings and sweaters, or completing puzzles with Jerome. Saturday afternoons, if the sun came out enough to soften the snow and take the bite out of the air, he and Jerome would bundle up and traipse out to the barn for another repair or woodworking lesson. To his surprise, Sterling was finding that he enjoyed such work, that it helped to relieve tension, and that he had a latent knack for it after all. Jerome, too, seemed to flourish in the role of teacher and opened up more and more with Sterling as he grew increasingly at ease with him. The boy's marks in school had risen significantly in every lacking area, and he was even developing a few friendships among his peers. Sterling was gratified to see the boy growing into a happier, more confident and able young man.

Mrs. Tomlinson never pried, but she did sometimes ask about Samantha: if anything more had happened, if he had heard from her. And to Sterling, it was a relief to be able to share the thoughts and memories of Samantha that he otherwise kept completely under lock and key.

He told Mrs. Tomlinson of his decision to find Samantha when school ended and apologize, a decision which Mrs. Tomlinson heartily encouraged and inwardly applauded. She felt that one way or another he must return to that town and have another chance to express his feelings to the young woman and see what came of it.

CHAPTER 19

FAMILY!

January 1902

During the quiet, dreary days following Christmas, Samantha brooded about the house, not feeling inspired or motivated enough to spend the hours writing that she had grown accustomed to. The first snowfalls in November had brought her exuberant delight with their sparkling beauty. But now she was tired of the endless cold, inside and out: the slippery wetness that prevented her from taking her usual walks and rides and the pressing gloom from cloudy skies that weighed down her spirits. Social events had slowed with the arrival of heavy snow, as it was more difficult to travel, and the options for possible activities were reduced. Samantha missed the sunshine. She missed green growing things. She missed...well, yes, she missed him too, but she had not heard from him since he left, so he must not be thinking of her in return. She knew she ought to forget him. Besides, she had Rupert. Dear, considerate Rupert. He was always so gentle and unassuming, so selfless and attentive.

The week after Christmas, on an early Saturday afternoon, Rupert took her on a sleigh ride with two other couples and was prepared not only with a heavy wool blanket for her but also a couple of hot stones that kept her feet warm all the way to their destination: an old cabin in the woods. At the cabin, the young men chopped wood, lit a crackling fire, and plugged a few holes in the walls where the chinking had fallen through. Samantha and the other young women tidied the one big room whose every surface was covered with cobwebs and a fine layer of dust, then made steaming mugs of hot cocoa to accompany the gingerbread they had brought.

The three couples spent a cozy few hours playing games and reading aloud funny stories, then when they grew sleepy, and before dusk fell, they bundled up again and headed outdoors for a snowball fight. When the six people divided into two teams, Samantha and Rupert ended up on the same side and quickly began building a wall of snow to protect themselves from the attack that was promised in ten minutes. They worked hard on the wall while the third member of their team, a young man, made a pyramid of snowballs, and soon they had an adequate fortress, ammunition ready. Rosy with their exertions, they crawled behind the wall and sat against it to catch their breath.

Samantha inhaled deeply a few times and tried to free her knitted mittens of the clumps of snow that clung to them. She quickly found this to be an almost useless exercise, however, so she removed them to pull her knitted cap down more securely on her head, then put them on again. Feeling eyes on her, she looked over at Rupert, who was smiling at her gently. He had nice eyes, she decided. Not the bottomless brown of Sterling's, but still a nice, clean blue that was true and honest.

"Are you ready to fight?" he asked.

"Are you ready to win?" she returned, a gleam in her eyes.

Rupert's smile widened, and he reached out a mittened hand to grasp hers in a brief handshake. "You've got it."

"Ready, set, go!" the other young man cried. And the battle began.

It was a close game, with each side taking a few hits and making numerous marks in quick succession. But in the end, the other team's wall suffered the most loss, and Rupert and Samantha's team was declared the winner.

Upon hearing this Samantha dropped to the ground and laughed in relief. "Whew!" she breathed. "That was quite a battle!"

Their team member returned to his girl's side and they watched as he received good-natured congratulations from the other team. Rupert lowered himself down beside her and nodded. They sat there together, laughing at the clouds of air they blew out with each hard breath until their heartbeats slowed to normal again.

"How do you manage to move so fast with all those skirts?" Rupert asked, removing his cap and shaking the snow off it. She could see where perspiration had dampened the hair at his brow, and his eyes were bright as he looked at her.

"I don't know," she answered, "but it was definitely tiring. You were pretty fast yourself."

Suddenly the mood changed and Rupert grew quiet. He reached silently for her mittened hand and clasped it in his own.

"Thanks for coming," he said in a low voice, looking into her face.

She nodded and searched his gaze. "Thank you for inviting me. This was the most fun I've had in a long time."

They continued looking at each other in silence until Samantha added, "But then again, I always have fun with you." It was true, but once she said it, she realized it might sound like she meant more than she intended.

But Rupert's eyes lit up and he seemed pleased by that. "Good," was all he said, though he looked as if he would like to say more. Then he got to his feet and pulled Samantha up beside him, and they headed back to the sleigh with the others.

Samantha thought about that day again as one afternoon in mid-January her boredom and despondency took her from room to room. She did enjoy spending time with Rupert and almost wished he would show up this moment to relieve her of the oppressive, shut-in feeling that was resting more and more heavily upon her. Before she realized what she was doing, she found herself searching through many of the dusty, unused rooms with their protectively draped furniture. She did not know what she was looking for but continued her wanderings. Finally, she ended up in her father's large, familiar library and absently began perusing titles. She glanced through the rows of books, not even sure why she was there. She had no interest in reading anything at the moment.

Then her eyes fell upon a worn, leather spine that said nothing at all. Plenty of the other books had no title on their spines either, but for some reason, she was drawn to this particular book. Perhaps it was its soft and shabby appearance, looking as if loving hands had opened it again and again. Whatever the reason, Samantha slid it from its place and smoothed a hand over its cover. She expected nothing, so when she opened it and read the first words, the shock of the discovery sent a jolt through her entire body. She let out a small cry, for there, on the slightly yellowed page in curled, upright handwriting were the words:

Journal

Lovenia Lewis Jennings

Samantha's heart stopped beating for a moment, then began to pound. She felt trembly inside and closed the book, clutching it to her chest and closing her eyes while she took a deep breath to steady herself. After a moment, she opened her eyes again and slowly made her way to the middle of the room, pulling her favorite overstuffed chair to a side window where there was more light. Then she sat, curling her legs beneath her in an unconscious effort to stay warm in the chilled room, and opened the book again. They were still there, those life-changing words she had never expected. *My mother wrote this with her own, neat hand!* The realization was thrilling and sad at once.

She traced the name gently with a forefinger as if she could draw from it the essence of her mother. The longing rose up within her as it had so many times before in the last few months, the longing to know her mother, to touch her and breathe in the scent of her. Samantha held the journal up to her face and drew in a long breath, but all she could smell was the mingled scent of worn leather, glue, ink, and old pages. She lowered the book, feeling slightly disappointed, but quickly turned the page with the hope that the words written there would bring her closer to the mother she had never known and help her better understand the woman she herself was.

May 9, 1876

I begin this journal as I joy to realize that Basil Jennings and I shall be wed in one month's time. I count him as my greatest blessing. Love, the kind I have dreamed of throughout my life and never truly believed would come, has come and its brilliance lights the path before me. Though I am not strong of body and may never be able to do for Basil all that he needs, he convinces me that the care I give him with my heart and my mind will be enough for him. He will make up the difference for what I cannot physically accomplish. But I feel stronger since I met my beloved than I have in a very long time! Basil is my strength and my happiness. The Lord is good.

Samantha stared at the page in wonder as she finished reading the first entry. Her mother had obviously been very much in love. The idea was as much a revelation as was Mrs. Dolittle's description of her father's loving care of Lovenia. For some reason, Samantha had never thought about her parents being in love. Now that thought delighted her, even as it surprised her. Not everyone married for love, she knew, and with the significant age difference between her parents, she had never been sure if theirs was a love match or not. She found herself wishing she knew this man that her mother had known and fallen in love with. Had the Basil Jennings of earlier years completely vanished or was that warm, affectionate part of him only in hibernation?

She turned to the next entry.

May 17, 1876

Time passes slowly and much too rapidly all at once. There is still much to do in preparation for the wedding and Mama has been such a dear to help so much. Without her skill and diligence, I could never be ready with my trousseau and make all the necessary arrangements for the wedding. It is a happy time, to be sure, but I am grateful I have all this to do but once in my lifetime. When I feel discouraged or despair of finishing everything, my thoughts turn to Basil once again and my spirits lift. To think of being his for the rest of my life makes my heart swell with such glorious hopes that I scarce can keep from lifting off like a bird in flight.

Samantha smiled and felt herself carried up in the ardor her mother described. She continued to read, savoring each word and turning the pages slowly, anticipating her parents' marriage as much as Lovenia had twenty-six years earlier. When she reached the entry written a few days after the marriage, she read eagerly.

June 13, 1876

I am now Lovenia Lewis Jennings. What a nice ring that has! It was such an honor and a pleasure to take Basil's name as he took my hand at the altar in the church. To feel his strong hand around my small, trembling one imbued me with a feeling of power. I have left Papa and Mama to cleave unto him, as the Bible counsels, and I know there is nothing better I could do with my life. The thought of creating a family with my dear husband fills me with awe. When he gave me his name and his heart, I gave him all that I am and all that I hope to become. It is as if I have been remade.

I feel content enough to burst, as if I have finally found my own nest, built just for me. Basil is so good and makes me feel like a queen. I continue to feel strong in body and spirit and bless the day he came into my life. I hope that I may make him as happy as he has made me.

Samantha sighed. The picture of their happiness was so lovely that she felt wrapped in a shawl of exquisite softness. This was her family she was reading about, when her mother had been only three years older than herself!

A light tap sounded at the open door, and Samantha turned, startled, to see Mrs. Dolittle standing there with a cup of tea in her hand.

"Excuse me for interrupting, my dear. I noticed you were in here and thought you could use something to warm your bones. I presumed to make up a warm fire in your room, if you care to move up there where you would be more comfortable." She walked over and held out the cup, a question in her dark brown eyes.

"Oh, that was so kind of you! Thank you, Mrs. Dolittle," Samantha murmured, grasping the warm cup in both cold hands. "I had not realized how cold it is in here, but you are quite right."

The older woman glanced down at the book in Samantha's hand and drew in a quick breath. Then she looked back at Samantha's flushed face and shining eyes. Slowly she nodded in understanding. "You found Lovenia's journal, I see."

"You knew about this?" Samantha asked, surprised.

"Your father used to keep it under lock and key—in a deep, dark trunk of his—until a time years ago when he lost the key for quite a few months and feared making the same mistake permanently. I somehow convinced him that the library would be safer, as it would never need a key to make it accessible."

Samantha looked at her, wondering why Mrs. Dolittle had never mentioned the journal during that first conversation about her parents' history. Her glance must have shown this troubling question, for Mrs. Dolittle hurried to say, "I wanted so much to tell you, but your father made me promise that if he allowed me to place it in the library, I would not tell a soul it was here. I prayed you would find it of your own accord. And I am so pleased to see that you have."

Samantha nodded and took a last sip of her tea. The way it warmed her insides was as delicious as its taste. She handed the cup back to the housekeeper and thanked her again, unfolding her legs to stand and feeling a momentary pain shoot through them as the circulation returned in a rush. "I will remove to my bedroom." As she followed the woman out of the library, she paused for a moment, holding up the plain, worn volume. "Have you read it, Mrs. Dolittle?"

Mrs. Dolittle shook her head. "I never felt it was my place." She reached out a slender brown finger and ran it tenderly along the leather binding. "Lovenia had a strong desire to leave a record for posterity and she kept it up faithfully as often as she could. I thought that was commendable—and I'll admit I have been curious--but not being family myself, it seemed intrusive to take a peek. So I never did."

Samantha hugged the journal close to her again and nodded.

"But I would tell you to enjoy it, Samantha, child, for it was written for you. I think it will help you to know your mother better—and your father too, for that matter—and will show you what a strong love they really had for one another."

"Yes," Samantha said softly. "It is doing that already."

Reading again in her warm, cozy room, Samantha sat comfortably on her bed and let herself become fully absorbed in her mother's journal. In so doing, she felt as if she had fallen into a treasure box that contained priceless gems and that in grasping them, her soul reflected their brilliance. Holding them, she held missing pieces of herself that filled a peculiar emptiness she had never understood; and knowing their value and the perfect way they fit into her life, she knew she would never loosen her grasp.

She read of her parents' early married life and how blissfully happy they were. Basil taught history at Ohio State University in Columbus and enjoyed it more than he ever had, for now he had someone to come home to, someone with whom to discuss his days and his ideas. They lived in a little house not far from the university, and though Lovenia missed him while he was gone, she kept herself busy with household chores, writing in her journal, and taking drives into the country a few miles away to visit her mother, or taking walks when she felt up to it. She delighted in caring for their home and preparing supper in anticipation of her husband's return, and listening to the accounts of his interactions with the students at the university.

About four months after their marriage, Lovenia wrote the following:

I hesitate to write this as I know nothing for certain, yet I cannot resist, for I am beside myself with anticipation. Could it be true? If not now then surely soon, but would to God I carry a little one inside me now. I have not spoken of this to anyone and will wait for a time before I do, but the certainty grows within me day by day.

Samantha smiled, joying in her mother's joy. But this happiness was overshadowed by a sudden remembrance, and she stopped breathing for a moment. Samantha knew what would come. She wished she could reach inside the book, reach back in time and stop the inevitable. But again, where would she be if fate had not been allowed its hapless course? Her own helplessness made her heart ache.

She read on as Lovenia finally became certain enough of her condition to discuss it with her mother, who directed her to see the doctor. She did so, and it was confirmed that she was, indeed, with child, two months along. When Lovenia informed Basil that night of their approaching parenthood, "His happiness," she wrote, "shone through his tears and he held me close for a long while as we discussed our plans for this coming child."

Now Lovenia had even more to keep her occupied while Basil was away teaching during the day. She enjoyed sewing tiny baby things and picturing little hands and feet and a cherub face. As she stated herself, "I could not be more content. This is what I have always wanted and now my dream is becoming a reality!"

Not until the eighth month of pregnancy did anything at all appear to be amiss. But in May, Lovenia's usual tiredness deepened, and she began to experience early signs of labor that were strong enough to frighten her. An almost panicked Basil sent for the doctor, who ordered bed rest and a day nurse. Lovenia's mother hurriedly moved in to take up this role, which gave Basil tremendous peace of mind. Being off her feet measurably improved Lovenia's condition and she enjoyed her mother's company while they both worked on little booties, nightgowns, and blankets together for a couple of weeks. The scare had apparently passed and Lovenia looked forward more each day to the time when she would hold her precious babe in her arms.

But that day never came. On a hot Wednesday in July, after more than twenty-four hours of tremendously difficult labor, a baby boy was finally born. But Lovenia was almost gone herself and could not touch the cooling flesh before he was laid in the grave.

As she wrote much later:

Every day since the passing of my dear baby boy, I think of yet another regret. Each day I think of the smiles I will never see him make, of the lisped words I will never hear him speak, and the halting steps he will never take. Every day I realize one more thing I will never see him learn. My womb and my hands are empty and so, it seems, is my heart. I know God has His reasons, but for now all I can wonder over and over is why I could not be allowed the completion of the dream I have wanted so faithfully all my life. Was this not a worthy desire? Did not God want this for my husband and me? And Basil, poor Basil. I know not how to comfort him.

Samantha choked back the tears in her throat and reached for the handkerchief she had used once or twice already. What tragedy! Why did such things have to happen to perfectly noble people who only wanted good out of life and brought good to others? She felt herself tremble in anger with the injustice of it. She wiped her eyes with a quavering sigh and blew her nose, wishing she could have been there to comfort her mother, even though she knew the thought was ridiculous.

As she turned back to the journal and absorbed herself in it once again, she barely recognized when Mrs. Dolittle crept in to lay a tray of food on the chair by her bed for supper. As she read, more questions filled her mind and, with their insistence, began to form themselves into pictures and ideas that kept her awake that night. A plan, both exciting and a little frightening, was forming in her mind.

CHAPTER 20

PLANNING A TRIP

January 1902

At the end of January, Sterling was invited by the father of one of his students to attend a Franklin County Committee meeting at the Sharon Township Hall on Granville Road.[23] The purpose of the meeting was to discuss how they could increase the education of their citizens, perhaps by exposing them to great literature, and also how they could offer more opportunities to share local writing. Knowing of Sterling's background in literature and writing, the man asked him if he would attend and offer his insights. Sterling obliged, pleased to be considered a part of the town and to lend a hand to such a worthy cause.

He watched in silence, content to observe the proceedings without comment until such a time as he had an idea that might benefit them. Someone made the obvious suggestion that the way to reach the most people would be through the newspaper. Worthington did not have its own paper, but many townspeople were subscribers to The Columbus Dispatch. Different ideas were voiced on the best way to include literature in the newspaper and how to most convincingly present the suggestion to the newspaper owner. Someone was nominated and accepted the responsibility.

Next, the meeting turned to the matter of how to create opportunities for local amateur writers and poets to share their own work. A few people had ideas, but the one everyone liked the most

---

[23] https://www.worthington.org/158/Maps-for-Download

came from Sterling. He suggested that the newspaper host a writing contest every few months that would print the winning entries from each category in subsequent weeks. If the newspaper could be persuaded to give two pages to an excerpt from canonized literature and one page for local writing (which would include Columbus writers, of course), surely that would be enough to pique citizens' interest, augment their education, and also, no doubt, increase the newspaper's readership as well. Then, if the project were successful, perhaps the newspaper would see fit to expand the literature section at some future point.

However, to begin with, the paper owner would probably require some cash to print the extra pages, which meant they would need to have a benefit of some kind to raise the appropriate funds. Sterling suggested that as long as they were raising money, they might as well raise enough to award small prizes for the contest award-winners to increase interest and participation in the contest. This suggestion was met with enthusiasm, and they decided on a plan of action.

The committee set a date for a carnival six weeks hence and Sterling, feeling obligated to continue his involvement in the project he had suggested, proposed to talk to several townspeople about donating their time or talents to the event. He had a few people in mind (including the Tomlinsons) whom he thought would be glad to contribute their talents to such a cause and wondered if he might even persuade his parents to donate a sum directly to the fund.

***

January, as Januarys often are, was a month of new resolves and renewed commitments for the year 1902. Included in Samantha's goals for the new year was the resolution to begin reading the newspaper again (an activity that had trailed off not long after Sterling's departure) so that she would know as much as possible about what was going on in the world. This really was no difficult goal for her, for though reading of crimes and tragedies saddened her, she felt edified and inspired when she learned of the newest discoveries and accomplishments. She had no wish to become someone famous who made actual discoveries, but she surely enjoyed learning about them.

At the end of January, it was reported that there had just been an accident during the construction of the subway tunnel in New York City. Opposite the Murray Hill Hotel a storage shed containing dynamite exploded and killed six people, wounded 125 others, and resulted in property damage of $300,000. The whole idea of building a road system beneath the ground had fascinated Samantha since its beginning two years before. What amazed her was that this was the first time an accident of such magnitude had occurred and that no more lives were lost. She prayed for the families of those who had died in the explosion.

The following day, on January 28th, a philanthropist named Andrew Carnegie funded a private, nonprofit research organization called the Carnegie Institution.[24] This sounded interesting to Samantha, and she tucked the information away for later recall, wondering if any great discoveries would issue from the research there.

---

[24] http://pubs.acs.org/cen/coverstory/8008/8008carnegie.html

But what shook Samantha the most was when she read about what the newspaper called "the barbaric practice of foot binding" in China. She was horrified: this was not something she had read about before. The article said that this binding (and often breaking) of little girls' feet to keep them small throughout the girls' lives was a practice that had probably gone on for almost one-thousand years. But on February 1, 1902, the Chinese Empress, Tzu-His (or Cixis), who was recently restored to power, issued several reforms for her country, including the forbidding of foot binding.[25] That relieved Samantha, but she also wondered how, after hundreds of years, such an imbedded part of the people's culture could be done away with in a mere word. It was also interesting to contemplate what different societies and cultures perceived as beautiful. *Who is right? Or does that matter?* she wondered. Unconsciously she wriggled her own toes in their stiff, narrow boots, grateful that her feet were free to grow as big as they liked, pain-free (though shoes were not exactly comfortable and she would have preferred to go barefoot if it weren't so cold). *I suppose beauty really is in the eye of the beholder,* she thought.

As a direct result of New Year's resolutions, the previously struggling Ladies' Quilting Society of Oberlin reformed with new leadership and made efforts to strengthen the ranks. Lists were drawn up of those needing quilts for weddings, new babies, or for the poor. Samantha and Katherine became official members and soon the society met for a quilting meeting once a week. Weekly and bi-weekly church activities began picking up again, too, as everyone recovered from the holidays and longed for direction during the cold, gray days

---

[25] https://www.chinahighlights.com/travelguide/china-history/empress-cixi-facts.htm

of February. The snow still continued to fall at intervals, but by now, everyone was used to it again and resigned themselves to traveling in it when necessary, except on particularly stormy or icy days.

In between meetings and activities, Samantha conversed with Mrs. Dolittle to discuss her latest questions and ideas about what she was learning from her mother's journal. She read of Lovenia's physical, mental, and spiritual trials as she struggled to regain her sense of self and her strength, and of Basil's grieving attention to his "Lovey." Once Lovenia felt strong enough, she began making almost weekly visits to her baby's grave, and that seemed to help her a great deal.

She wrote: *I know what the preacher says about un-baptized babies being lost, but I cannot believe that. Whenever I think of my baby and visit his grave, I feel very strongly that his spirit is somewhere in a heaven waiting for me. As I lay new flowers beside the simple headstone, I imagine him up there in heaven's garden, running, laughing, and playing, and this image calms my aching heart and brings me peace. Perhaps I may be able to see him again if I do all the good I can in this life...*

Samantha wondered for the umpteenth time where, exactly, her brother was buried. Is his grave near my mother's? She realized months ago, as her mind first began contemplating the life and character of Lovenia Jennings, that she had never seen her mother's grave, nor been told anything about it. Upon asking Mrs. Dolittle about its location, she was told that yes, as far as she knew, Lovenia was buried in Worthington. She remembered Basil saying something about his wife preferring as her final resting place that town where she had spent the majority of her life. Mrs. Dolittle had never been to Lovenia's grave nor had known of any time since Lovenia's burial

196

that Basil had returned to visit it. This added another question to Samantha's growing list, and it needled her more than almost any other.

She read on in her mother's journal, relieved as Lovenia gradually recovered not only her physical strength but also her strength of will to continue forward and make the most of her life. Lovenia still wrote of her lingering sadness and regrets over what would never be, realizing that those feelings would ever be a part of who she now was. Even through the pages, Samantha could tell that the tragedy Lovenia endured had further matured her, and had made her more thoughtful and deliberate. Occasionally she wrote of the hope that continued to burn within her, despite her near death and the doctor's solemn words, but she was careful not to discuss this with Basil, for it greatly upset him to talk about it. And she tried diligently to be happy with her lot in life, and to be grateful for what she did have.

As she looked to Basil to see what she could do to increase his happiness, she quickly realized that he was not as fulfilled in his role of teaching as he once was. He seemed restless and Lovenia remembered the desire he had once shared with her of teaching at Oberlin College. He was tired of the large university and yearned to try his hand at teaching in the small, innovative college instead. Lovenia could tell that Basil felt unproductive where he was and that he thought perhaps he could do more good in an environment where he would have closer contact with the students through the smaller class sizes and the small town.

As she began to bring up the topic more often and discuss the possibilities with him, she discovered that at one time he had actually come quite close to having this desire realized--something he had never told her before. Just a short time before meeting Lovenia, he applied to Oberlin in the hopes that, since he was qualified, had several years of experience at Ohio State University (and was not getting any younger), the school could employ him when a position became vacant.

Between the time that he sent off his letter and when he received a positive reply, he had not only met Lovenia, but secretly fallen in love with her. He felt in his heart that if he turned down the coveted position at the smaller college and stayed in Worthington, he might eventually win the greater dream he had so long coveted: that of marriage to a woman like Lovenia.

When Lovenia first began encouraging him to reapply, he would not hear of it and always changed the subject. He had vowed to put Lovenia's health and well-being first and foremost, he said, and would not consider making her take such a long journey, should he actually be offered a position again. But there were times when Lovenia would catch him staring off into space with such a wistful expression on his face that she knew he still harbored that dream, despite his strongest efforts not to dwell on it. Finally, after a couple years of Lovenia's gentle prodding and Basil's consistent refusals, Lovenia grew bold.

"It makes me tremble to think of what I have done," she wrote, "but I am still convinced it was the right thing to do." She had written to Oberlin College for Basil, inquiring as to their teaching vacancies and offering his services. Lovenia felt that this was what Basil needed and if he was not going to make the necessary steps, she would make them for him and see what came of it.

It took several months, but when the reply came, Basil's reaction was just as Lovenia hoped it would be, as she recorded later:

"Lovey!" he exclaimed after he read the letter, "the college is still interested in me! Can you imagine...?" I had never seen him so excited; it made me ever so grateful I dared do what I did. Watching the happiness with which he read the letter over once again brought tears to my eyes. I felt it was best to let him believe the administration at the college sought him out on their own. For in actuality, I had only let them know he was available again and still desirous to come. After finishing the letter for the second time, Basil looked up at me from the table, seeming stunned, and told me that the position they were offering him was better than what they had offered before, that it was the very position he had long yearned to have. I told him that, to me, this is evidence of God's hand in his life.

As we have discussed plans for the move, I think I have finally convinced him I truly am strong enough to travel all that way, and not only that, but that I want to. I love the way his eyes shine with the possibilities this new opportunity opens for him.

The "new opportunity" would have been very difficult to bring to fruition had it not been for the death of Basil's older brother and only remaining family member. Even as Basil grieved for his brother, receiving the large inheritance gave him and Lovenia the ability to travel much more comfortably than they would have been able to otherwise, and also relieved them of a great worry: they now knew they could afford to purchase a place of residence once they arrived at their destination, and that all other future needs would be met. Basil knew he would not have time to build a house before he began teaching and he wanted something nice for Lovenia, a place where she could feel at home, perhaps something large to grow a

199

children's school so she could fill a house with little voices after all. And so, the Jennings left Worthington and made the one-hundred-and-five mile journey by horse and wagon to Oberlin.

Samantha warily read of their travels, wondering how her mother had possibly made it through the rigors of living on the trail for two weeks. They took the trip slowly and easily and for the most part, Lovenia's strength held out, but only until they arrived in their new town and moved into the mansion. Then she relapsed and spent four or five months in bed.

At this same time, Mrs. Dolittle joined their household, which was a blessing for the Jennings, as Basil was often absent in his efforts to establish himself at the college. He disliked being away so much and thought of his wife constantly while he was gone, worrying for her. Lovenia yearned for her husband's more frequent presence at home also, but she tried to be understanding and always encouraged him to do his very best and to enjoy his work. And though Basil wished to be home to watch over her himself, it gave him great peace of mind to know that she was so well looked after by Mrs. Dolittle.

It was at this point in Samantha's reading and contemplation one day that there came a light rap on the door. "Yes?" she asked, looking up and blinking in an effort to bring her mind back to the present.

Mrs. Dolittle opened the door and poked her head in. "Samantha, you have a caller," she said, smiling.

"Oh!" Samantha was surprised but wondered if it might be Rupert.

"It's that Winton fellow again. He's waiting in the parlor. May I tell him you will join him shortly?"

"Oh. Yes, thank you. I shall be right down." It surprised Samantha how glad she felt at this news and how eager for such a pleasant interruption to her journal reading. She set the book aside and smoothed her dress and hair, stalling to give Mrs. Dolittle enough time to relay the message. Then, stepping lightly down the stairs, she suddenly realized she wanted very much to talk to someone about the things she was reading and thinking. And Rupert was just the person.

Hearing footsteps again in the doorway, Rupert looked up and saw Samantha's tall, straight figure standing there. He felt the butterflies in his stomach that always came when he saw her, and his heart warmed. He stood from his seat on the stiff, horsehair parlor chair and that slow, familiar smile brightened his face.

Samantha smiled back as she approached him and extended a hand. "Hello Rupert," she said. "I am glad to see you!"

"And I you." Rupert took her hand in one of his large, callused ones and held it a moment. "I hope you don't mind that I invited myself here once again. I... It has been weeks since I saw you and I wondered how you were. I wanted to come earlier, but work has had me tied up."

"I don't mind at all," Samantha reassured him, looking into his gentle blue eyes. "You are always very welcome here. Please take a seat." She motioned to the nearby sofa where she sat at one end and he at the other.

Rupert looked intently at Samantha across the space between them. "At our last outing, I did not ask you if you had an enjoyable Christmas."

"I did," Samantha returned, looking down into her lap. "The best in years, actually." She raised her head. "And you?"

He nodded. "It was good. I rode out to my brother's farm and enjoyed his wife's excellent cooking and played with their three children. It's a noisy home but also cozy."

Samantha nodded. "It was very quiet here as always but pleasant." She knew she was not offering much real information with this statement, but there really was not much to tell. Christmas had never been a large affair at the Jennings' mansion, though Mrs. Dolittle always did what she could to make it special before she left to spend a few days with her grown daughters in Amherst, a town eight miles away.

After exchanging a few more pleasantries, Samantha began telling Rupert of her discovery in the library and of the things she was learning about her mother. As he put himself in her position, Rupert became so enthralled in her story that without realizing it he soon closed the space between them.

"So I have been thinking..." Samantha paused and considered again. Should she voice this out loud? But she had mulled it over long enough and wanted another person's perspective on her idea. "I need to take a trip," she finished.

"A trip?" Rupert repeated, puzzled and curious.

"Yes. And you are the first person I have told this to. I simply..." Samantha waved a hand around for a moment trying to capture the right words, not realizing that Rupert held her other hand in his. "Rupert, the more I read, the more I learn, the more I have a profound desire to visit my mother's and brother's graves. I mean, I did not even know I had a brother until a couple of months ago. And I knew precious little about my mother until then, too. I suppose now I feel like I need to make up for lost—and wasted—time."

Rupert nodded slowly. "I see. And their graves are in Worthington?"

"That is what Mrs. Dolittle believes. I have not yet inquired about it to Father..." She turned her head to look at Rupert more directly and said ruefully, "He does not even know I have Mother's journal."

Rupert's expression was serious, his brows knit together in concern. "Will you talk with him?"

"Well, yes, I have been planning to. But I will wait a little longer until I know more and have better formulated my plan. I have so many questions for him! But he is not very...umm...shall I say...approachable."

Rupert thought a moment and then asked, "Would you like me to come with you when you talk to him? If that will make it any easier..."

"No." Samantha smiled at him and shook her head. "Thank you, but this is something I must do on my own, I think. It is not that I am afraid of him... I speak to him sometimes. But we do not speak often and it always takes effort." She paused a moment, thinking. "That sounds sad, I know. I never used to notice." Abruptly she did look sad.

"If I can offer any assistance, I do so gladly," Rupert said quietly, squeezing her hand just enough that Samantha became suddenly aware that her hand rested in his. She colored slightly and quietly pulled it away, hoping Rupert would not be hurt by the action.

Speaking quickly to cover the awkward moment, she said, "Actually, I *would* appreciate some help in one matter." She looked down at her hands now curled around each other, a little damp. Thinking about what she was going to ask of him made her suddenly feel over-bold.

Rupert waited expectantly, aware of his hand's sudden emptiness. "Anything," he said, touching her shoulder briefly in an effort to ease the hesitancy he sensed in her.

"It is a rather great favor for me to ask it of you and I do not want to presume upon our friendship..."

Rupert shook his head dismissively, his longish light brown hair swishing. "Tell me. If there is any way I can do it, I will."

Samantha looked away from him as she contemplated how to word this important request. "Well, as I said, you are the first person I have discussed this with, but..." She glanced at him again. "Well, I am hoping you and Katherine can accompany me to Worthington in the spring." As she said it, she was suddenly struck with the audacity of her question and looked at Rupert, biting her bottom lip.

Rupert inhaled sharply in surprise.

Samantha thought she glimpsed a certain worry in his eyes. "I will pay expenses for both of you," she said hurriedly. "But it simply would not be wise or proper for me to go alone, and I enjoy being with you two most of anyone in the world. I need someone to share this experience with. I have the feeling it may be difficult—as well as wonderful—and I will need your strength."

Rupert's heart quickened, but his eyes still questioned hers.

"Truly," she said, her own eyes sincere. "I would not say that if I did not mean it."

"It would be an honor, Samantha," he returned after a long moment of silence. "I need to make the necessary arrangements to take a leave of absence from work, which may not be easy, especially that time of year. But it will be possible, especially if we go early enough in the spring. I will make it possible," he said with conviction.

Samantha smiled at him in gratitude and rested her hand lightly on his arm. *He is a true friend*, she thought. "Thank you. It would mean so very much to me."

CHAPTER 21

FEELINGS

March 1902

Katherine Bodeen and Mrs. Dolittle put their heads together to throw a party to celebrate Samantha's eighteenth birthday in the first week of March. Both women knew Samantha would not enjoy being the center of attention in a large crowd, so they invited only those closest to her. The party was a success, and Samantha was both surprised that they remembered her birthday and touched by all the planning and preparations that had obviously gone into it. Rupert, Katherine, and the other few friends who were invited gave her thoughtful gifts and seemed to enjoy themselves as much as she did. And once again, Mrs. Dolittle outdid herself: the appetizers and desserts were simply divine, everyone agreed.

In honor of the upcoming occasion, and as eighteen was the official age when a girl had her "coming out," Katherine spent the better part of the morning before the party combing and arranging Samantha's long hair. Between the two of them and with Mrs. Dolittle's added input, they decided on a couple of new hairstyles that were quite becoming. Samantha was so used to simply braiding her hair—except for nicer or formal occasions when she pulled it all back in the way Katherine had shown her for the Christmas Ball--that it took some practice and more time than she liked to learn how to put it up in the new grownup styles. This was something a lady's maid could have done so much better, but she and her father had never used their wealth in that way, so she determined to learn how to do it herself with Mrs. Dolittle's help. And she did like the results, for not only did she look older, she felt more confident too. Somehow her long face did not seem quite so long when there were no braids on either side of it to elongate it further. And aware of the concentrated weight of all her hair piled on top made her carry herself a little differently. She was also surprised by how her hair shined as the red in it caught the light.

***

Sterling's efforts and those of everyone else on the committee, in addition to the many people they recruited to help, were rewarded by a successful carnival in early March. Held in the Sharon Township Hall on Friday evening and Saturday afternoon, it came at the tail end of an otherwise dreary winter. Perhaps that was why it was so well attended: the town had needed something to look forward to, with the Christmas holidays long since passed and Easter still a way off.

Sterling was glad for the involvement, which had taken up his few spare hours every week and helped him to feel more a part of the local community. Several of his students had agreed to involve themselves or their families and looking around now, he could see that most had taken it seriously. There were as many booths in the hall as could safely be crowded in, and such a variety of wares! Mrs. Tomlinson stood behind a booth piled deep with baked goods that were already selling rapidly. Jerome, in the booth next to hers, proudly displayed toys, walking sticks, and other wooden items that he had skillfully carved and fashioned himself for weeks. Other booths showed quilts, tablecloths and crocheted doilies, horse halters and other leather goods, candles, roasted nuts, wieners and sauerkraut, and even homemade candy.

It was such a warm, cheerful, bustling event that Sterling had to smile seeing it all. He spent hours walking from booth to booth, helping wherever he could by running errands and cleaning up messes, managing booths while the owners took breaks, feeling rejuvenated by the change of pace and grateful that he could participate.

By four o'clock Saturday afternoon, the last of the carnival-goers and booth-owners had bundled back into their coats and departed, leaving the members of the committee to tiredly shake hands and clean up the last of the clutter. Their final earnings counted, they happily discovered that they had made more than three times as much as they'd hoped. It was decided that the excess would be deposited into a Franklin County Committee fund in the bank, from which the prize money for contest winners would be drawn for many months to come, and which would cover any other unforeseen expenses that arose from the project. Sterling could plainly see the relief on everyone's faces, knowing that their financial worries for this endeavor had ended, at least for the time being.

After the carnival, the Columbus Dispatch actually agreed to make four pages available to them each week instead of the requested three, so taken were they by the committee's hard work and dedication to the citizens' educational improvement. (Of course, there had also been the matter of a tidy sum donated by Mr. and Mrs. Sterling.) The first literary excerpt already waited by the press to be added to next week's paper, as well as the announcement of the first contest, which would be held in two weeks. Sterling agreed to help choose excerpts from famous works and to review the amateur submissions if extra hands were needed, but he guessed that the contest would start out small before it gained enough publicity to really require his assistance.

***

Samantha glanced out the front window of the parlor and smoothed the bodice of her dress with slightly shaky fingers. In a fit of hospitality, she had invited the Quilting Society to her house for their monthly gathering and now she suddenly realized how very little she knew about being a proper hostess. But she wanted the challenge, to prove she was willing to accept all the responsibilities of being one of them and to prove to herself that she could do it.

Mrs. Dolittle stepped inside the room for one last glance around to be sure all was in readiness, and noted Samantha's nervous gesture. She walked over to her and put a hand on her arm. "Everything looks wonderful," she assured her gently. "You look wonderful too, my dear. There is nothing to worry about. It will all be perfect, just you wait and see." And then, as she turned back toward the door, she mused aloud, "Oh, I cannot say how long it has been since this house has seen guests like it will today..."

Yes, thought Samantha. *I wonder what Father will think when he hears all the female chatter down here.* She smiled wryly, imagining his surprise. *Let him wonder. He needs a little excitement in his life.*

Katherine Bodeen arrived first and Samantha greeted her with a smile, very grateful to see her and to have her support in hosting the group. A month had passed since Samantha had spoken to Rupert about her plan and still she had not found the appropriate opportunity to talk to Katherine about it.

Katherine had come a little early, bringing with her the quilt they would work on this afternoon, and the two girls quickly busied themselves, putting up the quilting frame while they waited for the others to arrive.

"I do not mind telling you how much I have looked forward to coming to this meeting in your home, Samantha," Katherine confided. Her dark head bent over the boards of the frame, but as she spoke, she lifted her face and smiled warmly up at her friend.

"Thank you," Samantha returned. She noticed that Katherine had not even stumbled over the word 'home' as others might have; she knew it was commonly referred to as the "Jennings mansion," with an air of odd mystery.

"I have lived in Oberlin most of my life and never caught a glimpse of the inside, so I've always been...intrigued, I guess." Katherine laughed softly and Samantha smiled back at her.

Samantha's nerves were beginning to calm, and she felt herself relaxing in her friend's company. "Don't tell me there are ghost stories about this old place," she said, raising an eyebrow.

"Well..." Katherine paused, her head cocked to one side. "Not exactly, but there is quite a bit of speculation." She held two of the boards perpendicular to one another while Samantha tightened the clamp.

"With only four people living here—Father and I, Mrs. Dolittle, and Martin in the room in the barn--there is very little of the house that is lived in. Most rooms are closed, the furniture entirely covered; it's quite dusty, actually."

Clamp in place, the girls moved to the next corner. "If there are ghosts in those rooms, they don't bother us," Samantha laughed.

"Oh, I know the ghost stories were only a way for us to scare ourselves, back in primary school. Now all I hear is the occasional rhetorical question, 'What does Professor Jennings do these days?' Of course, no one has an answer for that. No one seems to have seen him in years."

Samantha smiled a little ruefully. "That is something I ask myself every now and then. It does not surprise me the town would wonder." This time she held the boards while Katherine tightened the clamp. "You mean, you really never see him?" Katherine asked, almost in a whisper. "He is your father, and he never speaks to you?"

Samantha shook her head. "Not really. Not unless I seek him out. I didn't used to know I minded the lack of contact between us," she admitted, "but now I wonder how he can stand to remain so aloof, so isolated from society."

Katherine stopped turning the clamp and looked steadily at Samantha. She heard the regret in her friend's voice and recognized that Samantha saw a striking resemblance between her father and herself. "I never knew you while we were growing up, Samantha. But I'm glad I know you now." She laid a hand over Samantha's and squeezed it gently.

Samantha was grateful for the reminder to look ahead and not backward and to be kind to herself.

As members of the Quilting Society began to arrive, not one of the other women was straightforward enough to admit her own curiosity in the mansion. But they were all gracious and

211

complimentary of the glistening wood floors, the marble fireplace, the ornate light fixtures (whose sconces were bereft of candles, since no one had entertained here for all of Samantha's life), the elegant, raised ceiling. They praised Samantha's and the housekeeper's baking efforts and asked for recipes, which pleased them both. Mrs. Dolittle beamed like a young girl as she served everyone, and Samantha could tell she was enjoying herself more than she had in years.

By working steadily on the quilt that afternoon, the women finished tying and binding it in a few hours. These were such pleasant hours that Samantha did not want them to end. They all chatted easily about many topics, in the way of women, and Samantha felt included and happy.

Afterward, Katherine graciously stayed to help Samantha and Mrs. Dolittle clean up, as Samantha had hoped she would. When they finished, Mrs. Dolittle excused herself to the kitchen to prepare supper and Samantha turned to Katherine.

"Do you have another few minutes to spare?" she asked. "I have something I need to talk to you about." Suddenly she felt almost desperate, which must have shown on her face, for Katherine looked up at her with wide eyes.

"Yes, I have time," Katherine responded instantly. "Mother is not expecting me home for another hour or so." She searched Samantha's face and grasped her hand. "What is it?"

Samantha glanced around the room, which now seemed terribly empty after the bustle and chatter of the last few hours. "Come," she decided momentarily, "let's go to my room," and she led Katherine up the stairs to the room she had never invited anyone to.

Once inside, she closed the door and motioned to her nightstand where her mother's journal lay. "Please, make yourself comfortable while you look at that book there. It will explain some of what I need to say." She shivered involuntarily. "It is freezing in here! Sorry, I didn't think about that. Let me put a fire on and then I will join you."

Katherine's expression was still sober and questioning, but now curiosity burned in her blue eyes as she saw the book. She seated herself on Samantha's bed, then unlaced her boots and pulled them off so she could tuck her feet comfortably beneath her without dirtying the bedspread.

As soon as she opened to the first page and saw the name written there, she drew in a quick breath, held it a moment, and then let it out in a rush. "Samantha!" she said excitedly but with reverence. "Is this your mother's journal?"

Samantha turned from her position at the fireplace and could not keep from smiling as she saw the joy on her friend's pretty face. "Yes!"

"What beautiful penmanship!" Katherine said, tracing the first words with a delicate finger.

"I agree. Much better than my own," Samantha smiled wryly. She turned back to her task. "Please. Look through it," she told Katherine over her shoulder. "Read what you like." And then more quietly, "I am not the same girl I was before I found it."

"You *found* it?" Katherine asked. "Where?"

"In my father's library. It has been there for years, apparently, but I never knew it existed until I happened upon it in January."

"What a discovery!" Katherine breathed. "Oh, Samantha, this is so intriguing!"

"I am glad you think so too," Samantha told her gratefully.

Katherine concentrated with rapt attention on the worn journal in her hands while Samantha arranged the kindling and logs and lit the fire. She made sure the flames burned strongly and steadily and then stood and rubbed her hands together to rid them of a bit of soot. When she turned to her friend, she was gratified to see her genuinely enthralled in the words of Lovenia Jennings. Quietly she removed her own boots and sat opposite Katherine on the bed, throwing a spare blanket over their laps and waiting for her to finish what she was reading.

After a few minutes, Katherine looked up and her blue eyes glistened with a sheen of tears. "This is a treasure!" She indicated the page she had just read. "Your parents had a great love for each other... I can already tell that your mother was a wonderful woman."

Samantha nodded and blinked back the tears that seeped into her own eyes with the reminder of the tender things she had already read. "I wish I had known her," she said softly.

Katherine reached across the bed and touched Samantha's knee in a comforting gesture. She was silent a moment and then closed the journal carefully. "How lucky you are to have this." She handed the book to Samantha and folded her hands in her lap. "I am guessing you wanted to speak to me about something related to this book. Is that right?"

Samantha's mind returned to the present and she looked back at her friend. "Yes," she acknowledged. And then without any more preamble, she rushed to say, "I have made up my mind that I must find my mother's and brother's graves—"

"—Brother?!" Katherine exclaimed. "I never knew you had a brother."

"Neither did I until a few months ago. Oh, Katherine! I have found out so much so quickly that thinking about it all makes my head spin. But one thing that keeps coming back to me is that I need to find those graves, to pay my respects and feel that connection and...and closure. Maybe that sounds foolish, but it's the way I honestly feel."

"It doesn't sound foolish to me," Katherine said. "But how will you go about it?"

"I am still working out the details, but one thing I do know is that...well, I would very much like you to come with me. To Worthington, that is—at least, Mrs. Dolittle is fairly certain that is where the graves are."

Katherine inhaled sharply in surprise, reminding Samantha of Rupert's similar reaction. "Me? I would love-- What a fine adventure that would be! I have never been that far south."

Samantha could see that Katherine was already imagining and planning, liking the idea. "Of course, I would make the arrangements and pay all our expenses, so your family need not concern themselves with any of that."

"My family..." This thought grounded Katherine's fantasies abruptly and she groaned, looking into Samantha's face with a pained expression. "Oh, I want so much to say yes! But everyone knows how cautious and protective my father is and I doubt he will agree to two young ladies traipsing off on an errand like this."

Samantha was already nodding. "I foresaw that—and your father would be quite right; it would not be proper for us to go alone. That is why I presumed to ask Rupert if he would accompany us also."

Katherine's eyes widened again and then relaxed into a smile. "That would be perfect...as long as we had separate lodgings and made all other necessary arrangements. He is quite a nice young man, Samantha." After a pause, she added, "Not that you need my approval, but I do wholeheartedly approve."

Samantha's brows furrowed in puzzlement. "Approve? Of his coming with us?"

"Yes, that—of course." Katherine laughed and waved a dismissive hand, "But I mean... aren't you interested in him? Hasn't he been courting you?"

Samantha felt herself color. "I suppose he has been seeing me quite often lately. And I like him; he is a good friend." She frowned in thought. "But I do not think I feel that way for him... The way that you are saying..."

Katherine's graceful brows swept upward for a moment, questioning, then lowered and smoothed back into place. "These things take time," she said with a slight smile. "After all, you met each other only last December."

"I know, but..." Samantha had never spoken of Sterling to Katherine—or to anyone for that matter—and suddenly, she found herself yearning to confide in her friend. She knew without question that she could trust her implicitly, and she also knew that she would be understanding and empathetic. Perhaps she could even give advice from her own experience that would help.

Katherine must have sensed a change in Samantha's manner and the gravity in her words, for her expression, too, became more serious. She searched Samantha's face and leaned closer. "But you care for someone else?" she prompted.

Samantha hesitated a moment, then nodded.

"And he cares for you?"

"Well, I... I..." Samantha faltered, unsure of the answer, not certain how to put these things into words. She thought of Sterling, of his impetuousness and zest for life, his energy and enthusiasm for writing, teaching, horse riding, lively discussions... She could still conjure up his image in her mind's eye, the way his dark, wavy hair draped across his forehead, how his clothing always looked so neat. She pictured his tall, muscled frame and his handsome, kind face that always seemed to carry a trace of humor. But the picture was blurred around the edges and blurring more all the time. She looked down into her lap, suddenly feeling so miserable that she wanted to cry.

"Oh, Samantha," Katherine said sympathetically, moving across the bed to sit close and put an arm around her. "You don't know if this young man feels for you the way you do for him, is that it?"

Samantha nodded, not trusting herself to speak. In the background of her thoughts, she heard the fire crackling away merrily in the hearth and it was a comforting sound. She thought for several moments about what she wanted to say and then finally swallowed and cleared her throat. "I don't even know where he is now." She creased the soft blanket on her lap and then smoothed it absently a few times. "I really believe he cared for me, but then he left and I... I have not heard from him since. Now I know I really care for him too...and have no way of telling him so." Finally, she raised her eyes to meet the beautiful blue ones that were filled with such compassion.

"He did not tell you where he was going?" Katherine asked, a bit incredulously, and pulled a little away from Samantha so that she could face her again.

Samantha shrugged. "He did not even tell me he *was* going."

"But..." Katherine looked confused. "I don't understand. Who was—*is* he?"

"Lee Sterling." Samantha tasted the name as she said it, realizing she had not spoken it aloud for ages. "My writing teacher last summer."

Katherine mouthed the name a few times as if testing it for familiarity. "Writing teacher," she repeated. Then suddenly, realization dawned and her eyes grew wide. "Do you mean that tall, dark-haired young man who was looking for pupils last spring?"

Samantha nodded. "Yes. But as far as I know, I was the only pupil outside the College that he had while he was here."

"Oh," Katherine sucked in a breath. "I do remember seeing him—who could not? Samantha, he is one of the most handsome men I have ever seen!"

The corners of Samantha's mouth quivered as she again saw Sterling in her mind. "Yes, he is, isn't he?" she mused quietly. But then another thought struck her cold. "I know I am no beauty—like you, Katherine. Perhaps...perhaps he left because he realized he could not allow himself to become more deeply involved with someone whose appearance was so...incompatible...to his own."

"Nonsense!" Katherine straightened her back and spoke with firmness. "Samantha, I know you well enough to know that you see people as they are, past the facades and social graces. Above all, you are genuine. I cannot conceive that you would grow to care deeply for someone who would be shallow enough to place undue importance on physical attractiveness. Despite how good-looking he is, I know you did not fall for him because of that. And obviously he recognized the good in you--saw things in you that he liked and that interested him--or he would not have spent so much time with you."

"But—Katherine, I have a vivid imagination! Perhaps I only *imagined* he had feelings for me. He was my teacher, after all..."

"Yes, but he is only, what...five or six years older than you? I am sure his interests were not purely academic, not after he got to know you. Besides, you said you felt that he cared for you. What was it that made you think as much? I mean, if you don't mind sharing..."

"I... Well..." Samantha felt her cheeks redden, hoping her friend would not think less of her when she heard what had happened. "He seemed to enjoy being with me, we discussed our ideas and opinions with each other on so many topics, and he truly helped me improve my writing skills. We had such interesting conversations and had so much to say to each other about the world and everything in it!" She paused a moment. "And he also... The last time we met he...he kissed me." She looked tentatively at Katherine's face, wondering how she would react to this information.

Katherine's dark-lashed eyes widened, but instead of looking at Samantha in shocked horror, she slowly grinned and then began to laugh. "Yes, I would say he liked you—very much!"

Samantha swallowed. "You...you would?"

"Yes!" Katherine nodded, still smiling. "Maybe he was frightened by *how much* he liked you and that was why he left, to sort out his thoughts."

Now it was Samantha's turn to look at Katherine incredulously. "If so, he has had time enough to sort them threadbare!"

Katherine laughed again, as if this comment tickled her, and shook her head. "Oh, Samantha, you are a jewel," she said softly. "Wherever he is and for whatever reason he left, I am sure he still thinks of you. And I believe this is one of those times when what you need to do—all you *can* do—is trust in God. If you and Sterling should be together, God will make it happen. He will lead you both back to each other." She saw Samantha's dubious expression and added, "Truly."

"Well—" Samantha still felt frustrated. "If he really had to leave so abruptly and he really cares about me, why has he not sent any word? I have heard nothing!" She raised both arms in a questioning, frustrated gesture, unable to contain the conflicting emotions that only seemed to increase as time passed. "And if he did not care for me the way I thought he did, why did he make me think so?"

Katherine placed a hand over Samantha's agitated one and gave a half smile.

"I do not know," she said, shaking her head. "Perhaps he did write you and the letter never reached you. That does happen from time to time, you know. Especially this time of year, the roads can be treacherous and anything could happen."

Samantha knew she was just trying to comfort her, and she appreciated that, but she could not allow herself the hope that some long-waylaid letter would arrive on her doorstep. She looked at Katherine doubtfully and said nothing.

Katherine sighed and pulled her hand away from Samantha's, then lifted and dropped her shoulders in a gesture of defeat. "I do not know why he hasn't written," she repeated in a low voice. "I wish I did."

Seeing Katherine sitting there, sharing her uncertainty and pain, Samantha suddenly felt a swell of gratitude for having such a friend. "Thank you for letting me tell you about this... I feel relieved to finally share it with someone."

Katherine gave a wan smile. "What are you going to do about Rupert?"

Samantha sighed and shook her head. "All I know is that I do not want to break his heart, whatever happens. He is such a dear friend. I almost wish I could care for him the way I do for Sterling, but..." She paused, acutely aware of how difficult it was to express certain feelings. "Well, I feel none of that warm, trembly feeling deep inside me when I am with him that I felt with Sterling—and that I feel every time I think of him."

Katherine looked at her with sparkling eyes, and the corners of her mouth threatened a grin. "I have had a few beaux, myself, and I have not felt that way about one of them. You are a lucky girl."

As if to defend herself, Samantha added, "I know that feeling by itself is not enough to build a solid relationship on, but I think it is a necessary ingredient if one wishes to marry for love, like my parents did." She paused a moment, thinking of all the tender things her mother had written about her father. "Sterling has so many other admirable qualities. He is kind and perceptive, intelligent, and passionate in the things he believes in..." She drew a breath to continue, but Katherine's laughter interrupted her.

"You need not extol his virtues to me, my friend," she smiled. "I can see it written all over your face."

CHAPTER 22

NOT THE SAME MAN

March 1902

By the middle of March, Samantha had almost finished her mother's journal. When she thought about it, the reading had taken her longer than she would have expected. It was not a thick volume-- undoubtedly, she could have finished it in a few days if she read as much as she used to. But nowadays, besides all the social engagements Samantha participated in, she also liked to take time between each reading to ponder, to write her reflections in her own journal, and to talk to Mrs. Dolittle about what she learned. Besides, this journal was the only thing she had of her mother--the only words she would ever have directly from Lovenia--and she liked taking the time to savor each passage, enjoying the process and the discovery.

By now, Samantha had read beyond her mother's recovery from the journey to Oberlin, and her short years in the big house with Mrs. Dolittle and Basil, when he was home. She had read how Lovenia began to do more as her strength increased: how she joyed in the little garden she cultivated in the side yard that grew and produced under her diligent watch-care; how she looked forward to visits from her closest friends, Emma Ridgewood and Missy Phelps; how she enjoyed dusting or cooking or mending with Mrs. Dolittle. She never did quite feel up to the task of starting a school but still secretly ached for a way to fill the empty halls and rooms with the sounds of little voices and little feet.

Samantha reviewed the last part of what she had read the day before and shook her head, smiling. Her mother just would not give up, would she? *Have I ever wanted anything this badly?* she asked herself, and suddenly remembered asking a similar question of Sterling. Now she had to admit that, though there were things she wanted very dearly, nothing she had experienced matched Lovenia's desire and determination to have children. Even if it killed her, Samantha thought sadly. She turned the page and began reading anew:

April 11, 1884

> *Today I finally broached the subject with Basil again, something I have not done since Worthington. I have really tried to be content, for I truly have much to be thankful for, but lately not having a child of my own has become an unbearable sorrow. I expressed to Basil my desire to try again for a child. Surely the second time would not be so difficult! I promised to see Dr. Johnson and do everything he tells me, to rest and care for myself even more thoroughly than ever before. I pointed out that the doctor in Worthington could have been wrong, after all. "God loves us," I told him, "and I just know He intends for us to have a child that lives. I really feel that He would not deny me this one desire which permeates my every thought and action!"*

Basil knew his wife was prayerful and humble, and he did not doubt her ability to feel God's will. If, after all this time, she felt God would not deny her, how could he? And so he conceded, for he loved his wife as much as ever and wanted a child nearly as much as she.

Months later, as soon as Lovenia was certain she was pregnant, she began taking every precaution possible and Mrs. Dolittle was careful to watch out for her, lest she ever forget. As if she could! Lovenia never ceased thinking of her unborn baby and what the future could bring. She thanked God every day for the miracle of this precious little being growing inside her.

October 18, 1884

Lately I have had the strong feeling that the baby in my womb is a girl child and the thought makes me feel as if all I can do is smile. Sometimes I am afraid that this feeling is only a result of my wanting a girl so much, but the certainty of it grows within me as the baby grows. Yesterday I felt that particular fluttering inside that I had forgotten about. It is such a relief to feel that, to know that my baby really is alive, and that she is well—you see, I even think of the baby as a "she" without realizing it...

Samantha, sitting at the little desk in her room, paused in her reading, feeling again of her mother's love. Not only had Samantha been wanted, but her mother had specifically desired a girl! Unlike many other women Samantha had heard talk, her mother had not seemed particularly concerned that her husband still had no heir, no son to carry on his name to the future generation. Samantha imagined all the things she could have grown up doing with her mother—her very own mother!--and sorrowed again that it could never be.

She read on through her mother's next few months of pregnancy until she arrived at the beginning of January 1885. Then, earlier than last time, trouble struck again. The symptoms were the same as before and the same fear prevailed that the baby would arrive too soon. Just as the doctor in Worthington had done, Dr. Johnson tried all he knew to improve Lovenia's situation. But there was nothing for it and Lovenia had to remain on bedrest, seemingly keeping the baby inside by sheer willpower. Once again, she strove to keep a bright outlook on her situation and think optimistically. Her faith in God appeared never to waver and she urged others to believe in Him likewise. When her friends came to visit--as they often did--

they told her that she always lifted their spirits more than they ever did hers.

Samantha was impressed again by her mother's amazing ability to love and bless the lives that touched hers, even in her weakness and being bed bound, even in the face of impending tragedy.

Lovenia's last entry was chilling and heartbreaking in its finality. Samantha noted that the always-neat script looked shaky and significantly weaker than the last, as if writing had taken a great effort. She steeled herself for her mother's final words and reached for a handkerchief.

March 14, 1885

The thought will not leave me that I will not see this baby or hold her, as I never saw or held my son years ago. But I do feel I have God's assurance that my daughter's life will be spared, that this time it is I who will pass on to the next life. This realization brings with it only relief to leave this frail body behind and anticipation to see my little boy for the first time in heaven. Yes, there is a deep sadness in my heart too, sadness at leaving my dear Basil and never having the privilege of raising the daughter who is flesh of my flesh and whom I desired so long. Basil will take it so hard! I wish he only had the faith that I have, then he would be comforted. It will be such a challenge for him to care for the baby alone; I am so very grateful for my friend, dear Renee Dolittle, and how I know she will continue to bless this family.

I look forward to soon meeting my Maker and being carried into His bosom, to sing His praises forevermore. May my husband and my daughter, whom I wish to be named Samantha, ever know of my great love for them. A love so great, I would die for them.

Samantha took a great, shuddering breath as the tears coursed down her cheeks. She laid her head on her arms and sobbed until she thought her body would fall apart from the grief. She could not count the number of times she had grieved for her mother in recent months, but this was a stronger grief than she had ever imagined she could feel; it consumed all her senses. There was no room in her heart, mind, or soul for anything but the deep anguish that tore into her.

Samantha cried until tears would no longer fall, her eyes felt swollen, and her nose chafed from wiping it. She raised her head, trembling, and closed the journal that still lay propped up against the wall at the edge of the desk. She realized that her body was, in fact, still intact, and that everything about her surroundings was just as it was before. After the strength of the emotion she had just passed through, she felt as if the whole world should look different. The immense grief was still strong and heavy in her heart and had been only slightly abated by the flood of tears.

She sat for a long time, contemplating all that she had read and learned from her mother's journal over the past two months. So far, it seemed to her that her mother's death had been a waste. Neither her father nor herself had made of their lives and of themselves what Lovenia would have wished for them. Lovenia saw things in each of them that neither, it appeared, saw in themselves or in each other. But if Lovenia could love them so much, they must be worth it somehow! With more purpose than ever, Samantha resolved to make her life worthy of her mother's death.

***

Samantha was determined. She was going to do this, she needed to, and she was beginning to think it would really work out. After weeks of deliberating over the matter, writing down lists of things that needed to be done and arrangements that had to be made, and talking to both Katherine and Rupert a few times, she decided to finally face the most difficult hurdle.

So here she was, walking up the stairs to the third floor, to her father's room, holding her mother's journal tightly, as the talisman of strength, power, and encouragement it had become. She had come this way many times before in her life, but never regularly or with anticipation, and now she realized that it had been a very long time since she last visited him.

She knocked quietly but firmly and waited for her father's low, "Enter." When she opened the door of the sparsely furnished, slightly disheveled room, she saw only his back as he sat at his desk facing the window. Looking at him, his lanky frame bent tiredly over a book, his white hair thinning, she realized she no longer knew what to call him. She had always called him Father, but she was not sure if she could say that anymore. The Father she had been thinking of the last couple of months was the one she had come to know through her mother. And the Basil Jennings sitting before her was so far removed from the loving, devoted husband she had read about that she could not reconcile the two. Everyone in town called him Professor and that was what came to her mind most readily now.

There were only a few feet between them, but the space felt like miles, and the invisible wall between them seemed to Samantha so tangible that she could go no further than to step across the threshold. She stood there, suddenly uncertain about the thing she had been so determined to do only moments before.

Basil Jennings remained silent and still until the quiet seemed deafening. Finally, he lifted his head but remained facing the window. "Yes?"

Samantha swallowed. "Sir?" she said at last.

He stood slowly and turned toward her, barely masking his surprise. "Yes?" he said again.

A long-suppressed anger arose inside Samantha's breast and this time she did not try to quell it. Before she could be intimidated out of her mission or lose the courage that the anger gave her, she blurted, "Why did you never tell me about this?" She held up the journal in an almost accusatory gesture and her eyes demanded an answer.

Basil blinked and looked at his daughter as if unsure of who she was.

Samantha waited until she could stand it no longer. "Why have you never talked to me of my mother? Why have you never visited her grave?" Samantha felt her voice trembling and willed herself to be strong, but she heard her tone rise with the next question, higher than her normal voice. "Why did I have to find out from Mrs. Dolittle that I had a brother?" She knew she was verbally attacking her father and felt vaguely appalled at herself; this was not what she had planned. But she could not stop now. She took a few deep breaths as she watched him, willing him to say something.

But he did not.

"Why don't you ever talk to me?" she asked finally, feeling like a little girl again, ready to cry. This was not what she had planned to say at all! But looking at the old man standing silently across from her--the man who was supposedly her father and who still refused to speak—the anger returned again, and rather than say anything more hateful, she turned away, resigned to do this without his knowledge after all.

"Samantha!" She heard a note of desperation in his gruff voice that surprised her, and she turned back.

"I..." he faltered and stared at her with a different look in his bespectacled eyes than she had seen there before. "You... You look so much like your mother." He seemed to choke on the last word and Samantha saw a muscle twitch below one eye.

She was stunned and could only stare at him for a few moments. Then weakly she said, "I...do?" She felt her heart pumping quickly and yearned for him to tell her more. But he didn't.

Wearily he turned his desk chair around and sat again, gesturing for Samantha to pull the chair by his bed closer and take a seat also. "Samantha," he began and then stopped again. His eyes looked so sad that Samantha instantly regretted what she had said and began to apologize, but he shook his head to quiet her.

"I know I have not been the father to you that I ought to have been." He looked at her a moment with piercing blue-gray eyes that were unflinching, then looked down at the gnarled hands on his knees. "I did not intentionally keep you ignorant of Lov—of your mother, or of the fact that you had a brother." He sighed as if he carried the weight of the world on his shoulders. "I simply..." he looked up at her again. "It is still difficult for me to speak of her, even now. When you asked questions as a little girl I...I tried to answer as quickly and vaguely as possible...because the answers were far too painful." He cleared his throat as if the pain were lodged there still. "Eventually, you stopped asking. If I had known that you... If I had thought... Well, I am glad you found the journal after all."

Samantha nodded, a little wary still, and looked at him a long moment, thinking over all she had learned from the book. "I, too, am glad I found it, Father. It has shown me that I had a mother who was good and selfless, who...*adored* her husband and who loved the children she bore but never saw with her own eyes." She felt the tears rising in her throat but continued anyway. "It has taught me that I have a heritage, that becoming like my mother is the best thing I could possibly strive for. Now I *have* something concrete to strive for. My life has never had this kind of meaning before."

Basil Jennings' eyes glistened with unexpected tears and he blinked them a couple times, his chin quivering ever so slightly.

Samantha swallowed hard and then began again. "In the last few months I have both discovered my mother and lost her, grieving over her death for the first time in my life. And in finding her, I have found new things about myself—within myself." Then, even though she knew it might pain him, she had to add, "And the husband who called his wife 'Lovey' and who doted on her with all his heart does not seem at all the same man whom I call Father..." Then, feeling chagrined, she added, "I'm sorry. I probably should not have told you that."

Basil took a great shuddering breath and gave his daughter a pained smile that looked more like a grimace. "You are right. He is not the same man, I am afraid." He shook his head and looked away from her. "That man died with Lovenia... and was buried with her."

"Why have you not visited her grave, Father? Perhaps that would help you, bring a healing closure." Samantha heard the pleading in her voice and was startled by the new compassion she felt for the broken man sitting across from her.

"I cannot," he said. "No, I cannot." But there was a certain wistfulness in his tone, despite the finality of his words.

"But Father, *why* not? I am going—at least, with your permission," she hastily added. "I must go. I *need* to go!"

"Go, then," Basil said, looking up again and waving a hand. "I give you my blessing and whatever money you need to cover expenses. But I cannot go."

Samantha was startled. She had known money would not be an issue, but to have his permission so easily when she had prepared herself for a much more difficult scenario took her off guard a little. "Th-thank you," she returned, her heart racing. "This means a great deal to me. And I shall not be alone, so you need not worry about that." Would he have worried? She didn't know. "I will have two friends with me, one male, one female."

Basil nodded grimly.

He did not offer anything more and Samantha suddenly remembered what else she had been planning to ask him. "Father? Are...are the graves in Worthington?—that is what I have concluded, but I need to know for sure."

Her father said nothing for a few moments and then nodded slowly. "Yes. Somewhere in Worthington. I am afraid I don't remember the name of the cemetery." For a moment, he looked off into a very far distance and Samantha knew he was remembering something else.

The room was silent and Samantha felt like she should say something before leaving but was unsure what. Finally she said softly, "You are very welcome to change your mind and join us if you decide to... Father... Not that you need an invitation..." she trailed off, suddenly embarrassed by her boldness in this whole encounter. "I suppose I... should be leaving now..." She felt awkward and stood to depart.

"Samantha," he called her back for the second time and she turned to look at him. "Thank you." His frame looked as weary as before, but there was a different softness about his eyes and mouth.

She nodded slightly, feeling that the meaning behind the words was more than she understood.

"Would you..." He cleared his throat and swallowed a couple of times.

"Yes, Father?"

"Would you mind leaving the...the journal with me for a while?"

Samantha's eyes opened wide, not feeling in her heart that that was something she could give just yet. She searched his face as she searched her heart, wondering if she could do without it on her journey after all. In that moment, she realized that every detail of what her mother had written was woven into the deepest part of her, and she knew if there was any vital information in it that would help her on the trip, she would remember it when she needed to. Finally, seeing how sad and lost her father looked and remembering that Lovenia had been his first, after all, before she was hers, she returned to hand the journal to him where he still sat.

He caressed the cover gently and Samantha thought she detected a new brightness in his eyes. "I will not keep it," he said as if reading her thoughts, "but I find I would very much like to read parts of it again. Even if the memories are painful."

"Yes," Samantha returned softly. "Yes. That is good." Then she quietly left, closing the door behind her.

CHAPTER 23

A RESEMBLANCE

March 1902

Much to Sterling's surprise, the Franklin County Committee received a flood of entries for the March writing contest. He had not counted on how much publicity the contest would receive with the carnival or how eager the community would be to share their writing talents (or, in some cases, try their hand at it for the first time in an attempt to win a bit of cash). This surprise did not weaken his resolve to assist the committee, however. The members of the committee (of which Sterling, by now, was considered a part) each took a stack of papers to consider and agreed to meet again in three days' time.

When Sterling returned home to his room the first evening, after grabbing a bite to eat at the café down the street, he sat down with his stack of papers and diligently read over each one. Once he separated the quality entries from the amateurs, the real work began. As he read, he separated them into two piles until he had read them all. The next evening, he re-read those from the "good" pile and narrowed it down further. When this pile had shrunk to three poems and two articles, Sterling was satisfied and laid the papers aside so he could finish planning his lessons for school.

The following evening the committee met and exchanged with each other what they had each selected as the best work. They spent a couple of hours in this manner, reading and critiquing, weeding pieces out until they all were in consensus: one winner for each of three categories—Poetry, Essay, and Story. The three first-place entries would be taken to the press for printing the following week, the first of April, at which time the second contest date would be announced. Winners could claim their prize money by presenting themselves at the next committee meeting. So far everything had worked out fairly smoothly, though they did have a few kinks to work out of the process. For example, they had realized there was a need for specific guidelines on the length and format of entries, as well as a rule that once a person had won, he or she could not enter again for one year. But they would learn the best way to run things in time.

At the end of the meeting, one of the committee members mentioned that he had a brother-in-law in the printing business in Findlay, a few counties away and that he had mentioned the contest to him in a letter. The brother-in-law had written back, quite interested, and wondered if it might be possible to expand the contest to include more than just the one county; perhaps, in time, it could include the whole state. At this pronouncement, the committee was momentarily stunned, thinking of the incredible possibilities. Sterling was the first to offer his approval and the others quickly followed suit. With grand plans forming in their heads, the committee members adjourned until the following week, when they would put their various plans together and figure out how to coordinate a larger scale contest and work out all the logistics.

***

The morning after Samantha had spoken with her father, she turned to Mrs. Dolittle from the breakfast table and said, "May I ask you another question?"

Mrs. Dolittle looked up from buttering slices of toast near the stove and laughed. "So early in the morning and you already have questions?"

Samantha lifted her shoulders in a gesture of apology. "I'm sorry. But I had a talk with my father yesterday..."

Mrs. Dolittle came to stand near and eyed her across the table, immediately serious and attentive. "Did you now." It was a statement, not a question.

"I thought about our conversation all last night and I think I dreamed about it too. It...Well..." Samantha put down her fork and cocked her head slightly to one side as she thought. "Mrs. Dolittle, you know he never says much. But something he did say has me wondering what he meant."

Mrs. Dolittle nodded but said quietly, "Maybe this is a question you ought to ask him."

Samantha straightened and smoothed the napkin in her lap absently. "Perhaps, but I think you may know too." She paused and when Mrs. Dolittle did not protest, she continued, "He told me I look like my mother and I...well, I wonder if that is really true?" Samantha eyed her plate for a moment and then raised her head again to look at the beloved housekeeper.

The pucker between Mrs. Dolittle's black eyebrows eased and she smiled slightly. "Ah, yes. Perhaps I do know some of the answer to that question, my dear." She returned to the stove and resumed her ministrations to the toast, adding, "But what I see and what your father sees may be very different things. You may still try asking him sometime."

Samantha nodded, waiting for her to go on.

"All the while you've grown up, I have caught glimpses of your mother in you, but never have I seen as many similarities as I do now--ever since last summer, I think."

Samantha picked up her fork once again. She still had said nothing to Mrs. Dolittle about what really happened during the summer.

"When I think of Lovenia, what comes to mind first is her...mmm," Mrs. Dolittle frowned in thought, "I guess vitality would be the word." She chuckled to herself. "It may sound odd to apply that word to your mother—you know how sickly she was—but there was just something about her that was so...alive, despite it all."

Samantha nodded. She had had that impression herself.

"She had a way of lighting up the room with just her quiet presence. She was so unassuming and unpretentious—but when she wanted something important, she went after it in a way that no one could deny."

Mrs. Dolittle laid down the knife, wiping her fingers on a napkin, and brought the plate of toast to set it in the middle of the table, sitting across from her. She looked at Samantha's expression and saw the question written there. "Yes, child. I see those things in you too. Everything about you breathes vitality, and you do not make much of yourself either. I have also seen that you immerse yourself in whatever causes are most important to you. You are, perhaps, a little less gentle than was she, more able to say what is on your mind" —(Samantha blushed at this)— "but I would wager that is part of your father coming out in you too."

"Now, I do not know if your father sees that same quality in you that was so characteristic of your mother--since he and you are rarely in each other's presence—so I will tell you what else I see that he may also see."

Samantha chewed and swallowed and then sat still, fork unconsciously poised in the air over her scrambled eggs while she awaited Mrs. Dolittle's further observations. To her surprise, the woman leaned over the table and gently slipped off Samantha's spectacles, laying them on the table next to her plate. Then she leaned back in her chair and looked at Samantha for a long moment. A slow, reminiscent smile crept over her face and she nodded. "Yes, I daresay your father is right. Your eyes are exactly the same gray as hers. I can see that more clearly now. And your nose has that same delicate, upturned way about it that hers did. Your hair is different than hers, of course—you know her hair was brown--you have your father's coloring. And height like your father. But your facial structure and thin frame are decidedly Lovenia's." She paused a moment and then added, "And with your glasses off, the resemblance is clearer to me all at once."

Samantha nodded gratefully. "Thank you," she said, tears shimmering in her eyes, but still smiling. "It helps me to know that I inherited something from my mother." Then after a thoughtful pause, she reached across the table and squeezed the other woman's hand. "I am so glad you knew her, Mrs. Dolittle. She loved you, and it was so much easier for her to die peacefully, knowing you were here to take care of things—of me and father. She...she called you Renee."

It was a half-question and Mrs. Dolittle nodded in reply. "And I called her Lovenia. Ours was not the typical relationship between servant and mistress. I was blessed to never feel as if I were a servant."

239

The older woman's dark eyes grew moist, and Samantha gently let go of her hand as Mrs. Dolittle reached for her handkerchief.

After a moment, Mrs. Dolittle asked, "She really wrote of me, then?"

The question seemed to hold a hundred other questions inside it, and the one-word answer gave a hundred answers at once: "Yes." Samantha smiled at her, feeling her love for the housekeeper deepening every day. "She wrote of you as a 'godsend.' I think you were one of the best friends she ever had."

Mrs. Dolittle dabbed at her eyes with her napkin. "It does my heart good to hear that. Thank you for telling me. She would often express her appreciation and affection for me, but it has been so long that sometimes I forget how things once were."

Samantha nodded and then remembered something else. "A few times she mentioned two friends that would come by to see her. Do they still live in town?"

"Remind me of their names..."

"Emma Ridgewood and Missy Phelps," Samantha replied instantly, having said the names over and over to herself since she first read them.

"Ah, yes, I remember now. Kind women. Missy died about five years ago; consumption, I think. But Emma is still around, as I recall. I believe Lovenia meant a great deal to her, so I am sure she would appreciate a visit from you."

Mrs. Dolittle and Samantha chatted on for another few minutes while Samantha finished eating her breakfast (Mrs. Dolittle had eaten hers earlier) and then Samantha stood and gave her a quick hug. "Thank you for everything, Mrs. Dolittle. Among other things, you are a wealth of knowledge! And thanks for your patience with all of my questions."

Mrs. Dolittle beamed with pleasure and patted Samantha's shoulder. "Any time, child. I surely enjoy your company. Here," she added, reaching back to the table, "you mustn't leave these." She held out Samantha's glasses and Samantha held them in her hands, looking at them closely for the first time.

"I think," she said reflectively, "I think perhaps I will not wear these as often as I have in the past. I only need them for reading or sewing anyway, and I do less reading than I once did. Perhaps without them, I will look a little more like my mother."

Mrs. Dolittle patted her again and nodded. "That sounds fine, dear, just fine."

CHAPTER 24

SAMANTHA'S ENTRY

April 1902

With the contest and mid-term teaching occupying his mind almost completely, Sterling almost forgot the worry that had started nagging at him recently. He had hoped Samantha would have received his letter long before now and written something in reply, though he had not asked her to write him. Granted, it was probably still possible she had taken a while to send one and it just had not reached him yet. He hoped that was the reason for the delay.

At this time, he was also finally forced to think about a matter he had pushed to the back burner for months when Mr. Grover approached him before school one day to ask whether he intended to teach at the Boys' School the following year. Sterling was a bit taken aback by the question, though he recognized that he should have seriously considered the matter long before now.

He looked across his desk at the superintendent, who looked expectantly back at him, gray eyebrows raised, a half-smile lighting his features.

"I...I am afraid I do not have an answer for you right this moment, Mr. Grover. I have been so caught up in other things that I honestly have not...given it much thought."

Mr. Grover chuckled. "I've noticed how busy and involved you have become. I understand and I will not pressure you yet. We would greatly appreciate it if you decided to stay on here--you have been an asset to our faculty--but the decision is, of course, up to you.

I do need to know by April tenth what you have decided. April tenth, at the latest." He reached into a small satchel he'd brought with him and handed Sterling a sheet of paper. "Fill this out and leave it on my desk if I am not in my office."

Sterling nodded. "Thank you. I appreciate your offer to continue here and will give it serious consideration. This has been a good experience for me, and I feel more comfortable here all the time."

"Good." Mr. Grover reached across the desk and shook Sterling's hand. "We are glad to have you here, son. Let me know. And good luck with your lessons today."

"Thank you." As Sterling watched Mr. Grover leave, he realized he felt quite unsettled. In his attempts to push Samantha from his mind he had avoided all other thoughts of the future, but now he would have to face it head on and settle this one aspect of it, at least. He did not like the thought, but he knew it was necessary. Perhaps a walk through the cemetery would help him order his thoughts and priorities.

***

Samantha breathed in the sweet smells of greening spring and smiled softly to herself over her warm mug of cider. April had arrived gently, with no visible difference, so far, between it and March. She loved the expectation this time of year always brought with it, the excitement for the world to become new once again. For the past two weeks, the rain had come off and on, and now the women of the quilting group were enjoying refreshments outside while the sunshine lasted, chatting comfortably with one another. They normally met only once a month but had agreed to meet twice in April, as one of their members was engaged to be married and they wanted to make a special quilt for her, in addition to their other projects.

Samantha did not notice the conversations around her for a few minutes, but now one came filtering through.

"...I entered mine," one of the young women was telling her companion. "You ought to write something too. It couldn't hurt. And if you won, you would earn some spending money."

The other girl murmured something in reply, and they continued their conversation in more muted tones that Samantha could not quite make out.

A moment later, Katherine joined her, having finished serving everyone. This time the quilters met in her home, and she had suggested they take their break and refreshment outdoors. She sat in a wicker chair beside Samantha, shawl drawn securely around her, and carefully took a sip of cider while balancing a small plate of sugar cookies on her knees. Then she took a deep breath and closed her eyes appreciatively for a moment, much the way Samantha had done. "I just love spring, don't you?" she asked Samantha, opening her dark-lashed eyes.

"Yes, I was just thinking the same thing," Samantha smiled back. "When the rains slow down, and the flowers and blossoms have a chance to come out, what a wondrous sight the world is!"

Katherine took a dainty bite from a cookie and nodded. "Year after year, I never get tired of spring; it is one of those rare things in life that one can rely on. It always reassures me and makes me happy."

Samantha appreciated her friend's ability to understand what she herself was feeling and to express it so aptly. They both sat in silence for a few minutes, letting the slight breeze and the talk of the other women wash over them while they finished their cookies and cider.

Then Katherine suddenly brightened and confided to Samantha how much she was looking forward to their adventure the following week. "Every time I think of it and what we may discover, it makes me anxious to be gone already," she said in low tones.

Samantha nodded. "I am anticipating it with pleasure, too. I feel like it will give me a greater sense of closeness and closure with my mother. And I am so glad your father finally agreed to let you come."

Then Samantha remembered the snatch of conversation she recently overheard and asked Katherine about it. "Do you know what she meant by that? What is there to 'enter'?"

"Actually yes, I do know, and I should have mentioned it to you." Katherine brushed a few crumbs from her lap. "I read about it only yesterday. The paper said there is a writing contest expanding from Franklin County to include the whole state, and one winner will be chosen in each of three categories. Apparently, the deadline was originally this week, but they have extended it an additional week so that more people will have the opportunity to enter. I know how you love to write, Samantha. You should enter something!"

Samantha was intrigued. She had never heard of a contest such as this and never thought of sharing her efforts with such a wide audience. "Well...maybe I will. I don't know if anyone would really be interested in the kinds of things I write, but I suppose I could try. And women's submissions are actually welcomed, as well as men's?"

"Oh yes, everyone's. There is no rule as to who can enter. I would try too, but," Katherine's laugh was low and self-deprecating, "I do not have any talent for it and would not want to waste the judges' time."

"Surely your writing is not that bad!" Samantha rejoined.

Katherine nodded sagely, "Oh, but it is." She shrugged slightly. "That does not concern me too much, though." She took a bite from her last cookie and chewed for a moment. Then she raised one graceful, dark eyebrow significantly as she added, "I know my talents must lie somewhere," as if exactly where her talents were hidden was a deep mystery to her and everyone else.

Samantha shook her head at her friend and laughed. "Now that is an understatement if I ever heard one, Katherine. You have the most beautiful voice of anyone I know, and you play the piano so well."

Katherine laughingly laid a hand on Samantha's shoulder. "Let it not be said that I fish for compliments, but I thank you all the same. You are a dear." She collected Samantha's plate and mug to take back to the kitchen with her own, and Samantha arose to help her collect others' dishes.

Later that afternoon when Samantha returned home, after having gathered the submission information she needed, she sat by the window in her room and began looking through the poems she had written over the last several months. There were quite a few of them, but she wasn't sure any of them was something she would want to submit to the contest. She could enter one of her essays, but for some reason (perhaps because poetry was the newer and currently more exciting genre for her) she wanted only to enter the poetry division.

Stilling the papers in her hands, she looked out the window, lifting a finger to trace the rivulets of water that ran slowly and crookedly down the glass. It was raining again (would it never cease?) and she was glad to be in out of the damp and chill. She hoped the journey next week would not be this wet! Sometimes the dripping drone of the rain seemed a cozy sound, but today--and many other days besides--it only made her melancholy. And melancholy feelings led to melancholy thoughts, which led to Sterling.

Samantha knew she was not being fair to Rupert as long as she held onto thoughts of Sterling, but all the same she could not let go, and she still did not know exactly what she felt for Rupert. All she knew for sure was that she did want to see Sterling again, to see if what she felt was real and to know if he still felt as he once had seemed to. But whenever her thoughts came around to this again, the worry returned. If he still cared about her, why had he not written? A small note would have sufficed. She had received no indication, even, of where he had gone. The possibility of seeing him again, therefore, seemed remote.

She sat for quite some time, organizing her thoughts while she gazed out at the bright green of the new-leafed trees and, beneath them, the grass that shimmered a thick emerald. Unbidden, a particular conversation with Sterling came back to her in a rush, and she remembered the oppressive heat of that day and what he wrote that had touched her so. A poem of her own moved restlessly inside her that she had wanted to write for a long while but never found the right words to express. Maybe now was the time. From her small pile of papers she pulled out a blank sheet and set the others aside, then picked up a sharpened pencil from the wide windowsill, and began to write.

The next evening as Samantha prepared a small plate of food for her supper (it was Mrs. Dolittle's day off), a knock came at the front door. She wondered who it could be as she wiped her slightly soiled fingers on her apron. Though she knew many more people now than she ever had, only a couple of them had ever come to her house besides Katherine and Rupert. Perhaps it is one of them, she thought.

When she heaved open the solid oak door, Rupert stood there, hat in hand, his face and hands pink from a recent scrubbing.

"Hello," she said in surprise. "How are you? Come in!" She drew him inside and closed the door behind them. "Sorry about the noise," she added, as hammering noises echoed from a few rooms away. "Martin is finishing up some inside work today. With all the rain making a mess of things outside, he decided to focus on neglected projects in the house."

Rupert looked at her, his back to the door, turning the hat in his hands. "I hope this isn't a bad time. I finished work early today," he explained.

"Oh, no," Samantha shook her head. "Mrs. Dolittle is off today, so I was just preparing myself a little supper. Would you care to join me? There is plenty."

"Well, I..." Rupert paused and then gave her one of his slow smiles. "I didn't try to coincide my visit with your supper, but I guess this isn't the first time." He shrugged and chuckled quietly. "Although, I would go to just about any lengths to have some of Mrs. Dolittle's delicious cooking."

Samantha smiled and took Rupert's hat and jacket. Hanging them up she said, "I will have to relay the compliment. I'm afraid Mrs.

Dolittle does not get the praise she deserves, cooking for my father and me. I am sure we do not express our appreciation of her talents as often as we should."

She ushered Rupert into the kitchen and while she prepared a plate of food for him, he stepped out to the side yard to split a few logs to add to the dwindling pile just outside the kitchen door. Then he washed up at the pump. By the time he re-entered the house, after scraping the mud off his boots, their meal had almost finished warming in the stove.

Samantha invited Martin to join them, but the old man was intent on finishing his project and asked that a plate be prepared for him to eat a bit later. So alone together, but aware of Martin in the other room, Rupert told Samantha of his work the last few days on the farm, and of his adventure when a couple of the yearlings had figured out how to open the doors to their stalls and given him quite a run trying to get them safely back inside. Samantha told him of her entry in the writing contest and how it felt to her like a bold step in the dark, but at the same time like something she needed to do.

Later, while they finished the last of their meal, Samantha suddenly realized she had not told Rupert of the little important things that had happened recently. She swallowed her bite of food, then patted her mouth with a napkin. "Rupert," she said, looking across the table at him, his light brown hair still slightly tousled from chopping wood out in the slight wind. "I forgot to tell you something."

He looked up from his plate, chewing his last bite, his clear blue eyes watching her expectantly.

"First of all, I don't think I told you that I finished reading my mother's journal."

He shook his head and swallowed. "You did?"

"Yes."

"Do you feel different for having read it?" he asked perceptively.

Samantha nodded. "Very much so. Reading my mother's words from her own hand was..." she did not quite know what words could express the life-changing event it had been for her. "It's difficult to explain how it affected me, but it was definitely an incredible experience. Now I know what a remarkable woman she was and how much she loved my father."

"Have you spoken with your father yet about our trip?" He looked a little anxious and Samantha was touched that he would remember her anxiety about approaching her father.

"Yes. That is the other thing I forgot to mention. He gave me his blessing and whatever money we need to cover the trip, and he confirmed that the graves are in Worthington, though he doesn't remember where."

Rupert nodded. "I'm relieved he did not try to prevent you from going."

"So am I," Samantha agreed.

"Did your conversation with him go well, then?" Rupert asked.

Samantha thought a moment, brows furrowed. "Relatively well, I suppose," she said finally. "He is never easy to talk to, but we were more open with each other than usual. And he asked me to leave Mother's journal with him."

Rupert's eyes widened. "Really?"

"I didn't want to at first, but then I realized that I had internalized the journal pretty well and that it would probably be beneficial for him to read it again. He still mourns for her and maybe reading her words would help him finish the grieving process." Samantha paused a moment in thought, then sighed. "At least I can hope..."

Rupert reached a hand across the table and placed it over one of Samantha's. "I bet it will," he said encouragingly. "I can tell that reading your mother's journal has been a great thing for you, so maybe it will be for your father too." He swallowed and Samantha sensed he was about to say something that he felt was important. "Samantha, I..." he faltered a moment, eyes lowered to the table, then cleared his throat and began again. "I wish I could have known your mother. She must have been a remarkable lady to have such a wonderful daughter."

He squeezed Samantha's hand and tears came to her eyes. "Thank you," she whispered. She cleared her throat and then added in a normal voice, "You don't know how many times I have wished I knew her too."

Samantha blinked back her tears, and after a quiet moment, slid her hand free of his. She began clearing the table and Rupert quickly followed, asking, "If you don't mind my asking, what impressed you most about what you read?"

"I don't mind," Samantha replied. "I have been pondering that myself ever since I finished the journal, so I think I have an answer for you."

Rupert carried their dishes over to the sink and Samantha began washing them while he cleaned off the table. Then he joined her.

"I guess my answer has two parts to it," Samantha began. "Throughout the journal I was most impressed by my mother's complete love and utter selflessness. All she ever wanted out of life was to have a family and to be able to show them her love. That was her dream: to have children." She handed a cleaned dish to Rupert and he began drying it.

"When that was denied her, she quietly tried to forget her disappointment and instead took up my father's dream of teaching at Oberlin. She wanted whatever would make him happiest. But once she had helped that come to pass, she again took up her old dream." Samantha fell silent and Rupert dried dishes quietly, patiently waiting for her to continue. The only sound was the swish of the water as Samantha washed.

Finally she said, "I suppose Mother could not help returning to it. I don't think it would have been a real dream if she had not."

Rupert nodded in agreement. "True."

"And that is the second part of my answer. I thought I had good, worthwhile, strong dreams, but when I read about Mother's I realized my so-called dreams were mere fancies. She was truly dedicated to her dream and had faith that somehow God would make it happen. Someday." Samantha's voice cracked on the last word, and she swallowed a lump in her throat, handing the last dish to Rupert but not looking at him. Then she untied her apron and removed it, hanging it on its hook on the wall. Returning to Rupert's side at the sink, she placed both hands on the counter ledge, looking out the window and beyond to a place that Rupert could not see.

At last she spoke again. "Mother loved and dreamed to the extent that she was willing to give up her life to make her dream a reality. How many of us have dreams that powerful? Or have love that complete?"

Rupert felt his heart swell as he laid the damp dishtowel on the sideboard and looked at the young woman next to him. The weakening sunlight shone faintly through the window as it headed westward and lit Samantha's features with a yellow glow. He traced the line of her face with his eyes. From the high forehead, down the slope of her nose to its delicately upturned end, the indent just above the thin lips, then the small, rounded chin. What a remarkable, insightful young woman she was! Inwardly he marveled once again at the blessing of knowing her--and that she considered him a friend. He did not know what to say, so he put an arm gently around her shoulders and they stood there together, watching the light fade into the oranges and pinks of sunset.

***

By the requested April tenth, Sterling turned in his contract to Mr. Grover, having come to the decision to continue on at the Boys' School for at least another year. He could not think of anything better to do with his life and he felt, after all, that he had actually made a difference, albeit a small one. He had had to admit that teaching in this capacity had truly been enjoyable and rewarding, though it had taken him months to realize it.

In addition, he felt that a difference had been wrought upon him and hoped that he was a more thoughtful, careful, and caring man than he had been at the beginning of the school year. He felt a greater sense of belonging here in this town than he ever had anywhere else he'd lived, and he liked the feeling. Why leave a good thing? There was still so much to learn and do and be a part of.

Of course, there was another particular town toward which he yearned, but by now he doubted there was anything there for him. He knew the time was fast approaching for him to return to Oberlin and make his apologies to Samantha, but he dreaded the thought even as he longed to see her again. Despite his conversations with Mrs. Tomlinson and her reassurances, receiving only silence in the wake of his letter was still unsettling, to say the least. His distressing nighttime dreams had never ceased completely, and at times the effort of keeping Samantha from his conscious thoughts during the day was more than he could withstand. It all made him so tired. He wanted the whole ordeal over, but he still felt a certain reluctance to initiate it. School was rapidly coming to a close, however, and he knew that its end would leave him with no excuse not to return. In the meantime, he had final exams to create and then there would be corrections and the assigning of marks. A teacher's work was never done!

CHAPTER 25

A TREASURE

April 1902

The impending journey grew quickly closer, and Samantha felt anxious for its arrival: anxious in that she had a deep sense of excitement at seeing new things and finding her mother's final resting place. But she also felt some concern over how well the journey would go and what it would be like to have Rupert close by for a whole week. Since the beginning of their relationship she had sensed that he was interested in her as more than a friend, and the more time they spent together, the stronger his feelings grew. She could tell by the way he looked at her; those blue eyes of his were nothing if not ever-honest. Though they had only known each other a few short months, Samantha often had the feeling that Rupert would like to say much more than he did and was holding back, waiting for Samantha to indicate that she, too, would like their relationship to progress and to lead to something more.

Sometimes she thought she would like that. Rupert was such a good, kind, gentle, and unselfish person. He was everything a girl could ask for in a husband. But whenever she felt her mind leaning in that direction, her heart reminded her of someone else and she would realize once again that for her there was no spark with Rupert. As a friend, she cared for him deeply, enjoyed being with him, and was grateful for him. But she did not feel romantic toward him and didn't think she ever would—and she knew what it felt like to have those warm, exciting, romantic feelings that made a person excited just to be alive.

When she thought about all this, she wondered if she was being foolish, if she should not simply take the opportunity before her and learn to love Rupert the way he wanted her to. For all she knew, Sterling might be on the other side of the world and he would probably never return to Oberlin. So why was she hanging on to him, to the memories?

He is a good man too, she thought in Sterling's defense. *He is good and intelligent and he always listened closely to my thoughts and ideas. After all, he saw something in me from the beginning that I didn't even know was there! He is a little impulsive sometimes...but he always pushed me to try harder and be my best—he wanted the best for me. And with him I did feel that spark...*

Samantha was honestly afraid that the question she saw in Rupert's eyes would come out at some point during their trip, and the thought of breaking his heart made her so sad she felt sick to her stomach. But in the long run wouldn't it be even worse to commit to him while her heart was very much with someone else?

She was not certain what she should do when this inevitable moment occurred, but she kept a prayer in her heart that God would give her wisdom when she needed it most.

As she finished the preparations for her journey, such as purchasing train tickets and wiring for hotel reservations in Worthington, she decided that she must speak with Emma Ridgewood, if she could, before leaving. The idea of meeting another person who had really known her mother was very compelling, and the notion pulled at her so that she could not ignore it.

Thus it was that two days before leaving for Worthington, Samantha walked carefully up to the stately old house on East Vine

Street. She tried to avoid the puddles, carefully holding her skirts up with one hand, and pushed open the low white picket fence gate. The paint was peeling and the hinges gave out a protesting squawk as she passed through and up the walkway to the front door. Ivy covered the house and draped over the front porch so thickly that if the house had not been facing east and enjoying the first frail warmth of the day, Samantha would have been plunged into darkness.

Even after the encouraging words she had told herself on the way here, she still felt a little nervous and took a moment to lower and smooth her skirts, and to pull her gloves up more snugly. Wanting both to give a good impression and to be completely proper, she had decided to wear an outfit which had only recently been made. Katherine had seen the pattern in a catalogue and persuaded Samantha to order the fabric and hire the work done at the Oberlin Tailor. It was a long skirt in navy blue satin, the matching blouse with sleeves that billowed slightly just below the elbows. As the weather was still cool, she wore a dark shawl around her shoulders that draped down to her hands. On her feet she wore her nicer pair of smart black boots that laced up to mid-calf, and her hands and arms were graced with white kid gloves. Pinned to her neatly piled hair she had placed a large feathered hat that complimented the dress and which Katherine had called 'wonderfully elegant.' The result was very fashionable and gratifying, Samantha had to admit, and she actually felt quite dignified wearing it.

She glanced back at Martin, waiting in the street with horse and buggy, and felt further encouraged by his wave. She was glad she had followed Mrs. Dolittle's advice to have Martin drive her, for the roads were even more muddy than anticipated and would have made her entirely unpresentable had she walked. Taking a deep breath, she rang the bell and waited.

After several moments Samantha was about to ring again when she heard quick, light steps and a young maid answered the door. "Hello?" she asked, peering through the screen at her. "May I help you?"

"Hello," Samantha answered, trying to see the young woman through the darkness without appearing as if she were prying. "I came to pay a call on Mrs. Emma Ridgewood, if she is available this morning. Is this where she lives?"

The maid nodded. "Yes, Miss." To Samantha's relief, she opened the screen, becoming suddenly visible, and invited her into the parlor to be seated. The room smelled slightly of dust, but more obviously of lavender. "Please wait here while I see if she's disposed to speak with you. May I give her your card?" She had a faintly German accent and her speech, though slightly guttural, was easily understandable.

"Yes, thank you." Samantha handed her a card from the small case she carried, feeling awkward and grown up at the same time. This was the first opportunity she had had to use the cards she had received for her birthday.

The maid left the room, closing the door behind her, and while Samantha waited, her nervousness returned. What would this woman be like? She had imagined many different personalities for her, but she really had no idea what to expect. All she knew was that Mrs. Ridgewood visited her mother during those few short years before her death and that Lovenia had written of her as "a good friend."

Before long Samantha heard quiet but purposeful steps coming toward the room where she sat, and then the door opened. A tall, stately woman dressed in a neat gray gown, with brown hair graying at the temples, and a stern, handsome face entered the room.

"Good afternoon," she said in a deep, no-nonsense voice, looking at Samantha with an unmistakable hint of curiosity. "You are Samantha Jennings?"

Samantha stood and nodded. "Yes, that is correct," she replied, squaring her shoulders and willing herself not to tremble. The woman seemed friendly enough. "Thank you for seeing me, Mrs. Ridgewood. I am very pleased to meet you." She took a step forward and then stopped, unsure of what to do next. Swallowing against a suddenly parched throat she said, "My mother wrote such nice things about you that I...I wanted to meet you."

Emma Ridgewood stood still, searching Samantha's features for a full minute before her face blossomed into a smile and she crossed the few remaining steps between them. She grasped Samantha's hands in hers and squeezed them tightly. "Then you *are* Lovenia's girl!" she cried, tears suddenly springing into her eyes. "The only Jennings I have known personally are those of your particular family, so when I saw your name on the card I hoped that was who you were."

"You...you did?" Samantha asked. "Then you do remember my mother?"

"If I did not remember a *soul* I would remember her," Mrs. Ridgewood said emphatically. "My dear girl, your mother was a pure inspiration to me, and the most Christian woman I have ever met in my life."

She let go of Samantha's hands and motioned for her to take a seat while she also settled herself in a chair.

"My relationship with Lovenia was tragically short. Oh, those were brief years, though we did not know it at the time." She trailed off for a moment and pulled out a handkerchief to dab at her eyes, then blinked a few times and straightened up in her chair. "Indeed, though I only knew her a short time, the impact she had on me has stayed with me almost as if it were yesterday. I even named my oldest daughter after her. Did you know that?"

Wide-eyed, Samantha shook her head.

Mrs. Ridgewood looked at her with those piercing brown eyes and said nothing for a long moment. Then quietly she asked, "Why is it that you seek me out now, Samantha Jennings?"

Samantha collected her thoughts for a moment and then told Mrs. Ridgewood how she had grown up knowing very little about her mother or her family's history and had not known she could ask, and then how she had come to find her mother's journal last January. She concluded by telling the older woman of her arrangements to take the trip to Worthington to locate her mother's and brother's graves. "I wanted to meet you before I left. Somehow I did not feel that I should wait until afterward," she admitted.

Emma Ridgewood smiled a fond, sad smile. "You were right to follow your feelings," she said in that low, firm voice. "Trust them, for your heart will never lead you wrong."

Samantha was surprised by this statement, and then an idea of what she was really saying gradually sank in. "You mean that you will not be here when I return?" Samantha guessed hesitantly.

Mrs. Ridgewood shook her head and gestured a graceful hand across the parlor. "This is the last room I have yet to pack. Everything else is either boxed or will remain here, covered." She sighed. "I have been a widow for four years now and all six of my children are scattered throughout Ohio and Pennsylvania, attending university or busy with jobs or children." She gave a small, wry smile and raised her shoulders slightly. "Life in this empty house with none of my family nearby has made me feel lonely and useless."

"So, you go to visit them?" Samantha asked.

The woman nodded. "Yes, and if I find that I fancy living somewhere else I may sell this place. However, you did not come here to listen to me talk about myself. Come with me; there is something I think you would like to see."

Samantha followed as Mrs. Ridgewood led the way down a dark hallway and up two flights of narrow stairs. Finally, she stopped at the attic door and turned, one hand on the knob. "Pray I do know where it is," she told Samantha, grimacing slightly. "With all the packing I have done lately I am not quite sure where anything is anymore."

She opened the door, which creaked a little, and Samantha stepped into the shadowed room. A full-length window on the south side let in a broad stream of morning light, but the farthest corners of the room remained dark. Cobwebs hung from the rafters and a definite smell of mildew and age permeated the air.

Mrs. Ridgewood motioned to her. "Step this way. I believe it is in that trunk over there."

Samantha followed after her, making her way through tall stacks of boxes filled with old periodicals and odds and ends, still wondering what the woman was looking for.

Mrs. Ridgewood bent in front of a huge, old trunk with a large, tarnished lock and opened it with a key pulled from the pocket of her dress. "This is my trunk of treasures," she told Samantha. "Every item I have most valued throughout my life is in here." The heavy lid gave a long groan as she lifted it and examined the contents. She sifted through a few items for a minute and then let out a pleased sigh. "Ah, yes. Here it is." Gently she removed a gilt-framed drawing and blew on its surface to remove a light film of dust. After looking at it fondly for a moment, she handed it to Samantha. "You probably already have several pictures of her, but I do not think you have this one," she said.

Samantha turned the picture to catch the light from the window, her heart pounding as she stared at it. There sat three young women, arms linked, smiling as if in laughter. Samantha knew instantly which was her mother, for her face was at once familiar and dear, even in its novelty. Just as Mrs. Dolittle had said, there was the slightly upturned nose and the light-colored eyes, the slim form and the sculpted cheek bones. With her darker hair she looked like Samantha and yet different. Lovenia gazed directly ahead, as if she could see the viewer, her smile less pronounced than those of her two companions who sat on either side of her, but her expression content. The woman to her left looked slightly familiar, too, and Samantha realized this must be the young Emma Ridgewood. That meant the young woman on Lovenia's right was Missy Phelps. Samantha looked again at her mother, not many years older than herself, and felt the deep longing that swept over her so often these days.

Mrs. Ridgewood stood watching her closely, and when Samantha raised her eyes, the woman's gaze was perceptive. "I see I must rephrase my earlier assumption... Might this be the first picture you have seen of your mother?" Her tone was soft and gentle.

Samantha nodded, tears filling her eyes.

"I thought you must certainly have others...but I can see I was wrong. That makes me very glad I remembered this one."

"Me too," Samantha whispered, looking again at the precious picture in her hands.

"It will be of much more use for you to have it than for it to be locked away in this old trunk. I pull it out every so often, but you need it much more than I do. I only wish I had thought of it long ago." She hesitated and Samantha saw a struggle in her expression before she decided to continue. "Seeing you all grown up and just now learning about your mother, I feel how we failed you, Missy and I, and others in this town. We did help with as much as we could when Lovenia died. Prepared her body for burial and boxed up her things... We tried to care for you as well, but your father and his able housekeeper didn't want to relinquish you often. I think, in their grief, caring for you helped soften the pain." Mrs. Ridgewood swallowed and Samantha could see that her memories still held grief too. She looked off in the distance, remembering.

"After the funeral, after her body was transported to her hometown, Missy and I came by a few times, but it seemed that everything was in hand and your father didn't care to see us anymore. I think it hurt too much, seeing his wife's closest friends, so he preferred we stay away." She returned her gaze to Samantha's face. "But we should have tried again and again as the years passed." She spoke a bit harshly, her anger at herself making her words rough. "You should not have had to grow up without a knowledge of and a connection to your mother."

"It's all right," Samantha said, laying a hand on the woman's arm. "You did the best you could at the time. You didn't know."

"No, we didn't," Mrs. Ridgewood acknowledged. "But we should have tried harder. I am very sorry we did not."

"Thank you," Samantha whispered. "There are things I wish I had done differently too, but we cannot go back." She swallowed a lump in her throat and dashed away a few tears. Then regaining her voice she managed, "Thank you so very much for the picture. I have wished countless times to see my mother's likeness."

Emma nodded. "She was a wonderful person. You can be very proud to be her daughter."

"Thank you. I am. Finding her journal is one of the best things that has ever happened to me. It has changed my entire perspective about the world...and myself."

Emma Ridgewood nodded again, as if she understood perfectly.

Samantha looked again at the picture she held. "She is...much the way I imagined. But...it is different to see her with my eyes instead of merely inside my head. She is more real, somehow. It makes me realize more fully that she really did exist, human like I am."

"Yes," Mrs. Ridgewood agreed. "She was very real. And now her memory lives on immortally for those of us who knew her."

"Thank you," Samantha said yet again, her heart bursting with gratitude. "Next to finding my mother's journal, this is the greatest treasure I have ever received." She clasped the frame to her breast and hoped that Emma could understand the depth of thankfulness she felt. "I will cherish it always."

"I know you will," Mrs. Ridgewood replied with a smile. She crossed the space between them and then, though Samantha sensed it was uncharacteristic of her, held out her arms. Samantha accepted the embrace, clutching her mother's picture with one hand as the two held each other for a long moment.

"It is truly an honor to meet you, Samantha Jennings," Mrs. Ridgewood said softly.

CHAPTER 26

DREAM NO SMALL DREAMS

April 1902

A few days later, Sterling found himself walking to the Tomlinson's home. It was a crisp spring evening and a gentle breeze played about his face and through his hair, somewhat calming his troubled spirit. He always made too much of things, he knew, but knowing that did not help him take things easier. And he was feeling so distracted by his worried thoughts that he could not concentrate on planning lessons and grading papers. So, half-unconsciously, he had resorted once again to Mrs. Tomlinson's cozy kitchen and wonderful wisdom.

Jerome opened the door at Sterling's knock and his freckled face broke into a broad grin. "Hi!," he said and opened the door wider so Sterling could enter. "We are eating supper—want some?"

Mrs. Tomlinson appeared in the doorway to the kitchen and dining area, her cheeks flushed from cooking over the hot stove. "Come in, come in," she said welcomingly, gesturing with a hand for him to follow. "I'll dish up another plate." She returned to the stove, expecting him to follow.

Sterling smiled, feeling more relaxed already. He felt the natural, easy way of this place that he had come to expect but still appreciated, and it warmed him. "Thank you," he told Mrs. Tomlinson. "I'll go wash and come join you."

Over a simple but tasty fare of creamed vegetable soup and whole wheat biscuits, with applesauce for dessert, the three of them chatted and laughed, enjoying each other's company. Sterling noticed again how Jerome had grown since the beginning of last term, how much more open he was with others, and especially how much more content he seemed with himself. The boy had a very developed sense of humor and was also quite clever, so that often his mother and Sterling had to swallow their food quickly in self-defense, in order to avoid choking before laughter made them almost helpless with mirth.

After one particularly funny episode that Jerome related about something that happened in the play yard at school, Mrs. Tomlinson wiped tears from her eyes with the edge of her napkin and advised Jerome to cease--at least until supper was over and the dishes cleaned.

Jerome grinned at his mother and obliged, quickly downing the remaining food in his bowl. "Thank you for supper, Ma," he told her as he stood to take his dishes to the sideboard. With his back turned he added, "Since Mr. Sterling is here to help with the dishes, would you mind if I...?"

Mrs. Tomlinson glanced ruefully at Sterling and then back at Jerome who was returning to the table. "Son, Mr. Sterling is our guest, no matter how often he visits us, and it is not polite to pawn your chores off on him."

"No, it's all right. Really," Sterling said, chuckling. "I don't mind helping. In fact, I would prefer it. If Jerome has something else he needs to do, by all means..." He motioned a hand toward the door.

Mrs. Tomlinson gave Jerome a firm look and then nodded and the boy vanished. She shook her head and smiled. "He is involved in another one of his building projects out in the barn and I keep having to remind him about chores and homework. I hope his schoolwork isn't suffering."

"No," Sterling said, picking up his own dishes and taking them to the sink. "He does not answer every question correctly, but he is doing much better than at first." He started pumping water at the sink to fill the kettle on the stove. Once the water started flowing, he turned to Mrs. Tomlinson and added, "Actually, it is gratifying to see such progress—and to see him so happy."

Mrs. Tomlinson set the empty soup pot next to the other dishes on the sideboard and went back to the table with a dishrag. "I hope you know that, in large part, that is due to you," she said.

"I don't claim any credit," Sterling replied, "but I'm glad something has helped." He set the filled kettle on the stove and began stoking the fire so they would have hot water for dishwashing. "You have a fine son in that boy. He will grow up to make you proud."

Mrs. Tomlinson nodded, "He already does make me proud. He reminds me of his father more every day." She sat down at the newly cleaned table and watched as the fire began to lick at the wood Sterling had added. Once it was crackling merrily, Sterling closed the stove door and Mrs. Tomlinson's eyes followed him as he stood up.

"Sterling, I could see in your face when you walked in that you have something on your mind...and on your heart." She motioned for him to join her at the table and Sterling sat on a chair across from her.

"Yes," he admitted. "I knew you would." Suddenly all his former worries and wearies rushed back upon him and he brushed a heavy hand over his face. The prickly stubble on his chin and cheeks reminded him that he had not shaved the night before—something he rarely neglected.

"Is it about Samantha?" Mrs. Tomlinson asked, knowing from the look in his eyes and the taut line of his body that there could be only one answer.

"Yes," Sterling said again. "I told you months ago that I decided to go back to Oberlin, to face Samantha as soon as the term ends."

Mrs. Tomlinson nodded and searched his face. "But...?"

"But now I am second-guessing myself...again." Sterling raised his hands in a gesture of self-exasperation. "I know you must think me a fool, Mrs. Tomlinson. I *am* a fool! But I have not heard anything from her since I sent off that note in December—not a word. Surely if she had any interest in me at all she could have scribbled off a line or two in response!"

"I thought you were going back to offer apologies, regardless of how she may feel about you," Mrs. Tomlinson reminded him quietly. "And it is possible your letter never reached her."

Sterling sighed and lowered his head. "You are right, of course. I guess I just needed to hear it from you...one more time."

Mrs. Tomlinson reached across the table to pat his hand comfortingly. "Life for me has not gone the way I thought it would, or the way I wanted it to go. But now as I look back, I can see that God knew what was best for me and ordered things for my good, in the long run. He has watched over me and helped me become stronger through the hard times. And He will sustain you too, if you let Him."

Sterling didn't know what to say. He had never given religion serious consideration before, or ever thought of God on a personal level like that.

But Mrs. Tomlinson just smiled at him. "May I suggest a couple of scriptures to read, should you feel so inclined?"

"Alright," Sterling said slowly, thinking about it. "I suppose I can do that."

"Proverbs 31:10-31 and Matthew 19:26. There are so many more that could help you in your situation, but those two will suffice for now."

Sterling wrote down the references on a small piece of paper from his pocket. "Thank you."

"And one more thing," Mrs. Tomlinson continued. "This one I know you can appreciate, connoisseur of good literature that you are. It is something I have remembered through the years, something I read once...back when I had time to read." Her smile was a little wistful, but her laugh was genuine.

Sterling nodded, curious to know what she had read that would affect her enough to remember all this time.

"Goethe once wrote: 'Dream no small dreams for they have no power to move the hearts of men.'"[26]

Sterling nodded slowly. "I seem to recall that quote."

Mrs. Tomlinson leaned across the table to look him closely in the face and her words were serious and full of feeling. "'Dream no small dreams, Sterling. I know in the past you have dared to dream big. And I also know that it is only lately you have feared to build castles."

---

[26] https://www.brainyquote.com/quotes/johann_wolfgang_von_goeth_121252

Sterling looked at her, his eyes serious as well. He was a little surprised she recalled the brief mention he had made to her once of Thoreau's words about putting foundations under one's castles.

"But you need not fear. Some big dreams are worth holding onto, and sometimes all that is needed to build that foundation under your castle is the right person to help you see what kind of mortar to use."

Sterling gave her a half smile of appreciation. In a low voice he said, "You should be the teacher, Mrs. Tomlinson—or the writer."

She shook her head. "I have learned a few things in my time, that is all. I hope you do not mind me sharing them with you."

"No, not at all. Thank you. I appreciate it very much." He felt gratitude and emotion rising in his throat. "It is a welcome experience to receive sensible motherly advice."

Mrs. Tomlinson patted his arm. "You really will feel much better when this whole ordeal is cleared up and you and Samantha have discussed things. You are worrying yourself sick about it and that is not doing you or her any good."

"I know." Sterling sighed again and then stood. "Only a few more weeks and I can put this demon behind me."

"Have you decided on a departure date yet?" Mrs. Tomlinson asked, also standing. The kettle would soon begin to whistle and then she would be able to wash the dishes.

Sterling shook his head. "No. But I will." He saw doubt pass fleetingly through her eyes and repeated firmly, "I will. I know I have to go."

271

Mrs. Tomlinson moved to the sink and Sterling made as if to join her there, but she waved him away. "Why don't you go on home," she said. "Finish grading papers or whatever you need to do. I know you are busy, and it is already growing dark. I can finish these up myself."

Sterling hesitated a moment, then nodded. "Thank you for supper and for letting me drop in on you unexpectedly so often."

"We love having you," she returned simply. "You know that. And Sterling," she put a hand on his arm and squeezed firmly, "everything will turn out right. You will see. You must believe it and work for that end."

CHAPTER 27

TRUST

April 1902

Samantha stood between Katherine and Rupert on the train platform, a little nervous but also relieved to finally be leaving on the trip she had thought about every day for months. They were prepared for rain, but for the first time in days the clouds parted and allowed a bit of cool sunlight to peek through, as if to offer a bit of assurance to Samantha on this important day.

On her left, Katherine linked an arm through Samantha's, and Rupert on her right offered his arm. They stood there, quiet and pensive in the midst of the train station bustle, all three anxious for the beginning of their journey. Samantha thought they must look a bit comical, in a row like that, in order from tallest to shortest.

After a few minutes, Samantha drew in a breath and let it out slowly, forcing herself to relax. Both friends turned to look at her and gave her reassuring smiles.

"Thank you for coming with me," Samantha told them seriously. "I can already tell this would be very difficult to do on my own."

Katherine squeezed Samantha's left arm and Rupert patted her right. "That's all right, Samantha," he said, "we're glad to."

"Worthington seems so far away," Samantha mused. "I think it is partly because it represents the seeming fantasy that my parents were a part of once upon a time."

"Yes," Katherine agreed. "Or perhaps because you know it took your parents two weeks by horse and wagon to make the same journey, and that is all your imagination has to go on."

Samantha nodded in agreement. "Maybe so. All while I planned for this trip, I felt that I would be leaving the world I know. But," she laughed, "we are not even leaving Ohio! What a sheltered life I have lived."

"Likewise," Katherine concurred. "But I like it that way. I do want to see as many other places as I can--but in the end, Oberlin is home and home is where I like to be the most."

Rupert smiled appreciatively. "I agree with you there."

Soon they heard the whistle of the approaching train and felt its rumble from the rails a few yards in front of them.

"Worthington is just over one-hundred miles away and we will only be gone a week or less," Samantha observed, "depending on how long it takes us to find the graves."

Rupert nodded. "Thanks to modern transportation, this journey will only take us a few hours."

"I know," Samantha replied. "It amazes me to think that we will arrive there only this evening and that by at least the beginning of next week we will return. But...I still feel like I'm stepping forth into unknown darkness." She sighed. "I don't feel as brave as I did earlier."

"We'll be by your side to step there with you," Katherine replied comfortingly. "The outcome of the next few days is unknown to all of us, but who is to say it is not light we are headed toward, instead of darkness?"

Samantha gave her a small smile. "You are right. I need not fear. I have you two here with me and the Lord will guide us all."

"'Perfect love casteth out all fear,'" Katherine quoted cheerfully, "and love is what has brought you this far."

Samantha looked off into the distance and her smile grew a little sad as she thought back to the sacrifices her mother had made, and of the great love that Samantha felt for her now that she knew her better. Then she turned back to Katherine and the brightness returned to her face. "It has," she agreed. "Love has definitely brought me here."

The train drew closer and chugged slowly into the station. Then it groaned to a grinding halt and released a long, piercing hiss. Locomotives had existed for as long as Samantha could remember, but she had never actually stepped foot on one before. The steam engine seemed huge and powerful up close, but Samantha felt more excitement than fear now. She was truly ready to begin this little adventure!

Once the doors opened, Rupert turned to the girls and asked, "Well, are you ready to board?" They nodded and he grinned at them, his simple features lighting up with his own excitement. "Then, Worthington, here we come!" he cried, and manfully led the way, managing all three of their suitcases at once.

The train ride was pleasant enough, but tiring as journeys are. Rupert had traveled by locomotive a few times before, but like Samantha, this was Katherine's first such trip. Both young women exulted in the ease with which they could simply sit back and watch the landscape rush by in a whirl of greens. The speed was exhilarating—faster and smoother than even Champion, Samantha observed. Traveling this fast she could almost travel anywhere in the country and see whatever she wanted!

Before they had gone very far, Samantha opened the bag she held and reverently removed the framed portrait that Emma Ridgewood had given her. She handed it to Katherine without a word and waited to see what she would say.

Katherine took the frame in her hands and looked it over curiously. Then her eyes stopped and she inhaled sharply. "Samantha? Is this who I think it is?" she asked, looking up at her friend with wide eyes.

Rupert watched them intently from his seat opposite them, and after Katherine had taken another look at the picture, she handed it to him.

Samantha watched him peruse the drawing, his expression changing from curiosity to near incredulity. "Is this your mother?" he asked. "The one in the middle?"

"Yes," Samantha answered softly.

"But I thought you didn't have any portraits of her," Katherine said, puzzled.

"I didn't," Samantha replied. "But two days ago, I visited one of her dear friends from years ago and she had this tucked away in a big trunk in the attic."

Katherine reached for the picture as Rupert handed it back to her. "Priceless," she said.

"Yes," Samantha nodded, "that is exactly what it is to me. Next to my mother's journal it is my most prized possession. I feel a little more connected now that I have had a chance to see her with my own eyes."

"After eighteen years of not knowing what your mother looked like..!" Katherine trailed off. "I can only imagine what this must be like for you."

"I think you look like her," Rupert offered.

"Really?" Samantha asked eagerly.

"Yes, I see that too," Katherine mused. "You don't look exactly alike, but anyone would agree that you resemble each other."

"I'm glad. My father and Mrs. Dolittle also told me I look like her, and now I can actually see it with my own eyes. There is no one I would rather take after."

"How amazing that your mother's friend had this to give to you! After all these years..." Katherine handed the portrait back to Rupert for another look.

"But what is even more amazing is that I went to visit her when I did," Samantha replied. "If I had waited until after our trip, she would have been gone and I do not know when—or if--another opportunity would have presented itself."

Katherine and Rupert were duly impressed by that.

"It would appear that God is in the details," Rupert said reflectively.

Katherine smiled, "I was just about to say the same thing myself."

Samantha nodded and took back the offered frame, feeling warmed and loved by her friends' support and empathy. Quietly she slipped it into the bag again, comforted just knowing it was there, close by.

After a time, Katherine found that watching the scenery made her feel very strange. And when Rupert and Samantha turned their heads from the window to look at her, they immediately noticed how pale her face had become.

"What's wrong?" Samantha asked in alarm.

"I don't know...exactly," Katherine replied slowly. She swallowed and closed her eyes for a moment. "I suddenly feel very nauseated."

"Here." Rupert's plain face showed concern but also understanding as he stood from his seat opposite the girls and reached across the space to take Katherine under the elbow. "Lie down on my bench and we'll raise your feet." Samantha took Katherine's other elbow and together they eased her onto the padded bench.

"Thank you," Katherine murmured. "I'm sorry. I don't know why... Just a few moments ago I felt perfectly fine."

Samantha placed two cushions beneath her friend's feet and looked up at Rupert, who was still standing. He saw the confusion and worry in her eyes and responded with reassurance. "I think you're suffering from motion sickness, Katherine. It may make this trip uncomfortable for you, but it's nothing to worry about in the long run."

"Motion sickness?" Katherine repeated. "Oh dear. Then perhaps there is a reason I have never traveled far from home." She gave them a weak smile and they laughed.

Rupert turned to Samantha. "Fan her face with your notebook and I'll go find the conductor. I know some food is available for passengers, so perhaps they have a few extra crackers or toast. A friend I've traveled with gets motion sickness too and those things help him."

Samantha nodded and Rupert moved up the aisle in search of the conductor.

As Samantha began waving the notebook in front of Katherine's face, she remarked, "I am glad he knew what to do. I had no idea what was wrong."

"Me neither," Katherine said, her eyes closed again. "Thank you, Samantha, that feels good."

Samantha continued to fan her for a couple more minutes and then asked, "Are you feeling any better yet? A little color is starting to seep back into your face now."

Katherine opened her eyes and Samantha was struck for the hundredth time by how blue they were. "Yes. My stomach feels like maybe it will stay where it belongs for the moment." And then after a pause, "Samantha?"

"Yes, Katherine?" Samantha kneeled now, almost level with her friend while she fanned.

"Rupert is such a good, gentle young man. You could not do any better than him." Her eyes twinkled and Samantha knew she must really feel improved.

"I know," Samantha replied honestly, surprised by her friend's comment. "Sometimes I think I should just give in and learn how to turn my friendship for him into romantic love. In many ways it would be much easier than what I dream of."

"Well," Katherine mused, her eyes serious now, "I think God wants what is best for both of you...but I suppose that does not necessarily mean whatever is easiest or most convenient. I am sure He will guide you."

"Thank you," Samantha said gratefully. "That is what I need to remember. And you know, I have been thinking about that a lot lately, how all we really need to get us through the trials of life is to trust in God, and follow His guidance. It's like it says in Proverbs 3:5-6."

Katherine nodded in understanding and promptly quoted the verse from memory: "Trust in the Lord with all thine heart; and lean not unto thine own understanding. In all thy ways acknowledge him, and he shall direct thy paths."

Samantha smiled. "Exactly."

"That is my favorite scripture."

"I like it too," Samantha agreed, "and it makes sense to me." She stopped fanning to rest her arms for a moment. "But sometimes that kind of trust is so much more easily said than done! Particularly when times are especially difficult."

"It is not always easy for me to trust like that either," Katherine admitted. "But when I do, it brings peace into my life that isn't there without it."

"It's funny when you really think about it," Samantha said thoughtfully, her eyes far away. "Why should it be so difficult to trust in the only Being who is all-knowing and all-powerful? If we can put our full confidence in anyone, it is Him."

Katherine gave a wan smile. "I guess because we are human and weak, and because we cannot see Him. I have learned that faith and trust really go together."

"Yes," Samantha said, still lost in her thoughts.

Rupert suddenly reappeared then, and they helped Katherine sit up so she could eat the crackers he had acquired.

"Thank you." Katherine smiled at him and took a nibble from one cracker. "I think I will be all right now. You could be a doctor, Rupert!"

Rupert shook his head while the tips of his ears turned pink. "Oh, no," he said humbly as he seated himself opposite the girls again. "Not me. The only things I know are farming and building. But I do learn from experience."

"That is more than a lot of people can say," Katherine replied.

Their journey to Worthington was met without further mishap, though Katherine had to lie down a couple more times, and incidentally slept for a portion of the trip. Rupert found it difficult to stay awake, also; the lulling rocking of the train was so persistent, and he was more tired than usual, with all the extra work he had put in the last couple of weeks to make it possible to come on this trip. So Samantha enjoyed the changing scenery and the time to contemplate by herself, to write in her notebook, and to begin reading Walden. This was one book she had heard much about but never read.

During last summer's time with Sterling and the many topics they had discussed, Sterling had brought up "H.D.T."—or Henry David Thoreau—several times. Sterling had quoted the naturalist and writer with a certain level of awe and respect as if the man were a hero to him. Though Samantha had read Thoreau's Slavery in Massachusetts and Civil Disobedience in the past, there was one quote in particular that Sterling shared with her that had reawakened her interest in Thoreau and his book *Walden*. She could not recall the entire passage, but the part she remembered still sent a thrill through her every time she thought of it:

"I went to the woods because I wished to live deliberately, to front only the essential facts of life, and see if I could not learn what it had to teach, and not, when I came to die, discover that I had not lived. I wanted to live deep and suck out all the marrow of life..."[27]

She remembered the way Sterling gazed off into some unseen distance and the fire that lit his eyes while he recited the passage to her. His dark hair was especially wavy in the summer humidity and a thin line of perspiration trickled trails down either side of his face.

---

[27] https://www.environmentandsociety.org/mml/walden-or-life-woods

Samantha was not sure how, so many months later, she remembered such close details--unless it was the writer in her--but she was glad she did, for as she sat there on the cushioned bench, watching the world go by outside the window, she could hold up Sterling's face in her memory and look it slowly over again.

But the dull ache that rose up in her heart as she did so forced her to realize once more that seeing the dignified forehead with that ringlet of unruly hair across it, the slope of his Greek nose, the expressive mouth and strong jaw—even only in her mind--did nothing to assuage the pain of the loss she still felt whenever she thought of him. Those brown eyes with all the breadth and depth of emotion they conveyed, the frequent smile, the good humor that poked fun at himself but not others, were not things she could ever forget.

And neither were the things he had told her, the way he had helped her to taste the fullness of life. To her, he truly seemed one who had taken Thoreau's words to heart, who lived deep and sucked out all the marrow of life. No one else she had ever met possessed such enthusiasm and excitement for life or had about him quite the air of controlled passion that Sterling did. Everything he did was done with his whole self. He was never a fence-sitter with each foot on a different side of the issue, unable to make up his mind. And sometimes that had gotten him into trouble, she realized with a quiet smile, remembering that one particular conversation about women's rights when she had unintentionally made him speechless by her contradictions. Everyone had his extremes, she supposed. That was part of the trials of life, to find and maintain balance and moderation to all things, even as one jumped into important matters with both feet.

She turned to *Walden* again, eager to find in it all that had so impressed Sterling. Just the act of reading the very words he had so often read made Samantha feel somehow closer to her former teacher. And for now, that was enough. Because it had to be.

CHAPTER 28

THE SEARCH

April 1902

Once they arrived in Worthington, Samantha felt an even greater urgency than before to find her family's graves and wanted to waste none of the short time they had. The three friends were travel-weary and a little hungry, but Katherine and Rupert agreed with Samantha that they would prefer a walk in the fresh air to sitting in a stale hotel room. So, once they had checked into their hotel and deposited their luggage in their respective rooms, they headed on foot to the nearest cemetery.

St. John's Cemetery was located on the southeast corner of Dublin-Granville Road and High Street, directly behind St. John's Episcopal Church. As they entered the gate, Samantha felt a quiet sense of reverence wash over her upon seeing the old, gray and brown headstones. She could not remember the last time she had walked through a cemetery, and had not expected this feeling.

As she and her friends slowly passed the headstones and read the dates--some of them one-hundred years old—her sense of awe increased. Questions began to arise in her mind and some of them she voiced aloud, though others she pondered silently. There were many markers of soldiers who had died in the Revolutionary War, the War of 1812, and the Civil War. Samantha wondered how the news of their deaths had reached their families and how those families had coped with the loss of their beloved fathers, sons, husbands, brothers, and friends.

Many other graves were those of the earliest settlers of Worthington, and all were intriguing to the three friends, but seeing the graves of children gave Samantha a different and sharper twinge of sadness every time. The earliest date they saw was of a baby who had died in the year 1800 when he was less than a year old. She thought of her brother who had died as a tiny infant and wondered if the bereaved parents had, like her own mother, turned to God to heal their sorrow.

Upon later reflection, Samantha realized how significant it was that St. John's was the first cemetery they should visit. They did not find the graves they were looking for, but Samantha felt that she learned much about the history and foundation of her mother's town from her time spent there. They wandered through the place into the early evening, searching, reflecting, and conversing in low tones.

Eventually they all became too tired and hungry to search anymore, so Samantha suggested they head back to the hotel for supper. As they left the cemetery and made their way to High Street once again, Katherine put an arm around Samantha. "We will have more luck another day," she said encouragingly. "Maybe even tomorrow."

Samantha nodded and sighed but smiled at her friend. "I guess it would have been too perfect to find the graves on the first try, but at least we made a good beginning."

"And this town isn't big enough for there to be very many other cemeteries," Rupert added, "so it's only a matter of time. We'll find them soon."

"Yes," Samantha agreed. "It's only a matter of time."

The next morning after a sound sleep and a hearty breakfast, the three were ready for another day of searching. They inquired at the hotel desk as to the location of two other cemeteries and then flipped a coin. Gardner Cemetery won and again they started off on foot, following the hotel manager's directions. After a while, they eventually found a path leading through a small wood with a bridge over a wide stream, and a very small cemetery on the other side.

Samantha felt the same tranquility as the day before settling over her and was soon absorbed in her search. The three friends worked carefully through the entire cemetery in a little less than two hours and then sat on a bench beneath a tree for a few moments of rest. Samantha and Katherine removed their hats to re-pin stray hairs that had worked their way free.

Rupert, balanced on the edge of the bench closest to Samantha, held his hat by the brim and rotated it between his large hands. "How is it going for you ladies?" he asked.

"All right," Katherine responded, a hairpin in her mouth. She glanced at Samantha.

"It is a little discouraging," Samantha admitted, smoothing a few hairs back in place and pinning them securely. "Yesterday the search was exciting, but today I feel like it is taking too long," she said, feeling like she should apologize. "I wonder if there is a more efficient way to go about this..."

Katherine and Rupert nodded in agreement. "I know some cemeteries keep a list of the names of the deceased and the location of their burial plots," Rupert said thoughtfully. "But we appear to be the only people here, and the caretaker's office looks deserted."

"I guess maybe we should have asked about that at the hotel too," Samantha said regretfully. "There is just too much I don't know."

"Well," Katherine offered with her characteristic optimism, "at least we have not been impeded yet by rain, like we would be in Oberlin. That would make our search miserable."

"Yes," Samantha agreed. "You are right. At least the weather is pleasant."

Rupert got to his feet and placed the hat back on his head. "I think I just saw someone walk through the gate on the far side," he told them. "I'll go talk to him." He strode away from them with quick strides and called over his shoulder, "Be back in a moment!"

A few minutes later Rupert returned with an elderly man who told them he was the caretaker. He said the hotel manager had informed him that a small group of young people would be in his cemetery this morning and appeared to be looking for a particular grave. "Thought I might come by and see if I could be of any service," he explained.

Several minutes after that found Samantha, Katherine, and Rupert sitting in a tiny office, pouring over the cemetery's records. The man was helpful and the records well kept, but the name Lovenia Jennings did not show up anywhere in them, and neither did her maiden name, Lewis. The caretaker did not remember a Jennings burial occurring in his cemetery either, and he had a good memory, he told them.

"Well, thank you for coming by just when you did," Samantha told the man gratefully as they prepared to leave. "And thank you for letting us look through your records. At least we know now we didn't miss it."

"Do you have any suggestions of where we might look further?" Katherine asked.

"You know about Walnut Grove, no doubt," the caretaker replied, pausing with lifted white eyebrows to verify that they did. "Well, I would try there next; it is quite large. After that, there are a few others scattered around as well. Very small ones, more obscure and less cared for. But you might try them. Let me draw you a map." He reached for a sheet of clean paper and pulled a pen from his breast pocket. "Been here my whole life, so I could probably draw this for you with my eyes closed," he chuckled, his white whiskers turning up with his smile.

After clarifying what the man had drawn and thanking him once more, the three friends left, hoping again that this time they would find what they were looking for.

CHAPTER 29

THE CEMETERY

April 1902

After a long week of teaching restless boys who were ready for the summer holidays, and with evenings spent laboring over his students' homework, Sterling finally allowed himself a break: he needed it if he was going to be of further use to anyone.

He picked up a sandwich at the café for his supper and ate it while walking thoughtfully to the cemetery, a place that now seemed as familiar as his own room. Evening was drawing near, and shadows spread across the ground beneath the trees as the sun made its way westward. The night would be a chilly one and it felt like rain, but Sterling's suit coat would suffice for now. Approaching the fence that bordered the cemetery, he slipped through the place where a board had fallen crosswise and stepped into the peaceful confines of trees, grass, and headstones.

His stomach rumbled contentedly, and Sterling breathed deeply of the scent of blossoming trees and new grass. Spring was such a beautiful time of year! It forced itself into one's consciousness, demanding attention away from the worries and busyness of life. This thought reminded him of his conversation with Samantha, prompted by the singing meadowlark that day in early summer when they took their first walk to begin the day's lesson. Since then, he certainly had not always done very well at taking time out of the cares of life and work to notice birds and flowers as he had told Samantha everyone ought to do. He wondered if she had...

He walked on, contemplating all that had happened in the past year and what interesting turns life had taken. If someone had asked him a year ago where he thought he would be in twelve months' time, both geographically and in his career, it certainly would not have been here. But, despite his concerns over Samantha and the way they had gnawed at him during his time in Worthington, he was glad to be where he was. If he had never come, he would not know the Tomlinsons or any of the other people he had grown to respect and care for, particularly his students. And this kind of teaching had grounded him, somehow. He felt older and less idealistic than he had been at the start of the school year.

Sterling paused in his thoughts, thinking he'd heard something, then shook his head and continued wandering. A few moments later he heard it again and his feet faltered. He rarely encountered other people in this cemetery because of the odd hours he came. But now he heard the unmistakable murmur of voices, and one in particular which brought him to a halt. It sounded like Samantha's voice. But that was absurd! He almost laughed out loud at the thought. Wishful thinking did funny things to the brain, that was for sure. Still...he would know that voice anywhere.

Curiosity piqued, he turned in the direction of the voices. He walked for a couple of minutes, the voices growing louder as he drew nearer. If Samantha were here, as impossible as that seemed, he had to see her! He did not mean to spy on someone's grief or interrupt anyone's solitude, but if this were the woman he had grown to love...

Suddenly the voices ceased and one lone woman's voice, young and vibrant, reached him through the space that separated them. Listening to its timbre, the fine hairs on the back of his neck stood up straight and a lump formed in his throat.

"This is it," the young woman said reverently.

Sterling heard a scraping noise, and he inched carefully closer, standing still behind a tree. If at all possible, he wanted to see without being detected. He moved forward a couple of paces, crouched behind a bush, and peered out.

In front of a modest marble headstone knelt a young woman in a deep green dress with a long, fashionable cloak draped over her shoulders. Again, he noticed the slight chill and the feel of impending rain. She had hair the color of lightly bronzed sunshine piled beneath a graceful green hat. Her back was to Sterling and he watched as she cleared away debris from around the stone. A young, brawny man to her left knelt to assist her and a small young woman with dark hair did likewise on her other side.

"I can hardly believe we found it!" the dark-haired girl exclaimed. "After so much searching, I started doubting we ever would."

"So did I," the girl in green agreed.

"We really found it!" the young man added in awe, his face bright with a relieved smile, as he turned to look at the young women.

A minute later, the three finished their task and arose, brushing loose grass from their clothing. The woman in green stood near the face of the stone and reached out a slender hand to touch its surface. Sterling silently read the carved letters as she said them aloud:

"Lovenia Lewis Jennings

1858-1885

Beloved wife, mother, daughter, sister,

Who brought beauty like a delicate flower

into the lives of all who knew her."

No one said a word and Sterling felt a growing ache inside his chest, his eyes glued to the woman's back. He felt sure this was Samantha! He did not know her mother's name, but he knew she had died. And the last name on the stone was Jennings. But even more than that, though he had yet to see the young woman's face, the tall, slim line of her figure seemed infinitely familiar. He felt drawn to this young woman in a way he had only felt drawn to Samantha.

"That word is because of *me*," Samantha said in wonder under her breath, pointing reverently to *mother*.

"Did you know all those people survived her?" the young man asked quietly, drawing closer to her.

She shook her head. "No, I barely thought... I mean, I have been so focused on the miracle of my mother that I never..." She shook her head again. "The idea of having other relatives still alive is...overwhelming! Still," she mused, "that is good to know. I must look for them...someday."

The young man nodded and turned to look at her with a gentle expression that spoke of such great fondness that Sterling's heart thudded painfully. The young man touched her on the elbow and said almost too softly for Sterling to hear, "Yes, Samantha. All in good time."

The young woman glanced at him gratefully and Sterling saw the profile of her face for the first time. No more braids, it appeared, and no more plain, worn cotton dresses. Hearing her called "Samantha" and now seeing the side of her face, Sterling heard his heart pounding in his ears. This was incredible! How could this really be happening? If only he could reach out and touch her, hold her in his arms and apologize for the losses she had been through and the pain he had added to them.

Samantha turned her attention to the much smaller headstone just to the right of her mother's. It read simply, Baby Boy Jennings and underneath that, 1880. "He would have been five years older than me," Samantha mused, her voice sounding thick with gathering emotion. And then, after a time, "What would it have been like to have a brother?..."

A brother! Sterling thought. *I guess there really are so many things I still do not know about Samantha. But I want to know! I do want to know them. We talked about so much and yet there are still many things we never even mentioned...*

Returning to Lovenia's headstone, Samantha slowly traced the numbers on its face. "She was only twenty-seven years old..." she said in a trembling voice. "Less than ten years older than I am now."

The other young woman leaned toward her and put a comforting arm around her.

"Father had her for a mere six years..." Samantha's voice still trembled. "So little time! And he has never moved on, still lives in his grief. Foolish, aching man. He still pines away..." Samantha's voice cracked and she was silent again for what seemed a long time before putting her head in her hands and beginning to weep.

As he watched her shoulders shake, Sterling's heart hurt for her. It took everything he had to resist the impulse to make his presence known. He knew he could not do that now without revealing that he had been here all along, spying and eavesdropping. It killed him to continue to hide behind this bush! But this timing was all wrong and he didn't want to ruin the fragile moment for her.

The brawny young man drew close to Samantha and tentatively placed one arm around her. In a moment, Samantha had turned to bury her face in his chest and both his arms went around her.

The young man held her so tenderly that Sterling's heart smote him as he looked at them, and the sudden joy he had felt at so miraculously seeing Samantha suddenly fled, leaving a gaping hole in its place.

I know what that expression means, Sterling thought, looking at the young man's face with sudden clarity. *And I can see how tightly Samantha holds him, too.* He looked at them a moment more, but the pain quickly grew unbearable. *If you stay any longer, you truly will be watching what was not meant for your eyes*, a voice in his head told him. And so he quietly and quickly left.

Rupert patted Samantha's back, unsure of how to comfort her but loving the feel of her in his arms. Katherine began gently stroking Samantha's hair. "It's all right," she crooned to her softly. "Just cry. We're here for you."

By then Samantha could not have stopped the tears even if she wanted to. She held on to Rupert's solidity, needing the sense of stability that his presence gave her. But after a few more minutes, she took a shuddering breath and let it out again as she pulled away from him and tried to dry her tears with his handkerchief.

She looked at her friends and gave them a watery smile. Katherine held out her arms and Samantha stepped into them, infinitely grateful to have two such caring friends. But now, being in Katherine's embrace and feeling the depth of her empathy, the kind that only a fellow woman can show, Samantha's tears began afresh.

Finally, after another several minutes, Samantha was able to regain her composure, and after a long last look at the two gravestones, the three friends made their way out of the cemetery together.

CHAPTER 30

THE QUESTION

April 1902

That evening, Samantha took her friends to nearby Columbus for dinner at Marzetti's Restaurant,[28] which the hotel manager had deemed one of the most popular in the city. University students preferred it to most, he told them, and "if you like Italian food, it is superb." None of them had experienced Italian cuisine but were very willing to try something new, so they caught the next streetcar into Columbus.

The décor at Marzetti's was nothing fancy, but the restaurant had done well since its establishment six years before. Samantha, Katherine, and Rupert agreed that the food tasted incredibly delicious, and the atmosphere was comfortable and lively, especially with the muted patter of rain on the windows to make them feel dry and cozy inside. Samantha had previously felt at a loss as to how to show Katherine and Rupert her immense gratitude for their moral support this day, in addition to all their previous kindnesses. Throughout their stay in Worthington, they had eaten at various restaurants, so this was nothing out of the ordinary, but Samantha had determined to at least find something special and different, something memorable, to end this day of all days. As they enjoyed the new flavors and the comforts of the restaurant, she felt that she had chosen well.

She also proposed that they spend tomorrow--their last day— in Columbus to see the sights and purchase a few souvenirs. She

---

[28] https://marzetti.com/our-story/

believed they should have a little fun, not just work their whole trip. Samantha wanted her friends to be able to go home feeling that they had not only accomplished something important, but that they had also seen new things and had an experience they would fondly remember. But she felt very limited in helping them truly know the strength of the gratitude in her heart.

After they had all eaten until they were pleasantly stuffed, Samantha reached across the table to grasp one of Katherine's and Rupert's hands in each of her own. "I want to thank you both again for your help today," she told them quietly, looking at them with eyes that threatened tears again at the recent memory. "This little trip would not have been possible without you both, and I especially needed you today."

Rupert's cheeks flushed slightly at the intensity of her expressed gratitude, but he lowered his gaze and nodded. "It was real special to be there with you, Samantha. Thank you for asking me to come."

Samantha reached for her napkin and blinked back tears. "I cherish both of your friendship so dearly that--" she lifted her shoulders in an expression of inadequacy "--I do not know how to fully express it. I wish there were something I could do to really show you..." She looked into Katherine's smiling eyes and shook her head in resignation, wiping her tears with the napkin.

"For me, this has been the trip of a lifetime, Samantha," Katherine replied honestly. "I don't know where Rupert has traveled," she added, glancing at him, "but, as I've said, this is the farthest I have ever been from Oberlin." Her smile grew. "My family members are all homebodies, but I've always longed to see other places—as long as I can go right back home." Her dark brows raised as she added, "So, really, Samantha, I should be thanking you. Being your friend has been such a wonderful thing that no thanks is needed in return for anything I may have done for you." She reached across the table for Samantha's hands and squeezed them. "I am very glad I came too."

Hearing this and the sincerity behind her friends' words, Samantha felt a little more settled, though she knew she would continue to look for ways to further express her gratitude to them in the future. "I thank God every day for you," she whispered to Katherine as they all made their way out of the restaurant a few minutes later.

"And I, you," Katherine whispered back.

***

Two days later, about an hour before the three friends were to leave for the train station for their return journey, Rupert knocked on Katherine's and Samantha's hotel room door. Samantha opened it and saw him standing in the doorway, smelling of soap and with his face newly shaved. His brown hair was freshly combed, and his shirt newly pressed, but his nervous expression belied the order of his attire. Before he said a word, Samantha sensed that the encounter she had dreaded this whole trip was about to occur, yet she also felt a curious sense of relief at the prospect of getting it over with.

"Good morning, Rupert," she said cheerfully. "I hope you rested well?"

"Yes, thank you. And you?"

"Very well also. Katherine and I were just finishing our packing."

"Yes. I finished mine only a few minutes ago."

Samantha almost laughed at their awkwardness. After all the experiences they had shared, particularly in the past week, it seemed odd for them to be standing stiffly on either side of the doorway, talking like polite strangers. This could only mean one thing, just as she had suspected.

"We were about ready to go down for breakfast," she said, trying to keep her tone light. "Would you care to join us?"

Rupert nodded and said he would, but then added, "Would you mind stepping out with me on a short walk for a few minutes first?"

Samantha felt her heart pick up speed and turned to look at Katherine a short way across the room. Katherine winked at her so subtly Samantha almost missed it. "Go ahead," she said brightly, with a wave of her hand. "You and Rupert can meet me for breakfast as soon as you return."

"All right," Samantha agreed, trying not to show the reluctance she felt. Turning back to Rupert, she placed one gloved hand in the crook of his arm and they left the hotel. He had a buggy waiting and helped Samantha up while the driver held the door. After a short drive, they stopped and Rupert jumped down to help her out again. Samantha immediately noted that they had arrived at the Walnut Grove Cemetery gates and her heart thudded again, wondering if she had been wrong after all and Rupert actually had something very different in mind. Perhaps he had discovered some new information about her mother or brother?

Rupert asked the driver to wait and then led Samantha through the front gates and down one of the walkways. "It's a beautiful morning," he said softly.

"It is," Samantha agreed, willing her heart to slow and her breathing to return to normal. The poor fellow was nervous enough as it was without adding her nervousness to the mix.

They walked for a few minutes, chatting about nothing in particular until they came to a vast oak tree, with a bench at its base. Rupert led Samantha to it and they sat.

Samantha swallowed and offered a silent prayer that God would help her know how to answer this good, kind young man without breaking his heart.

"Samantha," he began. "I...I don't know how to say this... But I feel it's time for us to discuss some things."

Samantha nodded and gave him an encouraging smile.

He looked down at his lap and then cleared his throat. Finally he said in a choked voice, "Well, I guess I may as well just say what I'm thinking...if you don't mind."

"Not at all, Rupert." The words sounded confident and casual but internally Samantha was steeling herself for what she knew would come next. She hated this feeling of the inevitable pain that she would surely cause him.

"I... Well..." Rupert exhaled and raised his eyes to meet hers. "Ever since the first moment I saw you I have cared for you deeply, Samantha. More deeply than I ever have for any girl. You are compassionate and talented—and above all, genuine...and I enjoy being with you. You make me happy. I have never felt for anyone before, the way I feel for you."

Samantha felt the blood rushing through her temples and clutched her hands tightly together, the fingers intertwining painfully. Oh, if only he would not ask! This was the one thing she could not give him and still be fair and true.

"We have known each other for only a few months," Rupert continued, gaining momentum now, "but I feel as if I have known you for much longer. I can honestly say that you are one of my dearest friends and I love you as such." He laid one large, rough hand over both of hers and looked at her earnestly. "You have helped me in so many little ways and I want to thank you for that."

Samantha felt her anxiety ease slightly and she wondered at this reaction. Suddenly she felt that somehow there had just been a shift in the conversation, though it was so minute she could not be sure it had happened at all. What was he really saying?

Rupert was silent for a moment as he contemplated his next words, his hands in his lap again. "Samantha, I'm...I feel like I am more confident than I used to be, especially around young ladies, and I know that can only have happened because of your acceptance of me, and your kindness." His brow wrinkled with the desire that she comprehend what he was so haltingly trying to explain.

"You have been such a light in my life," he said quietly and with such pure sincerity that Samantha felt the prick of tears in her eyes. That was exactly the phrase she had often thought of in regard to Katherine!

Rupert looked away and clasped his hands together in a pensive gesture. He took a deep breath and let it out slowly before continuing. "To be honest, I have often entertained notions of what it would be like to have you by my side for always." He looked back at her, his glance searching her face for a moment, and then looked away again a little sadly, but as if he had received confirmation of what he expected. "If I could be sure that was what you wanted, too, I would ask you in a heartbeat. But I know that is not the case and I... I am all right with that now."

The tightness in Samantha's chest began to ease even as she felt the ache of having hurt Rupert without even knowing. She felt her breathing slow and deepen, and her body relax a bit more. He was not going to make her say no after all?! She had so dreaded breaking his heart, but it seemed now that God had heard her prayer and answered it in a way she had not expected--by helping Rupert understand, without her having to say anything.

"Part of your kindness to me is your honesty in word and action," Rupert continued. "You have never confused me as to how you felt about me, yet you have always treated me with respect. Our friendship has never been a game to you." He paused a moment and when he spoke again it was with a longing that he could not completely hide. "How I have wished things could be different..."

He faltered a moment and Samantha felt an ache for him rise up again, stronger, within her. So she would, after all, have to say some of what she had been forming in her mind for weeks.

"Rupert." She blinked back tears and turned on the bench to face him more directly. "Rupert, I am deeply sorry that things cannot be as you wish. But I do love you as a friend--very much. And I know it would only hurt us both in the long run if I said yes to something I don't feel is right."

She saw the pain in his eyes that he tried unsuccessfully to mask, and wanted to embrace him, to make it better. But she knew that wouldn't make it better, that she needed to just say what was on her heart. "Please understand, Rupert," she began again. "It is not that you are wrong, just that we are wrong, together. Ultimately, we would not be happy. And," she shook her head, "I could not knowingly inflict that unhappiness upon anyone, especially not someone I care about so much. I wish... I wish I could tell you differently..." She looked pleadingly into his eyes. "I don't want to hurt you," she added in a whisper, thinking of how she may have hurt him in the past by not responding to his love the way he wanted her to, how she must be hurting him now, but also how much more she would hurt him if she were not honest with him in this moment.

Rupert nodded and swallowed hard. "I know," he said simply. "I do understand—at least as much as I can right now. But it is your forthrightness which, in the end, has made this easier. And I am so glad to know that you trust me enough to request my company on this trip."

Samantha nodded.

Rupert paused again and after a few moments of silence, Samantha began to wonder if he were really all right. She had just about decided to ask him if he were ready to go back to the carriage when he said, a little abruptly, "I-I have something else I want to say—to ask you—but I don't want to sound like a cad." He looked away from her and after another pause shook his head. "No. Maybe I had better not."

What question? Samantha wondered, confused again. She placed a hand on his arm. "You can ask me anything. What is it, Rupert?"

Rupert lifted a hand to his head as if to remove his hat and then, realizing he had forgotten to bring it, ran a hand through his hair instead. Slowly he joined his hands together in his lap and looked at them. "There are many reasons why I am grateful to you for inviting me to accompany you here to Worthington... And one of them is because you also invited Katherine. For quite a long time..." he paused and cleared his throat, nervous again. "For years I have harbored a silent affection for her, and, uh... Well...being with her this week has opened my eyes further." A blush crept up Rupert's neck at this disclosure.

Samantha drew in her breath, suddenly understanding where this meeting was headed.

"But she is so beautiful," Rupert continued. "I have always felt so humble and simple in her presence. I *am* humble and simple. Besides, so many beaux swarm around her constantly that I have never had the confidence to approach her myself."

He raised his head and looked at Samantha again and she could see how vulnerable and exposed he felt. "I am but a plain farm boy who will never be more than a farmer and builder, and I...I have not felt that I have much to offer any girl, least of all her. But getting to know you has made me bolder. *You* gave me a chance..."

Samantha shook her head. "Simple? Nothing to offer?" she started, but Rupert held out a hand to quiet her.

"What I need to ask you, Samantha, is whether you think I have a chance with Katherine or not. I have debated over the matter so many times these last few days that I feel...worn out. And after another night of little sleep, I decided I could not do this another day."

Samantha had never seen him—so even-tempered and easy going--so worked up, or so intensely earnest.

"Katherine is such a kind, generous, and accepting person," he continued. But could she ever really see anything in me? You must tell me honestly what you think." His last words sounded hoarse, and he looked at her anxiously.

Without thinking through the sudden impulse, Samantha did what had not felt right only a few minutes before: she put her arms around Rupert and hugged him tight. "Oh Rupert," she cried, "I think that is wonderful! Really I do!" She drew back to look at him and was gratified to see a smile starting at the corners of his mouth.

"You-you do?" he stammered.

Samantha nodded excitedly. "Yes. Yes! I had not thought of it before, but now it seems just right, the two of you together." She hugged him again. "My two best friends in the world..."

She moved a little away from him and soberly confided, "She has told me more than once what a good young man you are."

"Then...then you think I do have a chance with her?" Rupert asked, the half-smile gone and the anxiety back on his face. "I don't think I am confident enough yet to risk defeat before I've even started. I would rather not try if she will only reject me."

"Oh, but you have to try, Rupert! Even if things do not work out between the two of you, don't you think you will make some good memories to look back on? And if you never try, you will always wonder. I keep learning that every experience we have in our lives— whether joyous or difficult—prepares us for the next experience. The attempt would only make you stronger!"

Rupert looked at her for a moment and then nodded slowly. "I see your point," he conceded, "I think you are right. And maybe with your confidence in me to add to the little I have, I just might be able to do this."

Samantha laughed, at once feeling relieved of the burden that had built over her for so long. Imagine, Rupert and Katherine! It just might be perfect.

***

Not until a couple of days later, at home in Oberlin again, did Samantha have the time and solitude that allowed her conversation with Rupert to come flooding back to her. It brought with it a rush of feelings she had not expected. She had known from the start that she and Rupert were not meant to be together and now she rejoiced in the possibility of Katherine returning his deserving love.

So why did she feel this sudden wave of sadness that he had come to accept reality, without even trying to convince her to the contrary? She should feel nothing but happiness and relief! Instead, she was crumpling in a heap on her bed and crying her eyes out. She didn't understand herself, but the pain in her heart was real. It was a different pain than she had felt before and she was not sure how to deal with it.

Not until her tears had abated and she started thinking through events from the beginning did she realize what she was feeling and why. And then, in an effort to put things into perspective for herself, she inevitably retrieved her journal from the bedside table and began to write.

April 19, 1902

Just now--now that he has moved on--I realize how much Rupert made me feel loved, appreciated, and admired, even though I knew it would never be right for us to be together. I love Sterling and I pray every night that he will return so that I may have the chance to tell him, to show him how I feel. But at the same time, I suppose I enjoyed Rupert's attentions more than I knew. Life seems a little less exciting now and, with the end of my long-anticipated trip to Worthington, it seems there is nothing more to look forward to. In the space of about four months, I have found and lost my mother and brother, gained my first beau and lost him to my best friend (perhaps: time will tell), realized what true love is after the object of my affection is gone, and still I have heard nothing from Sterling. I feel that I am adrift in a lonely sea and...

Well.... I wish one thing so hard it hurts.

I wish Sterling could feel my need for him, like a message in a bottle, and row out here to find and rescue me from drowning in this cold, cold darkness.

CHAPTER 31

FIRST PLACE and MEDDLING

May 1902

The students had finally finished the school year, but Sterling still had a few days left to correct papers and turn in grades to Mr. Grover. He shifted restlessly at the desk in his rented room, weary of the monotony. He had been so immersed in preparing final exams and then helping his students prepare for them that he had had time for little else, except for the deep sense of loss he felt every time a wayward thought drifted toward Samantha. He had not decided whether to still follow through with his plan to return to Oberlin at school's end or not. He had promised Mrs. Tomlinson he would—had promised himself months ago--but that was a few weeks ago. Before the incident in the cemetery had all but melted his resolve.

Knowing of Sterling's end-of-term schedule, the County Committee had thoughtfully bypassed him this time, not calling on his help to wade through the contest entries. Besides, they had added other capable individuals to their ranks who could assist them as they again went through the process of selecting winners for the suddenly state-wide contest.

Needing to give his mind a break for a few minutes, Sterling stood and stretched, and his glance fell on a small, crumpled piece of paper that had lain on his desk for weeks now. He reached for it, embarrassed that he had still not read the Bible references Mrs. Tomlinson so thoughtfully gave him. He smoothed the paper open and read the scriptures listed there, then decided there was no better time than the present.

He moved to the stack of books on the floor and looked down at their spines. His Bible rested toward the very bottom of the stack and when he fished it out, he realized how few times in his life he had read anything from it, particularly from a non-literary perspective. He had always had a copy in his collection because, despite his lack of particular religious convictions, somehow he still believed that everyone should own a Bible, and also because he considered the book good literature, if nothing else.

He sat again and, not being very familiar with the placement of the different books in the Bible, it took him a few minutes to find the two references. Marking the book of Matthew with one finger, he began reading in Proverbs chapter 31.

He read slowly and thoughtfully and was surprised when his heart thrilled strangely as he read verse ten: "Who can find a virtuous woman? for her price is far above rubies." Continuing on, he felt the hairs on his arms stand up as a warm feeling spread through him. Had Mrs. Tomlinson chosen these verses in connection to Samantha? For as he read, he saw Samantha in nearly every verse:

"... She girdeth her loins with strength, and strengtheneth her arms...Strength and honour are her clothing... She openeth her mouth with wisdom; and in her tongue is the law of kindness... Many daughters have done virtuously, but thou excellest them all... Favour is deceitful, and beauty is vain: but a woman that feareth the Lord, she shall be praised."

Sterling wondered fleetingly if these verses had anything to do with what Samantha had said about the fact that many women feel that they are making a difference, right where they are. From that statement he had caught her inference that women do not have to do anything spectacular to be spectacular, and that men's perception of what is spectacular might be skewed anyway. If a person is doing good in what she feels is the most important manner, and staying true to her beliefs, no one can do better than that, he realized. *Maybe happiness, wisdom, and success really are that simple...*

The words he read were so wonderful and the picture they created so beautiful that he had to read them over once more, slowly, just to savor each one again. The kind of woman described here was strong and powerful in her own right and her influence might be endless! That was the kind of woman Samantha was developing into. Sterling had not been able to pinpoint it before, but now he recognized it was true.

The verse in Matthew was much shorter, but even more powerful. The end of it read: "With God all things are possible."

Sterling's eyes grew wide. He looked up from the book and relaxed back into the chair, the Bible heavy in his hands. What did Mrs. Tomlinson mean by this? She had never met Samantha. Did she know things he did not? Well, of course she did. She was an intelligent woman with far more life experience than he. He was only a recently turned twenty-four-year-old young man with more imagination than experience. And another surprising thought suddenly came to him as well: With God's help he supposed Mrs. Tomlinson could be even wiser than she otherwise would be to help him in a time of need. Was that the case?

Sterling thought back quickly on the past year and all the emotions he had gone through, from the highest climes of exultation to the deepest abyss of despair. He remembered the many, many times he had felt alone and without hope, longing for that which he supposed he would never have. Through it all he had never once thought to ask for God's help.

Now, with the Bible open in his lap, seeming to stare up at him with consternation, Sterling suddenly felt sheepish. His family had always considered themselves Christians, but rarely talked of God, and he barely knew how to begin thinking of Him. But at this moment, with the words from Matthew and Proverbs fresh in his mind, Sterling did begin to think of Him. And he realized that though he had never consciously sought for God's help in prayer, there were several times when he had hoped somewhere in the deepest part of himself that there was Someone out there, greater than himself, who was influencing the world, subtly changing and fixing things that he himself could do nothing about. Without realizing it he had, to a certain extent, clung to that hope that somehow everything would end up as it should.

He read the passages again and felt a hundred chaotic thoughts rise up within him. His head whirling, he marked the two places in the Bible so he could easily find them again, cleared a place on his desk for the sacred book, and reverently laid it down. He stood and stepped to the one window in the second-story room, looking out across the street and over the houses and trees beyond. What did it all mean? And what was he to do with this information?

The questions piled up in his mind, one on top of the other. But standing there contemplating what felt like a simple yet great change in his life, he found no concrete answers. The only thing he did know for certain was that the hope those verses had just given him was as delicious as anything he had experienced in a long, long time.

As if Mrs. Tomlinson stood in the room with him, he heard the words she had said to him many days before: *"Dream no small dreams, Sterling, for they have no power to move the hearts of men."* It seemed that Mrs. Tomlinson wanted him to hold onto his dream of being with Samantha again and not give it up without a fight.

Samantha is certainly worth it, isn't she? a voice in his head asked.

He knew the answer to that question was a resounding yes and was astonished to feel a tear travel down his cheek. Maybe this was what Thoreau meant when he wrote, "Go confidently in the direction of your dreams!" and "Man is the artificer of his own happiness."

Even before the episode in the cemetery, Sterling had almost given up on his dream, he realized now. But maybe what Thoreau meant and what Mrs. Tomlinson wanted him to see in the Bible was that whatever one could do on his side of things he should exert himself toward with every effort, if he believed it would contribute to his true happiness. He must fight for it, in fact. And if he did truly believe in his dream and in the pursuit of happiness--if he, Sterling, really believed in and valued Samantha--how could he give her up so easily?

Well, he had decided long ago to return to Oberlin, to at least try, and he would do it!

But not quite yet. He still had papers to grade.

Sterling drew in a long breath, then let it out slowly and turned back to his desk. He shuffled absently through the newspaper he had bought days before and not yet had a chance to read. He knew he needed to get back to reading students' papers, but he still could not bring himself to do it. A little longer break was in order. So he skimmed the paper's headlines, turning pages distractedly, not noting anything of particular interest.

As he was about to turn back to grading, his eyes suddenly fell upon something that made him stop abruptly:

First Place Winner of the Ohio State Writing Contest, Poetry Division. And beneath that, the title "Song to My Love." It interested him, but that did not explain why his heart quickened so suddenly. He continued reading, startled and confused by his own reaction until he saw the name at the bottom:

Awaken, my love.

Awake and put on

thy rain-shawl,

and step out into the

sparkling diamonds with me.

Let us play among the heavy grasses,

and laugh like children--

shake exuberance from every

form of thy figure.

Taste the drops, my love,

gingerly trill each one

o'er thy tongue;

toss the dancing jewels

from thy fingers,

314

out of thy lashes--

and Look at me!

Look at this!

Dance, my love, and

kiss me sweet.

Let us not waste

heaven's tears.

-Samantha Jennings

Some might consider it scandalous—enough, he supposed, that the fact that it had succeeded in being printed at all was quite surprising and would no doubt bring up controversy (but then, Oberlin knew how to handle controversy). To him the poem was only beautiful. It spoke to the very center of his soul. It was not until he saw the poet's name at the bottom, however, that he knew why it had spoken so intimately to him. His breath caught in his throat with a gasp as he read Samantha's name.

Suddenly he remembered their conversation that day last July when the wet heat was so oppressive and draining that he and Samantha had had difficulty concentrating on their writing. When he asked her what she would do if it began raining that very moment, she said she would dance. And in his awkward poem about the rain, he wrote that he would want to be there with someone he loved and to kiss her. This poem of Samantha's was so much more gracefully formed than his own that it made him embarrassed to think of what he had written. But perhaps Samantha remembered it, for she had written of kisses in her poem as well, and of love. Perhaps she did still remember...

In his mind's eye he conjured up the scene again: the heat of the day, their perspiring faces, and his last-ditch effort to make a productive lesson of their time. He could almost feel the rough wood of the bench beneath him, could see Samantha across from him, the way her gray eyes had grown so tender as she read what he had written. And with a sudden shiver deep inside him, he remembered the one question she asked when she finished reading: "Who is she?" He had told her he did not yet know. But now he realized that he had known after all, that his dream had been forming that summer and he had just not recognized it for what it was.

How he wished he could go back to that day and give the simple answer that now meant everything to him: "You."

It did not surprise him that Samantha had progressed into writing poetry, nor did he stop to consider what this meant: That she was still writing, still learning, still practicing what she had learned from him. But of course she was; he had not expected less.

The message of the poem—the joyful depth of love--struck him right through the heart. Tears welled up in his eyes and he absently brushed them away. He did not know for sure if the poem meant anything about him personally, but another glimmer of hope lit within his breast. He acknowledged that she may have written it to express feelings she had for someone else—the young man he had seen with her in the cemetery, for example--but it truly seemed she had given him the chance to ask a question he had not dared think! And now he had to pursue the answer.

Whether he would fail in embarrassment or succeed in glory he didn't know, but he had to try. Now! He had to, or perish.

His old impulsiveness returned, then, as he stuffed a few things into a suitcase and a small case. Before heading out the door he hastily tore Samantha's poem from its place in the newspaper and tucked it into his pocket, along with the scrap of scripture references. He headed to the train station to buy a last-minute ticket, the papers on his desk forgotten and askew.

***

Mrs. Tomlinson sent Jerome up to Sterling's room while she waited in the wagon. They had not seen him for several days and, knowing he must be reaching the end of grading by now, they had stopped by on their way into town to invite him to supper that evening. But when Jerome flew back down the outside stairs without Sterling, his face wore an expression of confusion and worry.

"He isn't there, Ma," he said breathlessly. "There are papers everywhere and clothes on his bed, but he's not there. Where else would he go? He never leaves his things scattered around like that."

Mrs. Tomlinson frowned and handed the reigns to Jerome. "Watch the horses." She climbed down from her seat and started up the stairs to Sterling's room. *I wonder what could have happened...*

She did not have to wonder long. The room was just as Jerome had described and that was a reason for concern because, as even Jerome had noticed, Sterling generally kept his things very neat and organized. But what told her more than anything, and also relieved her worried spirit, was what she saw on the mess of his desk. Over disheveled stacks of papers, a newspaper draped haphazardly, and in the middle of one page gaped a tattered hole. Mrs. Tomlinson had a copy of that very newspaper at home in her living room and she knew whose poem Sterling had torn out.

317

That poem was actually one thing that had brought her to town to talk to Sterling. It had seemed to her like Samantha's poem was a way of reaching out to him somehow, and if Sterling had not realized that, she had determined to open his eyes to it. *But*, Mrs. Tomlinson smiled to herself, *it appears he is not so unaware after all.*

She stood there, thinking for a few moments, and then gathered the stacks of papers from Sterling's desk. It looked like most of them were corrected and she knew Mr. Grover needed them to determine grades, since Sterling was not here to do it himself. *I don't think he has shirked or relaxed in one duty this entire year*, she thought honestly. *Surely Mr. Grover will not begrudge him this one time, especially if I pick up the slack a bit.*

As she headed down the slightly wobbly stairs with the load of papers in her arms, Mrs. Tomlinson had another sudden thought. *I would wager he did not think to apprise Samantha of his coming, and I believe she needs to know in order for this thing to come to pass the way it should.*

"What are those papers? What did you find, Ma?" Jerome asked, when she returned to the wagon and took her place on the seat beside him.

"We are taking these to Mr. Grover, first of all. Son, drive us to the school. I think Mr. Grover will still be there."

"Yes, ma'am!" Jerome responded, with a grin and a happy toss of red hair. It was not every day his mother let him drive.

Mr. Grover stood when Mrs. Tomlinson knocked and entered his office.

"Why, Mrs. Tomlinson," he said, walking around his desk to meet her and extending a hand and a smile. "What a pleasure to see you. I trust you and Jerome are well?"

His voice was warm and she shook his hand, taking the seat he offered. "Yes, we are, thank you. Jerome is out waiting in the wagon." She saw no reason not to get straight to the point. "I came to bring these to you," she said, holding out the stack of papers. "They are Sterling's and he would have brought them himself, but something very important came up."

"I see." Mr. Grover's eyebrows raised in a gesture of curiosity. He took the papers from her and returned to his desk. After rifling through them briefly he looked up and stated, "Everything looks in order, as I have come to expect from Sterling. He is nothing if not dependable."

"I am glad you see that in him, sir. I noticed a few of the papers lack marks but I hoped you would overlook that slight failing on his part, this once."

Mr. Grover looked back down at the papers on his desk and sorted through a few more. "Y-yes...I can see that now," he said slowly. And then a little more briskly as he looked up again: "Well, these will not take me long to correct. I thank you for bringing them, Mrs. Tomlinson."

She nodded and stood, but before she could take her leave, Mr. Grover asked, "Does this, by any slight possibility, have anything to do with that girl he ran away from last year and who has continued to haunt him ever since?"

Mrs. Tomlinson looked at him in surprise. "You knew?" she asked. "I didn't think he expressed this to anyone but myself."

"No, no," Mr. Grover replied, waving a hand and shaking his head. "He said nothing, but I know a love-struck young man when I see one, and I knew from the start that his troubles were female related." He chuckled.

Mrs. Tomlinson nodded, impressed by Mr. Grover's perceptiveness. She suddenly saw him in a new light and felt a greater respect for him. And just as if Sterling really were her own son, she felt gratitude that his employer understood him so well, whether the boy knew it or not.

Mr. Grover raised a finger, a touch of amusement in his eyes. "As I always say when it comes to these matters, 'There is no remedy for love but to love more.' Henry David Thoreau."[29] He let out a small sigh. "I hope Sterling has finally sorted that out. When did he leave?"

"I really don't know," Mrs. Tomlinson admitted. She was further surprised by what Mr. Grover had quoted, and the irony of the author of the quote was not lost on her. "We only just now found his room disheveled and those papers waiting on his desk. I imagine it has not been more than a few hours, at most."

"Yes," Mr. Grover nodded again. "I am glad he went. High time he faced up to this, whoever she is. Thank you again, Mrs. Tomlinson." He shook her hand once more and gave her a wink that sent a youthful blush spreading slowly up her neck as she turned away.

---

[29] https://www.brainyquote.com/quotes/henry_david_thoreau_103440

She left, wondering that she should blush so easily. *A funny man, that Mr. Grover,* she thought. *But very kind and amiable.* She dismissed the thoughts and headed back to her waiting son.

When she climbed up into the wagon and took the reins from a reluctant Jerome, directing the horse further into town, he asked, "Where are we off to now, Ma? You're not heading home."

"No," she replied. "There is one more item I must attend to. I am never one to meddle, but in this case I must make an exception. We are going to the train station to find out when, exactly, Sterling left. And then, son, to the telegraph office--as my effort to bring together again what should have stayed together in the first place."

CHAPTER 32

THE TELEGRAM

May 1902

Samantha smiled in delight to learn that she had won first place in the poetry division. She had been half afraid to enter the poem at all, for she did not know how it would be viewed by strictly conservative minds. It was not meant to be scandalous or controversial—or anything other than joyful and heartfelt. Writing it had simply relieved an emotional load from her mind and given her the satisfaction she craved to express herself. With the rain this spring came enforced time indoors and, consequently, more time to reflect on her future—for change was certainly in the air, as was so common in spring--and to further sort out her feelings once and for all.

She knew she loved Sterling and that no other man she had met in nearly a year—including Rupert--could compare to him or ever would. She did not want anyone else, and she ached to see him again, to know if he even thought of her anymore. With the swirling of her thoughts and imaginings, as well as the incessant rain, images had developed in her mind that she needed to give voice to. Finally, the day before she entered it, the poem came bursting forth into a creation that expressed her longing, her aching, and her tenderness all at once.

Reading it again in print, she still hoped she would not regret submitting it to the contest. For now the entire state of Ohio would be reading the words of her heart and asking who Samantha Jennings was, and what kind of young woman she was to express such things so publicly. She wondered fleetingly if Sterling would be one of those who read it; she hoped so. Nevertheless, despite any misgivings, she viewed her poem with pleasure, tracing its outline on the page, still in awe that she, plain, quiet Samantha, was published!

The ticking of the clock over the mantle entered her reverie and pulled her sharply back to the present. With a jolt she checked the time and then fingered the paper in her pocket, the one she had kept on her person and touched almost constantly since she received it a couple of hours before.

Being published was a miracle and something, indeed, to savor, but this paper was the real miracle, especially precious because of how long she had waited for it—though she certainly never expected a message like this. She still felt unsure of its true meaning; telegrams were unforgivingly brief: "Sterling left Worthington for Oberlin today at one."

What was Sterling doing in Worthington, of all places? This weighty irony somehow added to the poignancy of her whole experience in Worthington.

And why is he returning to Oberlin? Her heart thudded in her chest as her mind raced through all the possibilities. Why was he contacting her now, after all this time with not one word? But rehearsing unanswered questions would do her no good, and she had thought through them a hundred times already. So, she willed her mind to stop and her heart to slow and she checked the clock once more. If the train were prompt there was no time to waste.

Samantha removed her glasses, stood, and moved to her wardrobe, taking out her navy blue riding habit. During the last few days, any time the rain let up for a few hours or for the afternoon, Samantha had saddled and bridled Champion and taken him for a chilly, though energizing ride through the countryside. She loved when the sun came out, making the droplets on trees and grass shimmer like diamonds, and steam rise from Champion's glossy coat. She would have enjoyed the countryside today too, but now their destination lay in another direction.

Once dressed, she hurried out to the yard and glanced anxiously up at the gray sky, placing her wide-brimmed riding hat snugly down over her hair as she went. If she got wet, it would not be the first time and she wouldn't mind that much, but at least the hat would keep rain out of her face and off the back of her neck.

***

Sterling's train pulled into the muddy station with a weary groan. The rain had washed the windows clean, at least, but when he looked out, all he could see past the rivulets of water were a gray sky and soggy greenery. It was a chill, miserable rain-soaked world.

The train ride had given him time to reflect, to mull things over...and to doubt again. Now he wondered if he were just being childish, acting on a whim like this. He still regretted the last time he acted spontaneously. Maybe it would only make things worse. *Why did I come back?* he thought, gazing out at the dreary train station. *And to this weather, too, which only deepens my sadness and frustration.*

Just the sight of this section of town brought a flood of memories that almost bowled him over. And he thought he had succeeded in forgetting!

As he stood with the other passengers, taking a firm hold on his luggage, his thoughts traveled back to the conversations he'd had with Mrs. Tomlinson (and with himself), that contributed to his decision to come back. He had felt strongly then that he needed to. But now... Now he wondered if he weren't just acting the fool. *I am not a young boy anymore. What will this really accomplish? What if I can't find her? Or what if she refuses to see me?* In his room several hours before he felt nothing but determination to see this through. Now a hundred uncertainties rose up to crush that.

Of course, at this point there was nothing left but to see the thing through to the end. *No small dreams* he kept telling himself. *She is worth it. I have to at least try.*

He spotted a closed carriage waiting under a storefront canopy to transport travelers from the train station, coachman hunched beneath an umbrella, horses' heads down, manes dripping. Securely donning his black derby hat, Sterling bent his head in resignation and stepped down from the platform. He'd remembered his coat and hat, but he had departed in such haste that he had not thought to bring an umbrella along. Which, considering how wet this spring was, just showed how preoccupied his mind was! He felt the rain falling heavily upon him now.

Slowly he made his way through the wet, milling crowd with "Pardon me ma'am's" and "Excuse me sir's." At last, he reached the coach and spoke briefly with the driver before stepping inside and closing the door. Two other passengers were already waiting inside and made room for him. He apologized for the water now dripping off him onto the floor of the carriage and sat near the window. Suddenly he heard something that made him glance outside and scan the area, wondering if he had heard right.

He felt the hair on the back of his neck stand upright and his pulse quicken. Had he really heard...? There it was again! But how...?

Then he saw them.

Her face was flushed, her eyes bright, and her hair curled damply around the temples. A dark, wide-brimmed hat covered the pile of gold hair with auburn highlights, and the smart navy-blue bodice of her riding dress fit snugly against the gentle curves of her body. He watched her in wonder as she trotted confidently into the station on...his horse! But how had she...? So, at least one part of his night dreams was true. Samantha and Champion had been together after all.

Champion whinnied again, the third time--such a familiar sound!

They pulled to a stop just short of the crowd and Samantha dismounted in one sure, fluid movement, eyes dancing, lips half-smiling. She said something to the horse and rubbed Champion's muzzle. Then she closed her eyes and lifted her face to the sky in a moment of apparent ecstasy, one hand holding her hat securely on her head.

Sterling could not take his eyes from her.

She turned back to the horse, then searched in the folds of her dress for a moment, pulling out a pair of glasses. (Ah...the glasses... So some things were still the same...) She put them on and glanced at what looked like a yellow telegram in her hands, then gazed past the people to the train. After a long moment of scanning the platform and surrounding area, her shoulders seemed to sag and she tucked the paper away.

Sterling watched as she carefully lifted the spectacles from her nose, hiding them back in her pocket. Absently, she rubbed the horse's ears for a few moments before looking up again to scan the crowd one last time. Then she shook her head.

One more person entered the carriage, filling it to capacity, and before Sterling could even process what he had seen or decide what to do, the driver started the horses in the direction of the hotel. Sterling had time only to see Samantha expertly remount Champion, and then his coach pulled out of sight. How did she come to be here just at this time, he wondered. Who was she waiting for? Someone who had sent her a telegram, obviously. Someone whom she was eager and happy to see; someone who apparently had not come.

Arriving at the hotel, Sterling stepped out of the carriage with the other passengers and headed through the streaming rain into the shelter of the large building. Inside the lobby, he waited in line for a few minutes, purchased lodging for a couple days, and headed up the stairs, key in hand.

After stepping inside the room and setting down his luggage, he took off his wet hat and hung it on a hook, then pulled the curtain aside and gazed out at the rain, which appeared to finally be losing momentum. He stood there, pondering, wondering what his what his plan of action should be. Finally, he decided to do something he had never yet done that he could remember: pray. Turning from the window, he stepped to the bed and knelt, unsure of the best way to approach deity. It felt strange to kneel and address someone he could not see, but he reminded himself of the feelings he had experienced while reading in his Bible this morning and took heart. He began tentatively, then gained in confidence as he poured out his dearest desires to God.

"Dear God," he started. "I know I haven't sought to know You before and have seldom truly acknowledged Your existence, but somehow I know now that You can help me. I also believe You know how I feel about Samantha. You know what is best for her and for me. I don't know if I did the right thing in coming back here, but I felt like I needed to face her and find out if she has any interest in pursuing a future together." He stopped and swallowed a lump in his throat, then began again, a little hoarsely. "She is precious to me, God, and I need your help to find her and talk to her. I learned from the book of Matthew that all things are possible with You. Please...help me know what to do. Amen."

He knelt there for another moment, head bowed, then let out a long breath and stood up. He would walk through town a bit and see if she was still here. Then if he could not find her, he would head to the Jennings mansion. He walked out the door and locked it, then strode quickly down the stairs, realizing he felt a bit better already, just having a plan of action.

CHAPTER 33

MY STERLING

May 1901

Samantha felt bereft. She was confused and very unsure of what to think or do. With a flick of the reins, she maneuvered Champion through the milling crowd, over puddles and cobblestones, and through a muddy sideroad to the edge of town where open pastures replaced houses. She had not taken Champion for a run in a few days and could feel his nervous, eager energy beneath her. At the forefront of her thoughts was the question of why Sterling had sent the telegram and then not arrived. Had he missed his train? Or was he here in Oberlin and she had just missed him? Tears of anger and frustration welled up in her eyes and began spilling down her cheeks. She tried to push the discouraging feelings away with the reminder that he had sent her a telegram, after all. But the tears continued to fall. As they neared the pasture, she flicked the reins, dug in her heels, and gave Champion his head. The black horse sped forward immediately and ran swiftly through the large pasture, impatient to stretch his legs and gain that speed they both enjoyed so much.

An hour later, as she turned Champion toward home and allowed for the horse to cool down at a walk, something occurred to her that she had not realized before. This was the same time of year she and Sterling met last year. Did he always make an annual visit to Oberlin to seek out new pupils? Or was he back to teach at the College?

Where is he? she wondered for the umpteenth time.

Despite her deep disappointment, confusion, and sorrow, she kept thinking of the scripture in Luke 1:37 that had given her hope so many times already: "With God nothing shall be impossible." And she remembered how remote the possibility of Sterling's return had seemed for almost a year now. Yet she had received that telegram! Perhaps God would still prove to be in the details. Maybe what Katherine told her months ago about trusting Sterling to God really was true. Katherine had said, "If you and Sterling should be together, God will make it happen." Samantha had not quite believed her that day, but her faith had come a long way since then, and now maybe, just maybe, she could trust this matter to Him.

As she and Champion turned into the long drive leading home, she was surprised to see a side door open and Mrs. Dolittle's round form running toward her. Samantha had never seen Mrs. Dolittle move so quickly, and immediately all sorts of frightening reasons for the woman's urgency entered Samantha's mind. She urged Champion forward at a trot and dismounted as soon as she reached the housekeeper. "What is it?" she demanded, "Is it Father? What's wrong?!"

Mrs. Dolittle, a little out of breath, panted, "Nothing is wrong, dear. Sorry to frighten you. But Mr. Sterling was here! I've been watching for you, all full of excitement and anxiety. I could not wait to give you the news."

Samantha stood there, holding Champion's reins, stunned. What did this mean?!

"What did he--? I mean, when..." She clapped a hand to her face. "What should I do, Mrs. Dolittle?"

Mrs. Dolittle laughed in delight and grabbed Samantha's hand to pull it down. She squeezed it between her own two hands and her dark brown eyes sparkled. "He was here about half an hour ago and said he would come back later this evening, if he did not find you in town."

"Then I must go look for him!" Samantha said, almost frantically.

"Now let's just take this slow." Mrs. Dolittle kept hold of her hand, rubbing it, and looked Samantha full in the face.

Samantha took a deep breath and willed her heart to slow. She nodded. "All right. You're right. I need to think this through."

Mrs. Dolittle nodded encouragingly. "Here is what I think we should do, my dear. I will find Martin to care for the horse while you go change and freshen up. Then, I can make you a quick lunch and you can wait for Mr. Sterling's return." She glanced up at the sky. "It seems the rain is over for now. With any luck, it will hold off for a few more hours. At any rate, I don't think anything will keep that gentleman from coming back here."

"Really?!" Samantha's breath caught in her throat and she felt the tears threatening again, this time for an entirely different reason.

"Yes, I don't doubt it!" Mrs. Dolittle stepped back and smiled again at Samantha's obvious shock, a combination of disbelief and thrill warring across the girl's face.

"Oh, my." Samantha could think of nothing to say for a moment and swallowed, hardly daring to feel the joy that accompanied Mrs. Dolittle's words. "All right," she said again, finally, willing herself to stay calm and follow Mrs. Dolittle's suggestions. "I *am* rather muddy and disheveled from that ride. But I don't think I could eat a thing right now!"

Mrs. Dolittle chuckled. "You are probably right. We will skip that, then. I'll go find Martin. Wait here."

Samantha was grateful for the housekeeper's intuitiveness, and for a moment to compose her thoughts while she stood there. Still holding Champion's reins with one hand, she rested the other hand under his forelock, between his ears, and rubbed softly where he liked it. The horse snorted and nudged her shoulder with his nose. "Good boy," she murmured, patting his neck.

Sterling, here? she thought wonderingly yet again. *Here? To see me?!* How was it possible? Slowly she started walking Champion to the barn, where they met Mrs. Dolittle and Martin coming her way. Martin grasped the reins and Mrs. Dolittle took her arm and led her to the back door and into the house.

Back in her room, Samantha changed into her olive-green riding habit and started on her hair. She knew she would not be able to simply sit around, waiting for Sterling to return. And she felt strongly that something wonderful was coming. It was as if she could feel the suspense, the tension waiting in the air around her. As soon as she finished her hair, she would head back out on Champion. The question was where she should go to find Sterling. As she brushed, coiled, and pinned her hair, she thought about all the places he could be. Where would he go? Immediately the answer came to her, quick as lightning and just as bright: the woods.

With so many thoughts and questions humming inside her head, she soon found herself on Champion's back, wind in her hair, watery sunshine in her face, heading there.

***

After an attempt at a meal at the hotel, Sterling ordered hot water to his room and bathed, shaved, and distractedly dressed. His fresh pants and shirt were a bit wrinkled from their travel in his suitcase, but he didn't notice. With barely even a glance in the mirror above the basin, he combed back his thick, dark hair, the usual unruly ringlet quickly flopping across his forehead again a moment later.

His determination nearly all intact again with his previous walk to Samantha's home and the favorable reception he had received from Mrs. Dolittle, he strode to the general store to pick up a few needed items, then walked around town for a while, hoping to catch sight of Samantha. He hoped the cessation of the rain and the weak sunlight through clouds now was a good omen.

It did not take long to realize Samantha was not in the main part of town, so he returned to his room, dropped off the items he had bought, and, before stepping out with his jacket and hat, picked up the clipping of Samantha's poem which he had placed on the dresser, and slipped it into his pocket again. Then, taking a deep breath, he stepped outside and shut the door behind him.

He walked at a good pace with as much confidence as he could muster. His shoes soon grew heavy with mud, and his pant legs spattered. He did not know why he had chosen this road exactly, or why he turned toward the woods now. It simply felt right, like all those walks to the cemetery in Worthington. But if he found her, he had no idea what he would say. There was so much he had thought through over the past several months, so much he wanted to say, but he really didn't know where to start! Whenever and wherever he saw her, he could only hope the moment would take care of itself.

Sterling's thoughts busied him so that he barely noticed his surroundings. Broad shoulders squared, he looked straight ahead, but his eyes were turned inward and he failed to notice that the clouds were starting to darken again. The temperature dropped slightly, but the air stayed untouched except for the faintest of breezes. Unlike the tenseness before a storm, the atmosphere remained peaceful, calm, and serene. Sterling, however, noticed none of this: he recited something just under his breath, absently continuing his long-legged stride through the forest.

***

Samantha tied Champion's reins to a branch and let him graze while she made her way to the meadow and the tree where Sterling sat so many months before on that magical, fairy ring afternoon. She noted the weather's change in temperament and looked up at the graying sky, but it did not worry her.

She stood leaning back against the tree, arms around herself, and closed her eyes to better feel the serenity that cloaked this beautiful place. She loved the peace she felt in these woods. It was hard to imagine that she never came here before Sterling brought her last summer, for now it was a refuge from the storms of the world, a change in scenery from her own intermittent emotions that at times threatened to drown her.

Lately, when she took the time to contemplate her life, as she did now, her thoughts of the future came up empty. Many times over these past months, she had struggled against feeling like she was sinking into a sea of sadness. But more recently, she felt that perhaps, instead, she waited in the midst of a barren desert. She fought against feeling ungrateful, for she knew she was very blessed, but she also knew that without he whom she loved most, her life was slowly beginning to dry up, bit by bit...and she with it.

But now he is here in Oberlin! The thought thrilled her yet again, making her heart pound with joy and wonder. She did not know if he would find her here, but she had great hopes that he would. To her, it seemed the obvious place; nowhere else felt right.

With a sigh she allowed herself to fully relax for a small moment against the tree. There was still that mysterious feeling that had pricked at her the last few days of something coming. Something good and important...

***

Sterling stood watching her breathlessly. Somehow he had felt she would be here, this place of their last meeting. And then, when he saw Champion grazing contentedly in the meadow, he knew he was in the right place. How gratifying to realize he had guessed correctly! Yet, he had to acknowledge that this was no coincidence. Was this how God worked? He didn't know for sure, but he did feel a warmth in his chest at the thought of his heartfelt desire, his prayer, and the feeling that had led him here. How lovely to see her here before him again! How she had matured and deepened in his absence!

He remembered the first time they met, and he realized she was no longer the pale, tentative flower, unaware that she could lift her petals to the sunshine. He smiled, seeing the old un-self-consciousness he had noted on their first meeting still intact. Though she did her hair up differently now, to be sure, and the straw hat and ill-fitting cotton dresses had vanished, somehow that did not seem to account for this change.

Most would not think her beautiful, perhaps, but that made little difference to him. He saw the slim, yet shapely, form he had seen in the Worthington cemetery, the confidence he had noticed at the train station, a peace and satisfaction that left no room for the backward girl of his memory. Even standing motionless against the tree with her eyes shut, she was so full of life and light!

Whatever could have happened? Had that young man he saw her with in the cemetery nurtured Samantha into this radiant woman he saw before him? But who else would have loved her that much? *Does another love her as completely as I? Can another?* he agonized.

But then he stopped himself. She had come to these woods, to the same clearing where he brought her on Champion's back that impulsive afternoon. That had to count for something. And in fact— he suddenly noted with a sharp intake of breath--she stood beneath the very tree he had sat under then.

He thought back again to the very first time he saw her. She had sat beneath a tree then and held a large book in her hands. Back then, she knew the pleasure of devouring information, but now, thinking of the poem in his pocket, it was obvious she knew the rewarding pleasure of writing, hungrily filling empty pages with all that was inside her.

And there was so much inside her!

Sterling continued watching from his discreet distance, wondering if now was the right time to approach her. He did not want to startle or frighten her, but his longing to touch her, to hear her voice again, to pour out his sincerest apologies and clear up any misunderstandings between them was so strong that it overwhelmed him. After eternal months of separation, his dream—his most

336

wonderful of secret dreams—stood only a few yards away! The wonder of this reality—finding her here after all--was too great to fathom.

Quietly he made his way toward her as raindrops began to fall again. The noise of their pattering masked the sound of his footsteps so that he drew close without her hearing his approach. Then he stood still and removed the newspaper clipping from his pocket, letting it sift slowly and silently to the ground near their feet. Shoving trembling hands into his pockets, he began to speak, his voice very low and heavy with emotion:

"Awaken, my love. Awake and put on thy rain-shawl, and step out into the sparkling diamonds with me."

Samantha opened her eyes wide in surprise and moved away from the tree. She stared at Sterling with a mixture of disbelief and wonder, as if he were a ghost from her dreams.

His voice rose a little as he steadily kept on, afraid if he stopped now, it would be forever. "Let us play among the heavy grasses and laugh like children--shake exuberance from every form of thy figure. Taste the drops, my love, gingerly trill each one o'er thy tongue; toss the dancing jewels from thy fingers, out of thy lashes-- and Look at me! Look at this!"

Trembling, Samantha took a step toward him. The rain gained momentum and its pattering down through the leaves became more insistent. Her response was immediate: "Dance, my love, and kiss me sweet. Let us not waste heaven's tears." In disbelief and amazement, she gave a soft laugh that turned into a sob. She clapped both hands to her mouth and stood there, gazing at him, still unsure that the moment was real, tears standing in her eyes.

Sterling's voice ceased, like the gentlest suspiration, giving way to the rhythm of the rain spilling through the myriad leaves overhead. Samantha's hair darkened slightly with the water, beginning to cling and curl against her head.

Slowly Sterling removed his hat in a gesture of appeal, fingers still shaking. He gazed at her, the mellow depths of his eyes filled to the brim with yearning and pleading. Yet still, he hesitated.

Samantha's heart swelled within her, and joy spread through her with a sweetness that was heady at its very beginning. She understood what he had not spoken, even understood far more than could have been spoken.

"Did you receive my letter?" he asked finally, in a choked voice, not sure why he chose to begin this way.

Samantha looked perplexed. "The telegram, yes, but no letter..." Her eyes held a question mark and she searched his face.

"Telegram?" Sterling asked. *The one I saw her holding at the train station?* Now he was the one confused.

Samantha shook her head faintly, the tears beginning to slide down her cheeks. "I wanted *so much* to hear from you," she whispered. "I wanted it more than anything."

Sterling could scarcely believe it, and yet at the same time, it felt astoundingly right. How could he have doubted so many times and for so long? He swallowed. "I'm sorry," he whispered back. "I did finally send a letter, but when I didn't hear back from you I...I was afraid."

As she heard this, the regret faded away, and seeing him there before her, a dream made reality, her heart caught in her throat. He was even more handsome than she remembered. She took in the dignified line of his forehead, the way his wavy dark hair turned curly as it dripped with rain, his brown eyes so compelling in their anxiousness. It looked as if he, too, were on the verge of tears.

She felt suspended in time, acutely aware of his nearness, yet looking on as if from a distance, drinking in the vision of his lean, well-muscled frame. A bit of the old shyness crept over her, but her gray eyes glowed warmly. "My Sterling," she breathed faintly. It was a tentative question.

"Samantha?" he returned, his tears beginning to mingle with the rain on his face. He lowered his arms, his hat dropping to the ground. He held out a hand and Samantha thought her heart would break to see the look in his eyes, as if he were asking for something that he was afraid she would never give. She wanted to comfort him, to heal the ache she saw in him, to pour all her love into him. Without another moment's hesitation, she crossed the few steps that separated her from his embrace.

He held her then, savoring her nearness. "Oh, Samantha, what agony I have been through--ever since I left last summer. Time has dragged on eternally." He whispered the words into her hair, inhaling its sweet fragrance. "I have been a coward and a fool. I almost did not return... I thought there was someone else... If only I had known that I did not wound you as I thought I had, that you..."

She looked up at him, and he down at her for one long moment. "You are the only one for me there will ever be," she said quietly. "But only after you left did I find out how much I need you."

There was too much to say and no adequate words. How do you tell another she is the air you breathe and that he is hope personified when you are just now beginning to understand it and to feel as if you had just begun to live?

Samantha clasped his face gently between her palms, losing herself in his eyes for a long, long moment. Then she raised up on her toes, closing her eyes and pressing her lips against his, pulling him close.

The shock was no less than it had been the last time, that first time. Rain beat upon their heads. When they drew apart, she kept her head tilted up and half smiled at him. His dazed expression almost made her laugh. "I have learned passion from you, Teacher."

Sterling swallowed. "And I temperance from you."

"At one time, I told you this was a magical place," Samantha said, taking his hands in her own. "Whether the fairy ring is still here or not, I think its promise is fulfilled."

Sterling agreed but did not know what to say. This was all too wonderful for him to verbalize.

Suddenly he felt he could not go on another moment without asking her forgiveness and clearing this burden from him completely. "Samantha—I-I want to apologize for that...last time. For any pain I caused you. And now, again, we have no chaperone. I should have--"

"Hush," she said softly, placing a finger on his lips. "There is nothing to forgive. Dance, my love, and kiss me sweet. Let us not waste heaven's tears."

ADDITIONAL READING

Walden Pond and *Civil Disobedience* by Henry David Thoreau

An Introduction to Poetry by X.J. Kennedy and Dana Gioia

Abigail Adams by Woody Holton

Roots by Alex Haley

Uncle Tom's Cabin by Harriet Beecher Stowe.

The Town That Started the Civil War by Nat Brandt

America in the Gilded Age and Progressive Era by Edward T. O'Donnell (lecture on audio)

About the Author

Katrina Lyman Jones began writing stories by age eight and novels at age twelve. From her earliest memories, books have always been great friends, and the library one of her favorite places. She loves many different genres, but her favorite is historical fiction because of all she learns about events in history, and how people in different times dealt with difficulty. She holds a BA of English Teaching from Utah State University, and is grateful to have been able to primarily focus on raising her children over the past 18 years. She has lived in Arizona, Ohio, and Utah. Currently she resides in southern Utah with her wonderful husband and five children, where she loves her faith, gardening, and being a flutist in the Southwest Symphony.

A Note from the Author

Dear Reader,

Thank you so much for reading this book! I hope you enjoyed the journey with Sterling and Samantha. If you could take a couple minutes to rate it on Amazon and/or GoodReads, it would mean the world to me! Ratings and reviews help indie books like mine become more visible to the general public, giving readers a better opportunity to know about them.

To review on Amazon, go to your account, find this book, and click on "Write a Review." Then select the number of stars you feel it deserves and write a sentence or two of review, if possible. Click submit and you're done!

GoodReads.com is a great place for book lovers to keep track of the books they've read, rate them, and give or receive book recommendations from friends. You can often find me there keeping track of all the books I read, too. ☺

If you would like to interact with me online, you can find me at any of the following places:

Email: katrinalymanjones@gmail.com
Instagram: @katrinajonesbooks
Facebook:
https://www.facebook.com/profile.php?id=100092388615223

Happy reading! I hope to "see" you again for the second book.

Sincerely,
Katrina Lyman Jones

Made in the USA
Monee, IL
23 September 2023

43291067R00195